WILDFLOWER
Second Edition

A Novel By
SIR PATRICK BIJOU

DESCRIPTION

Discover a Collection of Erotic Fiction Written Purely for Your Pleasure!

What is your heart's darkest, deepest desire? What if the vampire's bite is all you crave?

This fictional work of erotic art depicts all the intricacies of how werewolves and vampires satisfy their emotional and sensual needs. This series is written to bring up the fire burning inside every reader and stimulate your fantasies!

With these six stories, all your desires will come true…

This thrilling horror romance and steamy adventure will take you for an unforgettable ride through the world of darkest and deepest erotic desires set in a fantasy world.

In this collection, you will enjoy:

- The alluringly kinky tale of various emotional acrobatics from a group of werewolves and vampires that will most certainly tickle your imagination;
- The magnetically exotic story inspired by the old tale of those unknown creatures of the dark and their desire to love openly;
- The tantalizingly dangerous world that will immerse you in itself and connect you to your carnal desires;
- The temptingly frisky novel series will teach you a thing or two you can use in your bedroom;
- And much more!

Feel your temperature rise with excitement, for every page you turn will bring you new acters and their new adventures! Spice up your imagination with these erotic stories that will keep you hot & bothered all night!

Are you ready for steamy and kinky action? What are you waiting for?

Scroll up, click on "Buy Now with 1-Click", and Get Your Copy Now!

ABOUT THE AUTHOR

Sir Patrick has written over 20 published fictional and non-fictional books across several genres. He writes for the liberation of all people, focusing on those who are often left out the literary world of creative writing.

Sir Patrick's journey into content writing has allowed him to become an exceptionally motivated and enthusiastic author and professional communicator. He is a citizen of the world and this has greatly influenced his writing.

So, if you are already a fan, I appreciate you. If you are not yet one, then what are you waiting for? Read a book and then read some more. I create characters that resonate with you and infuse life into all I write".

Thank you again for purchasing this book, I hope you have enjoyed it!

TABLE OF CONTENTS

PART 5

CHAPTER 1

Liam hovered impatiently outside his cousin's house, waiting for Elina and Reasa to pack some clothes. He'd deliberately chosen not to go in. He didn't want to give Reasa an opportunity to call him to task for kissing her. The memory of their first kiss blew his mind. It had been so much more than he had ever dreamed imaginable. It was the single most perfect moment of his life and he didn't want anything to take that away, especially not his mate glowering furiously at him. No, Liam was happy to put of the inevitable for as long as possible so he could savor that magical moment. If that was a tad cowardly, he could live with it.

The sound of booted feet on the hard-packed earth had him turning his head towards the pack's large meeting circle. The wolves defending the outer boundaries were changing shift, the morning detail already out among the trees. Tired men trundled into the compound, some of them waving in his direction as they scurried home to get some much- needed sleep after a long night.

Liam waved back, feeling excitement as well as some trepidation about what they were about to attempt. They were going into uncharted territory with the wounded vampires at the Praetorian Compound. They had no idea if dream walking in their minds would be a help or a hindrance, but they had to at least try. If nothing was done there really was only one outcome for the vampires, and Liam just couldn't bear to think about that consequence.

"We're ready," Elina said behind him, and he turned back around to smile at his cousin and set eyes on his mate for the first time since they'd kissed.

How did she manage to look more beautiful with each passing day? The sun caressed Reasa's bronzed skin, making him feel jealous that it wasn't his fingers tracing each perfect feature, that it wasn't his lips tasting the satin smoothness of her cheeks. She'd tied her raven hair back in a short ponytail, the hairstyle not only making her cheekbones more pronounced, but also highlighting the gentle curve of her jawline.

She was glorious, and she belonged to him. He ached for the day that her shuttered green eyes finally looked at him, and she realized that he belonged to her as much as she did to him. It would happen. It had to happen. He just needed to be patient until she was ready to accept him. For now, her expression was neutral as she regarded him, her only acknowledgement a slight inclination of her head. At least she wasn't spitting at him as he'd expected.

"Is everything set?" Rafe joined them, his sons Ben and AJ at his side.

Both men had their father's tall frame, though Aaron junior's build was more athletic and his coloring favored his mother. His wavy, platinum blond hair was shorter than most of the male pack members, but it retained the unkempt look that was common among wolf shifters. He also sported a few days growth that further emphasized his wildness. His smile though was dazzling and took some of the edge off his appearance.

Ben was his father's double in just about all ways. He was as big and wide as the Alpha, and had the exact same coloring of dark brown unruly hair and deep brown eyes. The only thing he appeared to have taken from his mother's side was his nose. It was unusually long and elegant for so brawny a male. He, too, had a killer smile, and like his brother, was quick to display it. Both men smiled at them but didn't speak.

"We're all packed and ready to go," Liam answered, turning as Dayton followed the girls outside.

"Don't you need this?" The Beta held the book on dream walking in his hands, a half smile gracing his face when Reasa tutted under her breath.

"My apologies, I forgot to pick it up." She held out her arms for the book.

"I'll ride up with them," Dayton said to Rafe, his Alpha nodding his agreement.

"Ben and AJ are going too," Rafe informed the group, his tone firm. Not that any of them would have disagreed with their Alpha.

"Lily and Kal are already up at the other compound and the boys will be staying for the duration too. I think three extra Varcolac and a couple of strong wolves should be enough for security. The Praetorian Compound is being patrolled by the pack as standard anyway, so there will always be additional wolves to call on if needed. Let's just all make sure it isn't needed." His final words were directed at Reasa, who met his gaze without flinching.

"I have no intention of causing any further distress to your pack," the former vampire answered.

"Glad to hear it," Rafe replied, treating her to a warm smile. "If you and Liam can do what Annie thinks you can, well let's just say that will go some way to making amends for past actions. It's not going to absolve you completely, Reasa, but it will be a start."

She nodded her head, accepting what he said. The Alpha's honesty was something she could understand and therefore respect. She hadn't detected one lie from him and that was something she found surprising given the relationship between wolves and vampires in Europe. She had always believed they were liars and couldn't be trusted. It would appear she was learning many new things with her time spent in the Armand-Hanlon compound.

"Okay, everyone load up and get yourselves up to the Praetorian Compound."

They turned and headed towards the two waiting Jeeps at Rafe's command. Reasa had barely taken two steps when the air suddenly became tense and her head whipped around to see Pietro standing in the doorway of one of the other dwellings close by. For an instant she was frozen on the spot, her gaze locked with eyes blazing with hatred, and then she was pulled behind Liam's large frame, hidden from the vampire's view.

"Pietro... " Rafe growled... an unmistakable warning in his tone.

A loud hiss filled the air... a sharp clacking noise following quickly. Reasa didn't need to be able to see to know that the vampire had gone feral. Was today going to be the day that she died? She fervently hoped not. She wanted to try to heal the wounded vampires' minds. If she died after that... well at least she would have done something to try to repair the damage she'd caused.

She was there right in front of him. So close he could taste the warmth of her blood in his mouth, could feel her soft flesh parting in jagged tears as his talons shredded her body. So close, and yet, denied to him by the assembled group of wolves who protected her. Pietro hissed out in fury, his eyes darting quickly from one face to the next, cataloguing each position, as he worked out what sequence he would take to circumnavigate everyone to get to his target.

Liam he would leave until last. He would take down Rafe first, he was Alpha and the others would go to his aid without thinking about it. Elina would hang back to protect her cousin, so she would be next, leaving Liam in a moment's confusion over who to protect first. If he went to Elina's aid then good, Thereasa would be his for the taking. If not... he would have to deal with the huge Varcolac before he could satisfy his bloodlust.

The thoughts took barely a moment to careen through his mind before he was moving, ignoring the warning voices, his eyes black pools of rage as he flowed towards the Alpha. Sounds clamoured on the air, growls and voices, his name being yelled repeatedly, but he was blind and deaf to all. Instinct drove him, fury and vengeance blazing through his feral mind. She had to die and she had to die now!

Pietro swiped out a hand, batting away the two males who dived in front of their father. They crashed to the ground, instantly forgotten as he focused on the now dark brown wolf as the Alpha shifted to animal form.

"No! Pietro, no!"

The voice screamed at him, fought to be heard through the feral snarls growling from his lips. He knew that voice, had heard it whisper husky words of need and passion, but he ruthlessly pushed it aside. He would not be denied his kill.

The Alpha charged and Pietro lashed out, catching the huge beast in his arms and tossing it backwards. It was on its feet in a fraction of a second, coiling to spring again as he readied his talons to cut into flesh. The venom dripped from his fangs and he had the briefest moment of lucidity. He mustn't bite... he mustn't bite...

The wolf jumped, surrounded by a cacophony of sound, and Pietro struck out with his talons.

Pale blonde hair filled his vision, exquisite blue eyes filled with such fear. The wolf was behind her, shoved out of the way as she flowed into his vision, her stance defensive. His talons passed by her cheekbone by the barest of fractions, one nicking ever so lightly, causing the smallest of marks that instantly healed.

Cassia threw herself into his arms, holding him in a crushing embrace, so strong that he couldn't push her away. She wasn't fighting him, she was merely holding onto him, her words whispering in his ears. "Don't do this, Pietro. Please, please don't do this."

The urge to rid himself of the thing preventing his kill ran so deep it took everything in him not to plunge his talons into the soft, warm body embracing him. He wanted to... he needed to... but she was Cassia, and he could never do anything to physically hurt her.

"Pietro, be calm. Please be calm. Think about what you're trying to do."

As suddenly as the rage had overwhelmed him it died in the face of her words. Reason began to surface, and with that reason, he felt something else inside him die. He had been promised sanctuary with the pack. He had been promised so much, but when it came down to what he truly needed, he was very much on his own.

The one person he had come to rely on to understand him, was the very person who had stood in his way, using his attachment to her to thwart him. Cassia had to have known he could never hurt her. She had to have known that of everyone in the pack she was the only one he would have listened to in his feral state. She had known and she had used that knowledge against him!

"Release me, Cassia. I am once again in control of my actions." The words sounded dull to his ears and from the way she stiffened against him, he knew they did to her too. She held on a moment longer, long enough to whisper for his ears only.

"I'm so sorry... "

It didn't matter. No words she said could ever remove the feeling of betrayal he felt inside at knowing she had deliberately used his feelings for her against him. It was a hot knife in his gut, a pain so intense it eclipsed even the worst pain he could remember from Europe. Cassia had sided with the pack against him. She had betrayed him.

Pietro stepped back when she released him, avoiding looking at her beautiful face. He didn't want to look at her. He didn't want to see the remorse he knew would be there because that was who she was, someone who cared so much she would bleed inside at ever hurting someone she cared about. He didn't have anything left in him at that moment to forgive her. All he had was the knowledge that he was alone, as he had always been alone.

His gaze swept over the surrounding pack. The centre of the compound was now full of wolves, all looking at him, waiting for him to go feral again. Rafe was checking over his sons, reassuring himself they weren't harmed. Pietro hadn't meant to hurt them, just remove them from the fight. He knew they would recover quickly from any bumps and scrapes they may have taken.

There was no sign of Thereasa. From the ring surrounding one of the jeeps, he could take a guess that she was safely ensconced inside the vehicle. Nors was there as was Alexei, arms folded with disapproving frowns on their faces. They left him in no doubt that he would have to go through both of them to get to woman, and he had no illusions that they would hurt him badly if he tried.

Even Andrei was glaring at him from his left side, fury dancing in his friend's eyes. They were all condemning him, his friends of hundreds of years turning against him as Cassia had. With a long, loud hiss, Pietro spun on his heel, walking back into the home he had shared with his friends. He knew what he had to do.

"Pietro, wait... "

"Go away, Cassia. I have nothing to say to you." "You have to understand... we couldn't allow you to hurt Reasa. We just couldn't. I know she hurt you, Pietro. I understand your need for vengeance but it would kill Liam for anything to happen to her, and she's changing. She truly is changing, Pietro."

He wanted to shut out her voice. He wanted to ignore the plea that rang from every word she spoke. He wanted her to just be gone but this was her pack so that wasn't likely to happen. Spinning around, he impaled her with a look that contained all of his rage, all of his feelings of betrayal.

"I understand, Cassia. The pack will always come first with you, as it is what defines you. I am not pack though. I will never be pack or understand that group mentality. Thereasa ruined my life. She turned me into this thing I am now. I will never be happy until she is dead. Today you chose, Cassia. You chose pack over me and while I can understand that on a rational level, I can't on an emotional one. You betrayed me."

Pietro wanted to reach for her even as he said the words that he knew would cut her to the quick. Seeing the tears in her eyes filled him with so much misery that for a moment it almost overcame his feelings of betrayal. But those feelings were too ingrained in his heart and mind. He had trusted in her, he had let down his defences and let her close, and in that moment when he needed her to understand; she had turned against him.

"Tell Rafe I will be off pack lands within the hour. I don't want to spend another second longer here than I have to." Pietro turned away, hardening his heart to the pained whimper that came from the beautiful blonde wolf that had begun to mean so much to him.

"Please don't do this. Please, Pietro. Give yourself time to calm down. We can talk again once you've had a little time... "

"I don't want to see you ever again, Cassia. What we had is over." Misery overwhelmed him at his words and at the tortured sound that escaped her lips, but Pietro forced himself to keep walking up the stairs away from her. Though it hurt him to say it, he knew he wouldn't change his mind. What they had was truly over, whether he wept at the thought or not.

Pietro was leaving her!

Her mate was refusing her, denying her the only chance she had at happiness. Cassia tried to speak, tried to make him listen, but her tears were flowing too fast, the ball of pain inside so intense it felt as if it was choking her.

He had to understand... he couldn't mean what he was saying. She'd had to stop him from hurting her Alpha, from hurting Thereasa and in doing so, her pack. Why couldn't he understand? Why couldn't he just stay and listen to her?

"Pietro... " the word strangled out on a sob, her voice pleading for him to listen but he continued to walk away, never once looking back.

"Cassia, come on, honey. Come home." Dara was at her side, her sister feeling her pain and reaching out to enclose her in an embrace, to soothe her with her wolf's touch.

"Dara... Dara... oh God Dara... "

Cassia's wolf howled its grief inside her mind and she gave herself over to the animal, unable to bear talking any further. She shifted to wolf form, spinning around and racing through the open door out into the forest.

The wolf howled; the woman screamed internally. They raced through the trees, mindless of where they were going, heedless of any who followed. She crashed into trees, tumbling head over heels and then picking herself up to race off in another direction. All the while she howled her anguish, cried out against the torture that was her mate's rejection.

Cassia ran and ran and ran until she fell to the forest floor exhausted, panting and heaving as she whimpered out her distress. Soft hands stroked over her fur, a loving touch holding her shaking wolf form, whispering words tripping over themselves as they rushed out.

"It will be okay, Cass. I know it will. Pietro just needs some time. It will all work out, you'll see. Please don't weep so, honey. Please. You are strong and I am with you. I will always be with you."

Dara was crying with her, holding her wolf, and rocking her back and forth. She could feel her sister's pain echoing down their familial bond, knew she ached for her grief as much as she did. Dara, who had always been there for her, always been that second part of her from the moment she had been born and they'd first touched minds.

"It hurts so badly, Dara. It hurts so badly."

"I know, sweetheart, but you're strong enough to cope. Lean on me, honey. I've got you and I'll never let go."

Cassia surrendered to the grief of losing her mate, throwing her head back and letting out one long, anguish-filled mournful howl as her sister kept her word, holding her and never letting her go.

Pietro's head shot up and his gaze turned to the forest through his window, the awful howl ringing on the air for all to hear. He knew it was Cassia who was hurting so badly and he wanted to go to her but his feet wouldn't move. Instead, he turned back to his packing, throwing the last of his clothes haphazardly into his case.

"Are you proud of yourself?" Andrei growled from the doorway.

Pietro turned to look at his friend, seeing the signs in his body language that Andrei was barely in control of himself. "I take no pleasure from hurting Cassia." He snapped the suitcase closed.

"What the fuck were you thinking, Pietro?" His friend stepped into the room, fist clenched in an effort to hold back his feral side. "The pack took you in, gave you a sanctuary and this is how you repay them?"

"Some sanctuary," Pietro snarled back, his aggression levels escalating to match Andrei's. "You let the instrument of my torture live and breathe, Andrei. I can remember a day when you of all people would have ripped someone to pieces for much less but now you roll over and do whatever the wolves ask of you. And you ask me what the fuck I was thinking? What the fuck where you and Alexei thinking?"

The other male paused, taking a deep breath before relaxing his clenched fists. "It's not that cut and dried and you know it, Pietro." Andrei sighed deeply and ran a hand through his hair. "The pack is our family now and we have to consider the bigger picture. Believe me, I understand your need for vengeance. We all do, my friend. You have to meet us half way though; you have to understand that we're doing the best we can here."

"I can't!" Pietro hissed, turning away to grab his case. When he turned back, he'd wiped all expression from his face. "All I see is the people who always had my back are now protecting someone who is the cause of my disfigurement. All I see is those I call friend have aligned themselves against me."

"That's fucking bullshit and you know it! Where the fuck are you, Pietro? The man I know wouldn't wallow in self-pity and pitch a hissy-fit because things aren't going his way. And what the fuck did you do to my niece? Why are you breaking her heart? I should be kicking the shit out of you for that reason alone."

His reference to Cassia was too much, and Pietro dropped the case, hissing at his friend. "Then why the fuck aren't you? Go ahead... kick the shit out of me! Do it!"

Andrei's expression turned cold, the warmth dying from his eyes. "If I touched you right now, I would most likely take your head, Pietro. It's for that reason alone I'm ensuring that I retain a modicum of control. You're too weak to fend me off. It would be like slaughtering a Youngling."

Pietro glared at him a moment longer, before he reached for the case once more and stepped past his friend. "Thanks for the reminder of why we're all in this fucked up position in the first place. I never meant to hurt Cassia, Andrei, I truly didn't. She hurt me first though, but I guess that will always be a moot point with you and Alexei when it comes to one of your own. That I can understand."

"Pietro... "

He halted on his way out of the room, not turning to look back as Andrei called his name.

"I expect you back behind the bar at The Dive tonight. I suggest you use the apartment over the bar for a while until you're feeling more like yourself."

It was Andrei's way of telling him that no matter what had happened this day, he still counted him as his friend and would have his back to the best of his ability. Pietro was aware it was more than he probably deserved but he accepted it as gracefully as he could.

"I'll see you later then."

"Dara, let me, honey." Alexei's calm words belied the expression on his face as he ushered one daughter aside to reach the other.

She looked up through tear-filled eyes to see her parents beside them, her mother clearly having shifted into her wolf form at some point, as she now stood naked before them. "She won't stop weeping. I can't do anything to help her."

Her mother held out her arms, enfolding her in a tight embrace. "That's our job, sweetheart, not yours, though you are a credit to all of us that you have tried so hard." Gentle hands soothed down her back, trying to take the ache from her heart at her sister's distress. "Can you rustle me up something to wear, honey? There's a bit of a nip in the air."

Smothering down another sob, Dara fought for some composure and the concentration she would need to accede to her mother's request. She knew it was a deliberate attempt to redirect her, and she was grateful to her mother for it. She was no help to Cassia being an emotional wreck. She needed to be Cassia's strength right now.

Taking a deep breath and doing her best to tune everything out around her, Dara tapped into the well of power she had inside, conjuring up a sarong in deep forest green. It was easier to create single bolts of cloth as opposed to specific clothing, and it appeared her mother was content with her offering as Cedar wrapped the sarong around her body.

Turning back to Cassia, Dara watched her father kneel beside her, his hands gentle as they stroked through the wolf's tangle fur.

"Cass, honey, you can't hide within your wolf. I know it's hard right now but you need to come back to us. You need to let us take care of you." Alexei kept his words soft and low, all the while his hands continued to stroke the wolf as he talked.

"Come, daughter. Show me that wonderful strength I know that lives within your heart. Return to your family. Come home to us."

For a long moment it appeared as if she would refuse him, and then the wolf shifted into the woman, curled up on the forest floor. The second she shifted, Alexei scooped her up into his arms and she burrowed her face into the side of his neck, loud sobs wracking her body.

"He doesn't want me, Daddy. My mate doesn't want me."

Alexei's footsteps faltered as he started walking towards his mate and youngest daughter, a flash of fury in his eyes. His gaze fell on Dara after Cedar gave a quick shake of her head.

"Explain." The word ground out in a low voice almost over-shadowed by Cassia's crying.

Dara swallowed hard, trying not to shrink back against her mother, who continued to run a hand down her back.

"Alexei, please moderate your tone," Cedar remarked, a hint of censure in her tone. "Whatever is going on is not of Dara's making, and she deserves better than that from her father."

The rebuke in her tone was enough to get through her mate's initial fury, and he conceded her point, giving Dara an apologetic smile. "I'm sorry, Dara. I'm just concerned for your sister. Please tell us what you know."

Relieved to see a more normal expression on her father's face, Dara straightened up, giving him a tentative smile back. "I don't know much, Dad. Cassia told me that Pietro was her mate but that her wolf was acting a bit strange about it... as if it couldn't quite make up its mind one way or the other."

"That's impossible," Cedar interjected, a frown marring her face as she reached out to Cassia and stroked a hand through her weeping daughter's hair. "Our wolves always know - instantly."

"Cassia says otherwise," her daughter answered, shrugging her shoulders. "I wouldn't know personally as I haven't met my mate yet."

"One at a time... " Alexei muttered under his breath, his tone rueful as he cradled Cassia tenderly in his arms as they headed back towards the compound. She had finally stopped weeping, though it was apparent she was lost somewhere within herself. "Is Pietro aware of this?"

There was no mistaking the hard edge to his voice and Dara was glad the vampire would be gone by the time they got back. There was no telling what her father might do giving his current mood. "As far as I know, Cassia was taking things slowly with him, giving him time to heal from Europe before making her claim. I don't think he's aware of it despite the fact they've been spending a lot of time together."

"Lucky for him." Again the words were muttered, a dangerous edge to each one.

"Alexei," Cedar sighed, placing a hand on his arm to try to sooth the rage she could feel flowing through their mate bond.

"Look at her, Cedar. Look at our girl. Don't expect me to be rational about this when Cassia is hurting this badly. I just can't do it."

"Don't you think I'm every bit as concerned as you are, Alexei?" she answered quietly, unable to hide her disappointment. "Don't you think my heart is breaking seeing our daughter so distressed? One of us has to keep a level head about this, and of course, that person is going to have to be me, as it always it. I don't get the luxury of exploding into a temper and protecting my daughter because I'm too busy ensuring you don't do something stupid that will make things worse."

It was so unusual to hear the trace of bitterness in her voice that for a moment Alexei stopped walking, surprise crossing his face. Dara was equally surprised and uncomfortable witnessing one her parents' rare fights. She wasn't sure whether she should keep walking or stay with them.

Her father remained silent for a long moment, and then his expression softened and he leaned down to kiss his mate, brushing his cheek against the top of her head. "I'm sorry, I know you're just as concerned, honey. I'll promise to behave."

As quickly as Cedar had become irritated, her expression mellowed and she rolled her eyes in disbelief. "You don't even know the meaning of the word, Alexei Romanov, but I'm holding you to that promise."

With the disagreement over with as soon as it had begun; they broke through the trees and entered the pack compound. It was clear of most of the people from earlier, however Rafe was sitting on the steps to his house, his eyes pinned to them as they walked out of the forest. He rose and met them half way, his trouble gaze on Cassia.

"Is she okay? Do you need to use the safe room?"

Alexei looked to Cedar for the answer, relieved when she shook her head. "I don't think so, Rafe. Let us spend some time with her as a family. If we need you, we'll let you know."

The Alpha placed a hand on Cassia's head, leaning down to brush his lips against her cheek. "If you need us we are here for you." He said the words aloud and sent them down the Alpha link he shared with each pack member. There was no response from Cassia but he was certain she'd heard him. Straightening up, his concerned gaze met Alexei's and Cedar's. "Lacey will want to check in on her later."

"Lacey is welcome to visit anytime, as are you, Rafe. However, can we keep it to a minimum just now?" Cedar asked. "We don't want to overload Cassia with too many people around; not until she's had a chance to recover from today's events."

"Agreed. I'll have Aaron spread the word not to disturb you." Rafe nodded his head to Alexei, silently communicating that he wanted to speak with Cedar out of Cassia's earshot. The vampire continued on his way with his daughters, leaving his mate to discuss whatever their Alpha wanted to impart.

"Pietro left the pack a quarter of an hour ago," Rafe announced as soon as they disappeared into their family home. "I don't know if that's going to be a good thing or not for Cassia, but I thought it would be best if either you or Alexei broke the news to her."

Cedar's already concerned expression darkened further, her worried eyes turning towards her home. "Do you know where he went? If we can at least tell her that it may take some of the sting from knowing he's left."

"Andrei said Pietro will be staying at the Dive and taking over his responsibilities there from tonight, so he'll still be afforded some level of protection from the vampires that Andrei trusts while he recovers. Hopefully some time apart will show Pietro how much he misses Cassia. He is her mate, I take it?"

Cedar sighed and rubbed her hands across her face wearily. "It's certainly looking that way, though she did tell Dara that her wolf appeared to be undecided on the matter. I'm still reeling over that one, Rafe. I didn't think it was possible for a wolf to be confused."

"Neither did I," the Alpha frowned raking a hand through his hair, before giving his beta a reassuring hug. "I'll talk to Rayne before she leaves and have a word with Annie and Caleb too. Maybe there's something in their books that can explain it. We have to remember that the Varcolac are not like purebred Weres or Vampires. What applies to the rest of us may not necessarily apply to them."

With another quick squeeze, Rafe released Cedar so she could go to her daughter. As she disappeared from view, he pulled out his cell and dialled Rayne's number. He needed to have a last word with Gard and Rayne before they headed to Europe anyway. They had to decide whether it was wise to leave Kothari on his own with just Dara checking in with him. Given the turn of events with Cassia, Dara may be otherwise distracted.

The Jeep made its way up the mountain, Elina behind the wheel with Liam and Reasa in the back. The second Jeep shadowed them closely, Dayton, Ben and AJ bringing up the rear. Rafe's sons were unaffected by their tussle with the vampire. Pietro hadn't hurt them much and they'd insisted they were fine to continue with the task their father had set them. It had been a proud Alpha who had clapped each son on his shoulder and sent him on his way.

Liam's emotions were mixed, his heart going out to Cassia as he felt her pain as they all did. He was strangely detached when he thought of Pietro and his actions. He felt some level of anger towards the vampire for trying to harm his mate and hurting his friends, but he could also understand what had driven Pietro to act as he had, and that took some of the edge from his anger.

They could all understand and that was probably why, despite what had happened, there wasn't an overabundance of hostility towards the vampire. Liam had heard some mutterings from the younger pack members as they were heading off, but wiser, calmer heads in the pack would work to subdue any antipathy towards Pietro and the vampires in general. Aaron would probably assign some intensive border patrols so the more hot¬headed youngsters could blunt their anger. By the time they returned to the pack, the incident would have become just another story to tell on a balmy night sitting around a fire.

That left Liam with only one real emotion to ponder; his fear that his mate would have been hurt, and what he would have been prepared to do to prevent that ever happening. He was ashamed of the thoughts that had flooded his mind as Pietro struck out. All the gentleness that made him who he was evaporated on the spot, and the feral vampiric side of himself had taken dominance.

He had considered killing Pietro to protect Thereasa. The thought had actually crossed his mind, his vampire urging him to reach out and take the other male's head. How could he even think such a thing? He was aware that Cassia was attached to the vampire, knew now that Pietro was her mate given her reaction to his rejection. His friend had placed his needs and the pack's before her own, and he had considered doing the worst thing a wolf could ever do to another pack member.

What kind of monster did that make him? How could his family, his friends, every single pack member protect him, protect Reasa for him, when he wasn't worth their efforts? This couldn't continue... things couldn't go on as they were. Cassia deserved her happiness with her mate and that would never happen as long as he and Reasa remained at the pack. There really wasn't any other option. They would have to leave the pack once they'd done all they could at the Praetorian Compound. There would never be a place for them there. Recent events proved that.

"We won't allow it." Elina's cool words broke the oppressive silence in the car.

"You won't have a choice." Liam wasn't surprised that his cousin could guess at what he was thinking. She always seemed to know what was going on inside his head; she'd lived in it for long enough.

"What?" Reasa didn't look at him, her gaze remaining fixed ahead.

"Liam is coming to the conclusion that you will both be leaving the pack. I am just disabusing him of it."

Reasa's gaze turned to the man at her side and for a second she almost smiled at the stubborn expression she saw on his face. Once more she was struck by the strong familial bond between the cousins, and even if she hadn't been aware of their history from walking through Liam's memory, she would still have sensed their strong attachment.

"You need your pack," she said, turning away to look out the window. "You are not a solitary creature and would not thrive well without them."

"Pietro is Cassia's mate, Reasa. Today has proven that to all of us. She will never be happy without him, and he will never come to accept you. His inability to forgive you will continue his rejection of my friend. I cannot cause her pain so I can be happy." Liam's quiet words hung heavy on the air, a faint quiver in his voice.

Reasa didn't answer him. It was hard to refute his words. Pietro's need for vengeance was too ingrained. He was the kind of male others in her coven had aspired to be and could never attain that level of strength. She understood males like Pietro; she not only understood them, she respected them. Louis was one who held the same strength, the same determination as the wounded vampire back at the compound. He would mete out the same type of justice Pietro yearned for, and she would deserve it for her actions.

The situation was currently at a stalemate though. For one couple to be happy the other couple must suffer. From that point of view, Liam's logic made sense and while she couldn't argue with it, she was as determined as Elina not to allow it to pass. She would have to find some way to resolve the situation once they had helped the patients at the Praetorian Compound. She was aware of what she had to do, and she knew that Liam would do his utmost to prevent it. However, it wasn't his decision to make. When the time came, she would stand before Pietro alone and accept his judgement.

Elina also knew the truth of it, though she continued to deny it because she didn't want to lose her cousin. While she argued with Liam about his proposed course of action, her eyes met Reasa's in the rear-view mirror, and the former vampire could see that the other woman had an inkling of what she was thinking.

"The pack is strong, Liam. We have that strength because we stick together no matter what. Don't lose faith in us. We will find a way to resolve this." Even though spoken in a cold tone, there was passion in Elina's voice as she appealed to her cousin. Reasa heard the underlying words being spoken to her too, and her admiration for the other woman rose. If they had met under any other circumstances, Reasa was sure she would have called the other woman a friend.

Liam's expression remained stubborn, though he leaned back and rested his head, closing his eyes as he did. He was completely clueless about the unspoken communication between his mate and his cousin. "Let's just concentrate on what needs to be done for now. The rest is a while away. This is more important."

Reasa mirrored his position, closing her eyes and once more seeing Pietro standing in the compound, naked hatred oozing from every pore in his body, all projected towards her. She felt the same thrill of terror as she had then, followed by a feeling of disappointment as Liam had shielded her. Had she wanted to die in that moment? That thought had followed her around ever since she'd had her vampiric nature stripped from her. There had been times when she'd truly believed it was what she wanted and others when she'd wanted to cling to life.

The only thing she really knew was that it wasn't her decision or Liam's about what would happen in the future. There was only one person who had the right to decide her fate, and she only hoped she would be courageous enough to stand tall before him when he made it.

The Jeep pulling into the Praetorian Compound shook her from her musings, and she opened her eyes to view the large house that was home to the Praetorians. Elina pulled up close to the steps and pulled on the handbrake. It was strange being back. Exciting and yet terrifying. The last time Reasa had been here, she'd lost everything that had made her who she was. She wasn't able to contain the shiver that ran through her body.

"No one will hurt you here," Liam rumbled, his voice low, for her ears only.

"There is nothing further that anyone could do to hurt me than what has already been done," she answered, stiffening her back as the door opened and a large vampire with flowing black hair came out to greet them.

Mac greeted the arrivals with a touch of caution laced with optimism. He was relieved they were here and willing to try to help his injured people, but he was wary too, given his mate's involvement. Lily was happy and bright, so certain that Liam and Reasa were going to save the day with this new skill they'd discovered, but he was concerned about what would happen if they failed.

His mate's eyes held a hint of sadness every time he looked into them. Though she smiled and went about her life with the wonderful strength and resilience he'd fallen in love with, he could always detect that small hint of melancholy that lived within her because of Brandon. She missed her friend keenly, cared for him devotedly, and if this didn't work... if they lost him... he knew his beautiful mate would die a little inside.

"How sure are you about this?" He asked the question of Liam and Reasa, as they were the ones who would be performing the dream walking.

"There is no certainty, Mac, just the hope that we can affect a positive change." It was Liam who answered, his tone grave. "We know what's at stake. If it can be done... we will do it. That's the best we can give you."

"Fair enough." Mac wasn't feeling as comforted as he'd hoped he would. He nodded to the Weres who had escorted Reasa to the compound and motioned for them to precede him into the large house that was the heart of the Praetorians.

"We'll stay outside," Dayton announced. "There's nothing we can do inside and we're muscle rather than brains up here. We'll check in with the other wolves and do a sweep around the compound." He headed off into the trees, followed by Ben and AJ.

"I will attend inside," Elina said, walking up the steps into the house, patently ignoring the brawny blond vampire who was standing in the hallway as she entered.

"Good to see you too, Missy," Karn chuckled, blue eyes flashing with mischief as she sailed passed him and started upstairs.

"Idiot." Wafted back down the stairs and only made him chuckle harder.

"Behave," Mac growled, giving his friend a glare.

Karn's made a half-hearted attempt at looking sheepish but his attention was already diverted from the frosty woman intent on ignoring him, a speculative gleam in his eyes as he looked at Liam and Reasa. "I think I can do a little of what you can. Would I be in the way if I tagged along and tried to pick up some tips?"

Mac's head whipped around in surprise as Liam gave his friend a nod. "You're empathic? You never told me that."

"You never asked," Karn countered with a grin. "And why would I? We all keep our skills to ourselves. Perhaps that's why they're so diluted now. We're all so busy trying to be the biggest badass around that sharing unique talents has never been in our best interests. How the hell do you think I've managed to keep this motley crew in line for so long, Mac?"

It was a rhetorical question but the leader of the Praetorian's answered anyway. "You've had an inkling of what they were thinking or feeling." "Feeling," his friend confirmed. "When you can sense emotions it's easier to divert the ones you don't want to be predominant in any given situation." Mac looked stunned and a bit put out at only now learning what his second in command could do, but Karn was unrepentant. If this new knowledge of shadow walking hadn't materialised, he would have kept his mouth shut about his abilities.

"I have no objections to you observing, Karn," Liam said, his lips curling in a small smile. "The more people who can hone their skills the better." He glanced at the woman at his side before turning back to the waiting vampires. "Should we make a start?"

With a concerned expression Mac nodded and motioned for them to head upstairs to the infirmary.

"You doubt we will be successful," Reasa commented as she passed him, feeling oddly comfortable in his presence. He reminded her of Louis a little, with perhaps a tad less of a cruel streak in his eyes. She didn't doubt for a moment that the Praetorian leader wasn't capable of cruelty, just that he was less inclined to veer in that direction.

"Brandon is close to Lily's heart. If you try this and fail, her heart will break. In saying that, this is the lesser of two evils so I am willing to give it a try."

She could understand his position, and hoped they could affect a positive change on the vampires. There was a lot at stake, not only the hopes of all those who cared for the injured, but also the mental well-being of the Varcolac at her side. There was no accounting for what Liam would do if they failed. It didn't bear thinking about.

Reasa tried to convince herself that it was the emotional backlash of Liam's powers that concerned her, but she knew she was lying to herself. Though it was a strong factor to be considered, the kiss she had shared with Liam was still very firmly emblazoned in her memory. She should have been furious about the liberty he'd taken, and a part of her was, but mostly she longed for another taste of his lips, to see if his kiss had truly been as amazing as her memory told her it was. Shaking the memory from her mind as best she could, Reasa entered the door to the large infirmary, her gaze quickly sweeping the area.

Beside the very first bed that came into view stood Elina gazing down at the dark-haired male lying there. For all intents and purposes he gave off the appearance of being dead. Her expression was neutral, no sign of her inner thoughts as she watched the male for a moment longer and then walked gracefully over to the nearby window to rest against the window seat facing into the room.

Sitting in a comfy armchair beside the bed was Lily, a book in hand that she was reading out loud to the sleeping male. At their entrance, the Varcolac finished the paragraph she was reading and then turned grave eyes to them. "I hate this book but it's one of Brandon's favourites. Please wake him up so he can finish the damned thing himself."

Lily rose from the chair, smiling a sad smile as she dropped a kiss on Brandon's forehead. "See you soon, Bran."

She walked across to them, slipping effortlessly into Liam's waiting arms. For a moment they just hugged quietly and then Lily straightened and stepped back, acceptance in her expression. "I know you will do your very best, Liam. Don't do anything that endangers you though, not for Brandon, and not for the others. They were your protectors and they wouldn't want you to do anything that caused you harm. Keep that firmly in mind." She was silently granting forgiveness in advance... should they fail at their task.

Liam nodded solemnly, guilt threatening to overwhelm him again. He was the reason six souls lay trapped or destroyed within their host bodies, and his beautiful friend was granting him absolution if he couldn't rectify his grievous error. He didn't deserve it and he wouldn't fail. He would stay there for however long it took to bring each and every one of the injured vampires back.

"I think you should go be somewhere else, Lily," he answered, his gaze dropping to her abdomen. "I have no idea how much, if any, emotional leakage will seep into the room as we try this. It would probably be best if you weren't present as a precaution."

"I don't want to leave Brandon... " Lily started to say, her gaze sweeping back to her friend as she spoke. Her mate was already moving though to gather her up against his chest and pull her towards the doorway.

"You heard Liam, this has never been done before and we don't know what may happen. I will not countenance any harm coming to you or our daughter, Liliana."

She knew she couldn't argue with Mac. She didn't have any intention of it. It was right that she shouldn't be around so much empathy right now and she would never do anything to risk their child. As if she would even consider causing her mate to, once more, lose the most precious thing in his world. "You never let me finish," she smiled up at Mac, sending soothing love down their mate bond. "I had been about to say I didn't want to leave Brandon but it would be best if I wasn't around such charged emotions. I'm not completely stupid, my love."

His frown lightened and then his expression turned sheepish. "Overreacting again, uh?"

CHAPTER 2

Though his words were conciliatory, his tone was implacable and brought a loving smile to her face as she gave him a reassuring hug. "It's understandable. Let me know if there is any improvement."

Mac kissed his mate, long and slow, giving her as much love and reassurance as he could. He was aware that her heart was breaking and she was afraid to hope for a good outcome. He wanted to tell her it would all be okay but he truly didn't know if it would. He finally raised his head and cupped her cheek tenderly. "You'll be the first to know, my Lily Rose."

Satisfied, the pregnant Varcolac headed from the room, leaving everyone staring quietly at Brandon for a long moment.

"I think it's best if we try this on Brandon first," Liam finally broke the silence. It appeared the expectation was there from the Praetorians that his friend was to be the first attempt anyway, so he was merely formalising the thought. "We need another comfortable chair. I don't know how long this may take."

Karn left the room and Elina came forward to look up at her cousin. "I can shield the room as you work. It won't be the best of shields as I'll need to cast it across everyone present, but it should help if there is some emotional leakage."

Liam considered it for a moment and then shook his head. "That kind of shield would be mostly ineffective and not a good use of your talents." He glanced at Reasa and then back to his cousin. "Reasa's control is exceptional. I'm not concerned about any issues there. I think it would be best if you buffered my defences instead. You're used to my mind so it will be second nature to you."

"And you will feel more confident in yourself knowing I am doing so," Elina said telepathically for his ears only.

"Yes I would, Elle. I am so much stronger with the new shielding techniques I've learned but this... this will just make me feel a bit better."

Karn's return into the room with a second plush armchair halted their conversation and Elina once more returned to her spot at the window. As Karn set it down beside its matching companion, she let her gaze run over the vampire that had managed to break through the cold defences she'd honed to perfection. She was still perturbed that she'd lashed out at him with such violence. Her loss of control had been unforgivable, no matter what the circumstances had been. It was unfortunate he would be present during this exercise, when she needed all of her control, but she would find a way to ignore him.

As if realising he was under scrutiny, Karn turned his head to look at her, his lips curling in another insufferable smile as his pale blue eyes twinkled and seem to convey that he knew just what she was thinking. Looking away, Elina turned inward, feeling the link that connected her to her cousin and concentrating solely on that as she slipped into Liam's mind and wove a delicate net of spidery tendrils around his impressive defences. Her web looked flimsy but it was as strong as she could make it. If Liam's control broke, well there would be at least a small fraction of time for the others to run before total catastrophe occurred.

Turning back to her cousin, she watched him and Reasa sit down beside Brandon's bed, the ancient tome open in Liam's lap as he quickly ran his gaze over a couple of pages. She stiffened when Karn moved to her side, resting his back against the wall beside her.

"Can I shadow you?"

Every single part of her being screamed NO but she ignored her instincts to push him away and relaxed as best she could. "I am only an additional shield for Liam. You will not learn anything from that."

"Guess, I will be the judge of that?" he countered swiftly, and she knew he would cause a scene if she continued to thwart him and that was counter-productive to why they were all here.

"Fine." Elina allowed entry into her mind, trying not to lash out instinctively when she felt the pure male dominance of the vampire by her side slip easily inside and nestle close to her own defences. She ignored him as best she could, relaxing further when he didn't push at her inner defences but instead examined her link with Liam and followed that path to her cousin's mind.

"Impressive." There was such respect and awe in Karn's tone that the last of Elina's misgivings eased and she concentrated on what was happening before them as opposed to fixating on the male at her side. She was relying on Karn not to violate the trust she was giving him. She only hoped that she wasn't wrong to do so.

Liam glanced at the woman at his side, meeting her apprehensive gaze. "Do you need more time?"

Reasa shook her head, rolling her shoulders to relax some of the tension suffusing her body. "No, we should begin."

At her acceptance, the large Varcolac closed the book and set it down on the floor. "Mac, it might be best to clear the house of anyone who doesn't need to be here."

"That's already been done, Liam. Everyone who is here needs to be here," the Praetorian leader answered calmly, signalling the Weres and vampires who were tending to the others. "We can't afford to leave the others uncared for while this is happening. Everyone present has volunteered to be here."

Again, it was as if he was being absolved of any responsibility in advance, and Liam felt another moment's doubt that he could, not only, bring the vampires back, but deserved any forgiveness.

"We should begin, Liam."

Reasa's practical tone helped to balance him and he nodded his head slowly, turning to look at Brandon lying so peacefully in the bed. "Time to come back to us, Brandon," he muttered under his breath, feeling Reasa slipped effortlessly into his mind beside Elina.

Dear God it was hopeless!

That was the first thought that came to Liam's mind as he slipped into Brandon's and viewed the carnage that was there. Unlike everything he'd previously experienced, there was no long passageway with doors leading from it, straight or curving haphazardly as Reasa had described. He stood at the beginning of what appeared to be a maze, a ten-foot barrier of steel mesh in front of him.

"Reasa?" He couldn't keep the hopelessness from his voice and knew she picked up on it instantly.

"I've never seen anything like it before," she whispered, her tone horrified as she stood beside him. "Liam, this mind is gone. There is nothing we can do."

They were speaking aloud as they had done before, and he knew the others would be listening to every word they said. Despite concentrating solely on Brandon's mind, he could detect Mac's sharp, indrawn breath at Reasa's announcement. Liam refused to be defeated, refused to give up hope when they hadn't even tried yet.

"I don't accept that, Reasa. I can't accept that. We have to be able to do something."

"What? I have no experience of this. I don't know where to begin and that book didn't give us any answers for something as damaged as this. What can we do?"

Squaring his shoulders, Liam reached down and took her hand, to lend her strength and also to find some himself. "We can try, Reasa. We can try." Taking a step forward he pulled her through the opening in the steel mesh and deeper into the fractured mind before them.

The conversation between Liam and Reasa made Mac's heart sink. He had no idea what they were seeing inside

Brandon's mind but it sounded hopeless. He looked away from the bed, towards the window where Elina and Karn stood.

"Are you seeing what they're seeing?"

Elina shook her head, for once her serene expression clouded by a deep frown. "I can only feel their emotions, Mac. Whatever they're experiencing has stunned them. Reasa is convinced there is nothing they can do. Despite the fact she has more experience than Liam, he isn't willing to concede that point yet. Liam is determined they can prevail, but I'm not sure how much of that is wishful thinking on his part."

The Varcolac turned her gaze from the couple at the bed to the Praetorian leader. "Are you sure you can't clear out more people from the house? I'm unsure if I'll be able to contain Liam if this goes badly, Mac. Perhaps you should join Lily? We can't afford to lose you as Praetorian leader, let alone as Lily's mate."

A low growl from the male at her side had her head inclining in his direction.

"You should have more faith in your cousin... and yourself. Liam's shields are strong and the buffer you have in place buys us all a little time should something go wrong. Doubting Liam while you're in his mind isn't going to be of help," Karn remarked.

Mac considered their words when Elina didn't respond to his second in command, taking his time to digest the ramifications if things went wrong. Karn was right, they had an advanced warning system in place, and they could use the precious few seconds that Elina could grant them. For now, his place was here with his fallen, until such times it became too dangerous to remain. In addition, if Elina was right about Liam being unrealistic about their chances of success, someone had to be there to ensure neither he nor Reasa came to any harm. That was his job.

"I'm staying," he finally answered, his tone brooking no argument.

The Varcolac opened her mouth as if to say more but a hand on her arm diverted her attention and her frosty glare turned on Karn. "Do not touch me."

"Don't get excited, Missy. It wasn't that kind of touch."

Karn removed his hand, delighting in the irritated snort that escaped Elina's lips. He couldn't help baiting her at every possible turn, regardless of how dire the current situation was. There was something about the woman that brought out the devilment in him. It had been a long time since any woman had interested him on the level that Elina did. Mac's disapproving glare settled him down somewhat, and he settled back to let events unfold.

More steel mesh greeted Liam and Reasa as they moved forward into Brandon's mind. It bent and twisted, seeming to branch off into different paths. It was indeed a maze, one so twisted that they hit a dead end almost immediately and had to backtrack. Liam chose to go right, weaving through spaces so narrow he could feel steel barbs snagging at his arms. He ignored it, keeping his forward momentum until he hit another dead end.

"Back," he sighed, returning to the beginning and choosing the forward path this time. Liam refused to give up. The fact they were in a maze indicated some kind of order within Brandon's mind even if it was complicated. If the vampire's mind was truly destroyed then shouldn't there just be blackness or an absence of everything?

They continued forward, eyes flicking over every conceivable surface they could see. Liam had no idea what they were looking for and he doubted Reasa did too. He only hoped that they would recognise it when they did see it. The maze hit a dead end going forward halting them in their tracks again. They had the option of turning left or right, and Liam pondered which route to take first. Settling on the left, he turned to start off in that direction but Reasa resisted his movement.

"Wait! Stop!" she cried out, pulling him back, her gaze fixed on something on the ground at her feet.

Liam frowned, puzzled by why she had stopped him. He couldn't see anything other than grey stone and more steel mesh, but she was bending down low, peering at something just out of his line of sight. His gut instinct was to keep moving forward, however he had to concede that Reasa had been doing this a lot longer than he had. It was pointless bringing her with him if he was going to disregard her expertise.

Shifting his position to get a better vantage point, he saw what appeared to be a small dull glass bead. He had no idea what it was or why his mate considered it significant. It was clear she did as her brow was furrowed in a deep frown as she stared at it.

"Liam... " When she looked up at him there was a flicker of something in her eyes he couldn't quite make out.

"What is it?" He held his breath as he waited for her answer, hoping against hope it would be something positive. It just had to be something positive to ease the growing hopeless he was feeling.

"I think this is part of Brandon's psyche. Reach out with your emotions, as you did at the pack. You have to concentrate hard but you should be able to sense it stronger than I can. There's barely a flicker nudging at my senses."

It was difficult to bend down in the tight space beside her but Liam dropped to his knees uncaring that a steel barb scored down his back drawing blood. He reached out with his stronger senses, concentrating on the glass bead that looked so innocuous. At first he could detect nothing, and then, for the briefest of moments he sensed something, felt some kind of connection.

"I think you may be right," he whispered, the first tendrils of hope beginning to form within him. He called out to Brandon but there was no response, and yet, Reasa's hopeful expression helped to sooth his initial disappointment. If this was part of Brandon's psyche... if they could find more small pieces scattered throughout the maze...

"Can we fashion a receptacle? If there are more pieces splintered throughout the maze, we can gather them all together and maybe that will be enough for Brandon's mind to do the rest?"

As soon as he'd asked the question, a clear glass urn appeared before them, and Reasa reverently placed the glass bead into it. It looked so lost and alone within the huge jar, and yet, a little of the dullness appeared to have receded. Liam wasn't sure if it truly had, or if it was just wishful thinking on his part.

"We could be here for days looking for other parts of his psyche," Reasa said quietly, as they took a moment to pause and consider their options. "Perhaps we should split up? We can place a marker on each passage we've tried so the other doesn't waste time repeating steps already taken. If we find more of these beads we can add them to the urn by a simple thought command. The book said we could do that as long as we can hold onto the image we're transporting an object to."

Hope flared brighter within the Varcolac, his beautiful mate's idea brilliant in its simplicity. He had to dampen it down, had to try to put things in perspective. They were only surmising that they had found a piece of Brandon's psyche. It could be just what it appeared to be, a lone glass bead. However, Liam was sure they were on the right track despite his caution to himself. There had been that briefest flicker of consciousness. He was certain of that.

"I'll take the left and you take the right," he announced, standing up. He imagined a red ribbon tied into a bow against the steel mesh. "If you see this sign, I've been there already."

Reasa quickly imitated him, using a blue bow to mark her passage. They left the glass urn where they'd found the first bead so they would have a clear point of reference to project to if they found others. "Good luck," she said, turning and moving off into Brandon's mind.

"What the fuck?" Karn hissed out the words, drawing Mac's eyes to him.

"What?"

"There's blood on Liam's T-shirt!"

Elina flowed gracefully from her spot before the others could move, reaching to pull up the back of her cousin's t-shirt as gently as she could. Her alert gaze travelled the unbroken skin, a smear of blood being the only indicator that there had been an injury there. As they watched, Liam's skin tore open for a brief moment, and then instantly healed.

Karn's gaze was on Reasa, another hiss escaping as a long-jagged cut appear down her left arm. Unlike Liam, she didn't heal instantly. She no longer had vampiric healing abilities.

"Get them out!" Mac ordered, his voice terse as another cut appeared on Reasa's face, scoring down her right cheek.

"No!" Elina blocked him as he moved to shake Reasa, her steely gaze daring him to try to go through her. "Whatever is happening in there isn't life threatening. These cuts are shallow. Liam can heal himself. I will take care of Reasa. If there is any hope of them bringing Brandon back then they must be allowed to continue."

"How?" Mac demanded, fury dancing in his eyes as another shallow cut appeared on the former vampire's forehead.

Elina was unsure if she would be able to help Reasa but she was going to try. They had no idea what Anakatrine has done to her on a D.N.A. level when she stripped Reasa of her immortality. The pack had used traditional healing methods when Reasa had been injured earlier. Elina wanted to try something else.

Leaning forward, she pressed her lips against Reasa's forehead, feeling the other woman stiffen at her touch before she relaxed once more, an absent-minded acknowledgement brushing Elina's inner thoughts. Reasa was focused on what she was doing within Brandon's mind, but she was conscious of what Elina was attempting. Allowing her lips to part, the Varcolac ran her tongue over the scratch, sealing it in one pass.

"Fuck!" The word ground out of Karn, as if he couldn't contain it.

Elina ignored him, moving to the wound on Reasa's cheek and pressing her lips against it as she had before. She tried to ignore how good the blood tasted... tried to ensure that she was in full control as she healed the other woman's injuries.

Mac moved around them, leaning down to Reasa's left side. He reached for her arm but Elina moved so fast, he was knocked flat on his ass before he could touch her. "Fool!" The Varcolac hissed, cold eyes flashing with an emotion so feral, Karn took a step back.

"How do you think Liam will react to your scent on his unclaimed mate? How do you think he will react knowing you have tasted her blood?"

Neither of the two males had even remotely considered what a major fuck up that would be. They were both dominant, territorial males, who wouldn't think twice about overreacting should another male touch what belonged to them. Mac had reacted as the protector he was, so intent on helping Reasa he hadn't considered the fallout of his actions.

"Do not touch Thereasa while he is unaware," Elina continued in a more even tone, her feral expression easing as she moved to tend to the arm wound. She ignored Mac as he relocated back to his previous spot, intent on her task. When the wound was healed, she licked her lips with closed eyes, willing her inner demon to retreat to the cage she kept it in.

Seeing no further wounds on Reasa, she returned to her position at the window, aware that both Mac and Karn were staring at her as if she'd just grown horns. An exasperated sigh escaped her lips as she shook her head in cool exasperation. "Liam trusts me and therefore my scent on Reasa will not aggravate him, and neither will my taking of her blood. He knows there is nothing sexual in the act, that it is merely a healing gesture."

She shook her head once more, fighting the urge to roll her eyes at the disbelief on their faces. Stupid males! "Why is everything about sex with vampires? I mean, really, do you ever think above your waistline?"

"Perhaps because the taking of blood is always performed during some kind of sexual activity," Karn snorted, mockery lacing his tone.

"Idiot." Was the only answer he received, before Elina turned her attention back to the couple by the bed. When it became apparent things had settled down with them, the vampires returned to their watching brief, allowing the Varcolac to call the shots... for now.

Liam turned to his route, scouring everywhere as he walked at a snail's pace. He didn't want to miss anything and the beads were small and easily masked by the steel mesh. Despite his vigilance, he almost missed the next bead; some inner sense halting his footsteps as he walked past the area it was hidden. Turning back, his searched the area to his right more closely until the glass bead appeared within the mesh. It was as dull and lifeless as the first one, but he didn't allow that to dampen his hope.

"Go join the other part of yourself, Brandon." Liam called up his memory of the urn, emitting a small sound of surprise when he saw it already contained an additional two beads. It appeared Reasa had had more success than he'd had so far. With a proud smile, his bead joined the other three in the urn, and Liam turned once more to continue on his journey.

He had no idea that the work would have been so painstaking, so exhausting. Liam felt as if he'd been walking for hours on end when he finally started treading ground Reasa had already been over. Her pretty blue bows showed up sporadically for a while and then it appeared every passage he walked into contained her mark.

"Liam? I think we've completed the maze," he heard in his mind. His hand being squeezed in the real world accompanied the words. "I'm tracking routes you've already travelled." Reasa's mental voice sounded weary and he wondered if his did too as he answered.

"Same here. Let's head back to the urn."

It felt like it took forever to reach the beginning of the maze and the glass urn that was two thirds full of beads that were now glowing brightly. Reasa was already there, staring at the light her expression rapt. "Can you feel him, Liam?" The words whispered out, awe suffusing her voice.

It was only when she spoke that he felt the third presence with them, a distinctly male persona emanating from the urn. There was no conscious thought, nothing that indicated intelligence but there was something there, and it was getting stronger with each passing second.

Dropping to his knees beside his mate, Liam gripped her hand as they stared at the light, watching it pulse to a slow rhythm they weren't party to. It was as if the light was undulating to a beat they couldn't hear... a beat that was slowly picking up pace.

"Brandon?"

The light flared for a fraction of a second, and then it returned to its slow pulsing once more, a feeling of serenity washing over Liam. He could see that same serenity flowing over Reasa, the illumination from the urn bathing her exquisite features in an ethereal glow.

"We found him, Liam! We found him!"

Reasa threw herself into his arms, laughing and crying at the same time, completely overcome with the emotion of the moment. Liam held her close, tears mingling with his own laughter, the emotions mixing with a sense of disbelief that they had been successful at their task. True, Brandon wasn't fully with them just yet, but there was enough of his psyche gathered that, perhaps, with a bit more time, he'd be able to find his own way back.

Exhausted beyond belief, Liam felt his mate's own mental fatigue, and the way her body sagged against his. With a tired groan, he rose back to his feet, pulling Reasa up beside him. "We've done all we can for today. We can come back tomorrow if required. We need to rest, Reasa."

It was a testament to how exhausted she was that she didn't object to him ordering her about. When Liam slipped from Brandon's mind and turned to look at her, Reasa's head was resting on Brandon's bed, her body slumped over with tiredness.

He was instantly concerned for his mate, so much so that it took him a moment to realise that the room was practically empty, Elina and Karn being the only two remaining that weren't monitoring the patients. The room was darker, a handful of lamps casting a pale light around it.

"You're back." Elina's cool words didn't mask her concern. "You've been gone for hours, Liam. We didn't know if we should try to force you to leave or let you be." "What time is it?"

"Almost midnight," Karn answered, a frown marring his face. "I was all set to make you leave but your cousin here wouldn't let me. Just like she wouldn't let us remove you when you both started bleeding all over the place."

His scowl was for Elina who merely shrugged and turned her gaze to Reasa. She could see Liam was exhausted but he had the strength of being Varcolac keeping him going; his mate didn't. "Reasa looks wiped out, Liam."

"Wait, what do you mean bleeding all over the place?" Her cousin's concerned gaze turned to Reasa, gently raising her from her prone position and searching her face intently. Her eyes fluttered open briefly, and then closed again as if she was too tired to keep them open. "There isn't a mark on her," Liam breathed, suspicious eyes alighting on Karn.

"Don't look at me," the vampire growled, giving Elina a pointed look. "She ran the whole show today. You want to know why the girl's healed, ask your cousin."

For a moment, Elina really wanted to smack the smug look from Karn's face but she fought down the errant thought, keeping her gaze firmly on Liam in case he reacted unfavourably. She was relieved to see that his initial suspicion was waning, and it was more curiosity than anything else on his face. "We can talk more about it tomorrow," she answered neutrally, giving him the briefest of smiles.

Liam shot her another quizzical glance before his need to take care of his mate overcome his curiosity and he rose, sweeping Reasa into his arms and cradling her against his wide chest. "Where can we rest?"

Karn headed for the door. "You can use the room at the top of the stairs on the second floor. You can have the one to the right of it, Elina." He paused as they passed him, his Praetorian instincts coming to the fore. "Brandon?"

"We did what we could, Karn. The rest is up to him." Liam headed up the second flight of stairs and opened the door to the room they'd been assigned. The last of his strength was waning and all he wanted to do was crawl into bed.

Kicking the door shut, he clutched Reasa tightly and managed to pull down the cover on the bed. He sank down onto the mattress with her, laying his mate gently against the pillows. Fast asleep she was so vulnerable, and his protective instincts surged up within him. He found enough strength to pull off her boots and his own before he wrapped Reasa in his arms and pulled the cover over them.

He didn't care how pissed off she would be when she woke. She was his to protect, and nothing would make him leave her side until she was rested enough to take care of herself. Liam's eyes drifted closed, his heart slowing to beat in tandem with the woman's in his arms.

"Kothi, are you sure you'll be fine here on your own? Wouldn't you rather stay with someone for some company?"

Kothari searched his mother's face, seeing the tell-tail signs of concern that was never far when she looked at him. She tried to hide it from him, but he was adept at seeing through most subterfuge. That expression infuriated the monster that lived within him, but it also broke the heart of the little boy who craved his mother's love.

This morning it was the boy who held dominance, and the much softer side of his personality came forth, a side that only his parents ever witnessed. Giving his mother a tight hug, he pushed down his inner demon so he could savour the blissful moment. It wouldn't last, it never did, but he would take each precious moment when he could. "I'll be fine, Mother. You don't need to worry about me. Don't go to Europe looking back and worrying. You need all your attention on your task there."

In truth, he was livid that Rafe was sending his parents away. He knew if he asked them not to go, they would stay. However, he also knew he couldn't ask that of them. Somebody had to go to Europe, it was the only way to protect the pack. Logically he understood that but emotionally he wasn't ready for his parents to be thrust into the heart of the enemy. If anything happened to them...he was afraid of what his monster would do.

"We'll be fine, son," Gard said, entering the living room and setting down the packed cases he was carrying. "We haven't reached this age without knowing how to take care of ourselves. The most important thing is you listen to Rafe at all times and do what he says. If my memory serves me correctly, weren't you supposed to be up at the Praetorian Compound as an extra guard?"

Kothari tried not to bristle at the subtle rebuke in his father's voice. He was supposed to be up at the other compound. He hadn't wanted to leave until he'd had a chance to say goodbye to his parents though. Surely his father understood that? "I'm heading up there shortly. I just wanted to say goodbye." His tone was rebellious and only served to have his mother tightening her hold on him.

"We understand that," Gard answered, a resigned sigh in his words. His son always bristled against any kind of authority, even that of his parents. It was concerning and something they hadn't managed to correct no matter what parenting techniques they'd used over the years. "It would be best if you got yourself up there now. We'll be on our way soon." He took the sting from his words by giving his son a warm hug.

After a long pause, Kothari nodded his head and turned to leave the room. "Be safe."

"I'm worried about leaving him," Rayne said, stepping into Gard's embrace as their son disappeared. It would be the first time Kothari would be alone without his support system and it was hard for her as a mother to leave him.

"He's a grown man, Sarayne. There has to come a day when he needs to discover who he is and fend for himself. He isn't completely alone anyway. He has the pack." Gard's words made sense but she could hear his own concern. Only time would tell just how well Kothari fared left to his own devices.

Shaking off the sensation of doom that threatened to overwhelm her, Rayne smiled up at her mate, leaning in for a long slow kiss to settle her foreboding. "Did Rafe get you?" she asked when Gard let her up for breath. When Rafe had visited earlier to ask about any abnormalities in the Varcolac mating instincts, her mate had been visiting Rhianna and Caleb to get any last minute instructions they might have had.

"He did though I probably couldn't tell him anymore than you could."

Rayne had been quite flummoxed by the question of whether the animal part of a Varcolac could be indecisive over the mating pull. She had known that Gard was her mate quite soon into their relationship though it had frightened and confused her a bit at the start. However, that had been the woman's dilemma...not her panther. She could give no clear reason of why Cassia was experiencing indecision from her wolf, though from the girl's reaction to Pietro's rejection, it appeared the wolf had made up its mind.

"It is an interesting development," Gard continued, releasing her from his arms, though looping one around her shoulders. "But not one that we can influence in any way. Caleb had arranged for his friend Joshua to meet us in Scotland. He thought it would be best if we start where Pietro was found and see if we can track backwards to the source of the poison. He has also set another friend travelling to Romania to see if they can turn up any folklore about plants with unusual properties. He didn't say much about that friend but did say they would know how to contact us should they unearth something."

Rayne cuddled closer to his warmth for another moment before she straightened and moved to pick up her case. "I guess we should get this show on the road then."

Gard followed her, retrieving his case and casting one final glance around their home. He was worried for Kothi and equally worried about what they might find when they reached Europe. One thing he was certain of though, nothing would happen to Rayne while he was alive. He'd let her down once before, many centuries ago, and he would never allow that to happen again. Looping his arm around his mate once more, they set off for their car and the trip to the airport.

"Cassia?" The sound of her father's voice seeped through her sleepy mind, pulling her from the endless nightmare of Pietro's harsh words. She didn't want to wake up, and yet, staying asleep wasn't doing her any good either so she forced her swollen eyes to open. Her father was sitting on the edge of her bed, his brown eyes so full of concern that for a moment she thought she'd start weeping again.

She could remember bits and pieces of the preceding day after Pietro had gone, enough to know that she hadn't been alone all through the night. If Dara hadn't been lying beside her, then her mother had, and laterally her father. They had held her as she wept, surrounding her with so much love both physically and mentally that she'd finally fallen into a sleep full of nightmares.

Cassia was exhausted but she hadn't gone rogue. Perhaps the Alexander family had a deep layer of strength that protected them when they lost their mates? Her Uncle Dayton had survived the loss of his first mate. Perhaps Cassia would be able to endure her loss too, because Pietro had been certain in his convictions. He wouldn't forgive what he saw as her betrayal.

More tears came unbidden and she felt her father's arms wrap around her as he rocked her gently. "Let it out, sweetheart. I know it hurts but let it out so it doesn't fester inside you. We are here and always will be. We will love and protect you, my beautiful daughter."

The deep love in his words, the hidden tenderness that lived within her father's hard exterior, was so overwhelming her sobs became louder as she clung on for dear life. She was floundering, drowning; she didn't know how to stop of the tears. Her heart ached so badly she was sure it was going to burst and there was nothing she could do to prevent it.

"Daddy..." Cassia couldn't get any more words out, just that one word so full of anguish she could feel his tears against her neck as he continued to rock her.

"I know, sweetheart. I know."

Cassia cried herself into another restless slumber, waking once more to find her father still beside her bed only this time he was sitting in a chair, his head resting on the cover as he slept. He looked so exhausted that for the first time since Pietro had left she felt an emotion other than misery. She felt ashamed.

Her entire family were suffering because of her weakness. They were probably terrified that they would lose her and she was doing nothing to dissuade them of that. Self-loathing rose up deep inside her and her shame escalated as she imagined what they must be feeling. How could she subject them to that fear? How could she be so weak?

"I'm sorry," she whispered, reaching out to touch her father's golden hair with a shaky hand. His eyes opened instantly, and he blinked sleepily for a moment before his vision cleared and he took her hand in his.

"Never be sorry for needing us, Cass. We are family and we will always be here," he whispered back, gently squeezing her hand to reassure her of that.

She didn't deserve them, not after what she must have put them through in the last twenty four hours. She would show them how strong she was. She would take that awful expression of fear from her father's eyes. "I guess I needed a timeout there," she managed with a shaky half-smile.

"I guess you did," he smiled back stroking a hand tenderly against her tangled curls. His expression turned grave and a dark scowl crossed his face. "Do I need to be having a chat with Pietro?"

Instant fear suffused her at his words. She could imagine just what kind of chat her father was talking about and that was something she didn't want to see happen. Pietro had his reasons for how he was feeling. He had suffered enough without being punished for being justifiably angry about things. "No, please don't, Dad. This is between us. We need to work things out ourselves."

Cassia expected him to argue more but instead his expression cleared and he shot her a rueful smile. "Your mother's been telling me the same thing for hours. Only she hasn't been as polite about it." The open amusement in his eyes was a good indicator of just how vocal her mother had been on the topic. Her father always got that expression of love and admiration when his mate put her foot down about things.

"She's right, Dad. Pietro has no idea that my wolf is claiming him. I didn't tell him because at first my wolf was undecided and also I wanted to give him some time to heal. It's not his fault my stupid animal has decided to overreact to his leaving." Cassia was beginning to feel stronger the more she rationalised things in her mind. Saying the words out aloud appeared to settle her wolf down a lot, its anxiety levels decreasing sharply.

Alexei pondered her words for a moment and then acquiesced. He had to concede that his daughter was the best person to know what was happening and how best to resolve things. It didn't stop him wishing he could take some of her burden as his own, but he knew he had to leave it up to Cassia. "So, you're wolf is certain that he's your mate now? Dara told us that it was undecided before."

Forcing herself into a sitting position, Cassia nodded. "I think this little episode has hammered the point home," she sighed, scrubbing a hand tiredly over her face. She could do with some restful sleep but that didn't appear an option at the moment.

"What are you going to do? You did hear your mother when she explained last night that Pietro has left the pack?"

Cassia nodded again, muffling the half sob that threatened to escape. "Yes, he's gone to The Dive for now," she sighed, working to build her defences as she thought through the issue. "For now, I'm going to get up and have a shower and some breakfast. I'll decide what I'm going to do after that. Maybe all he needs is a little time to feel the effects of the mating pull. I'm not really sure, Dad. I just know that I need to get out of this bed and stop feeling sorry for myself."

Alexei couldn't have felt any prouder of his beautiful child. He was proud of all his girls; they were each amazing in their own ways. He loved Cedar so deeply only death would ever separate their link. His daughters...he cherished them as an extension of his and Cedar's souls. Balancing his own feral nature when one of them was hurting wasn't easy but he tried his damnedest to be the kind of man they could love and respect.

It was frightening to realise his girls had grown up so quickly. Oh, he was aware they followed their mother and the demands of their animal halves. He wasn't that naive that he wasn't aware of their dalliances within the pack. Still, mating was something so very different...and mating to one of his oldest friends? It took him a moment to process that thought before he burst out laughing, startling Cassia.

"What?" Her quizzical expression made him laugh louder.

"I was just remembering the hard time I gave your Uncle Andrei over his reaction to Lily mating with one of our oldest friends. I'm only now realising the boot is on the other foot. He's going to have a field day getting payback."

The subtle way her father gave his approval of her choice of mate wasn't lost on Cassia. Her eyes sparkled as she giggled at his words and she couldn't resist the urge to throw herself into his arms in a tight embrace. "Thank you, Dad." She didn't need to tell him what she was thanking him for.

"You're welcome, sweetheart. Just be happy. That's all I've ever wanted for my girls."

Alexei stayed a little longer with Cassia before he headed back to his own room. It was still early and Cedar was sleeping, having only gone to bed a few hours before. Now that he was sure his daughter would be okay, he gave into the need for a few hours' rest himself, quickly throwing off his clothes and climbing into bed with his mate. Cedar muttered under her breath, rolling over to instinctively wrap her limbs around his tall frame. He hardened in an instant, as he always did when he lay beside his woman.

"Is it Dara's turn?" Cedar murmured, stroking her hand down his back as she sleepily brushed her lips against his chest.

Her touch had his breath catching and he couldn't have stopped himself from tangling his fingers in her curls if he tried. Tilting her head back, he silenced her with a passionate kiss, moaning quietly as her lips parted to his touch and her tongue battled lazily against his.

"Alexei...?"

"Cass is fine, sweetness." His words were muffled as he trailed his mouth down the graceful arch of her neck, laving his tongue greedily against her soft skin. His teeth nipped hard and she moaned and brushed her body against his.

"Really?"

There was still very much the mother in her tone and he sank his teeth a little harder. "Yes, she is. She's showering and making breakfast so that gives us a little time to... "

Cedar arched as his fangs elongated and sank into her neck, pressing her aching breasts against his torso, muffling a cry as one large hand engulfed her flesh and squeezed hard. "Alexei!"

He drank deeply, savouring the hot blood flowing down his throat, his talented fingers moving lower to his other favourite spot on her body. Sinking his fingers deep within her body, he raised his head again to capture Cedar's lips to muffle the sound of her climax.

His heart thundered in his chest as her body shuddered in his arms. She was so beautiful when she came apart for him. It was a view he would never tire of watching.

Barely giving her a moment to catch her breath, Alexei rolled on top of his mate, moaning against her mouth as he joined them together. "Hmmm yes, we have enough time to enjoy this and have a little nap afterwards," he laughed, stroking languidly into her hotness, savouring the feel of her body sheathing his in the most intimate of caresses.

Cedar's arms wrapped around his neck, her teeth nipping at the spot when it joined his shoulder. "Then let's dance, lover," she all but purred, rocking her hips up to meets his as she bit down hard.

Cassia heard Dara before she felt her sister cuddle into her from behind. She held still to allow her that moment, knowing she had scared Dara badly. Putting the teapot down carefully, she turned around to hug her sister tightly.

"I was so scared, Cass." Dara whispered the words, and Cassia felt dampness against her neck where her face was burrowed.

"I'm sorry, I didn't mean to scare you like that," she answered running a soothing hand down her sister's back. "My wolf just got a little overwhelmed by things and needed some time to come to terms with what had happened. I'm fine now, Dara. I promise."

Her sister clung to her a moment longer and then she pulled back and wiped at her wet cheeks. "Are you sure?"

Cassia shot her a rueful smile, a trace of melancholy in her eyes. "I'm still hurting, that hasn't changed, but I'm not wallowing in it any more. I've been racking my brain trying to think of how best to confront Pietro but haven't come up with anything concrete yet." She motioned to Dara to sit and then plated up a cooked breakfast for both of them. Sitting beside her, she ate some of her cheese omelette and sipped at her tea.

"What are you options?" Dara asked between forkfuls of egg and bacon.

Her sister shrugged, staring pensively ahead as she considered her answer. "I suppose I can give him some time and see if the mating pull kicks in. Or, I could pack a bag and move in with him whether he likes it or not."

Dara's eyes widened with shock. "Would you really do that?"

Cassia shrugged. It was something she was considering given the circumstances with Thereasa. "I can't discount it, Dara. I know I would have to discuss it with Mom and Dad, as well as get approval from Rafe, but with the hostility between Pietro and Reasa I may have no choice but to leave the pack."

Her sister's dismay increased. "But...what about researching the antidote and your healer's training? What about the pack? Cass, you're so pack orientated I don't think you could ever be happy being apart from us." Dara was aware that she sounded selfish but nobody knew her sister better than she did. She had no doubt that Cassia wouldn't be happy on her own, even if she was with Pietro.

"What's the other option, Dara? Should Liam and Reasa leave the pack so Pietro and I can stay? What makes my needs more important than theirs? Liam has always needed the pack more than I ever have. Now that Reasa is human she is too fragile to be out there alone even with Liam. We have to consider everything before a decision is reached. You know that in your heart, honey."

Dara did but that didn't make hearing the words any easier. Yesterday she had been afraid she would lose Cassia to turning rogue. Today her relief at finding that wasn't the case wasn't eased any. She didn't know how she would handle her sister not being a part of the pack. They had always been together, always looked out for each other. However, Cassia's happiness had to come first. If things couldn't be resolved between Pietro and Reasa then one of the Varcolac would have to leave. There was no escaping that fact.

"Maybe once Pietro accepts you as his mate it may help him find some forgiveness in his heart."

Cassia sipped at her tea before giving her sister what she hoped was an encouraging smile. She wasn't so sure of that but it was a hopeful possibility. "Let's wait and see what happens, Dar. For now, let's finish breakfast and then I'm going to head over to the lab for a little while and do some work while I think things through."

They sat together in silence, each locked in their own private thoughts. Cassia knew that whatever happened Dara would be fine. Yes, it would be a change for her but her sister was just as strong as she was. Hell, she managed to keep Kothi in line when most others failed. It took a very strong woman to do that so she knew with certainty that Dara could cope with anything life threw at her. Dara just needed to believe that in her own heart.

Reasa woke slowly, feeling the warmth of Liam's body heat beside her long before she opened her eyes. It was hard to miss as she found herself wrapped protectively in his arms with one hard thigh flung over her hip, and her head resting on his wide chest. She should have been outraged at him taking liberties, but it felt so good that she just lay there savouring the sensations his touch inspired.

She felt safe for the first time since her circumstances had changed. It was hard admitting it but she couldn't deny it. Everything that Liam did revolved around keeping her safe. Every decision he made was done so with careful consideration on how it would affect her. The Varcolac was claiming her as his mate and he made no bones about it. As far as he was concerned, it was inevitable and she would just have to get used to that fact.

Liam frightened her as nothing or no one had for a long time. He frightened her because his strong determination was winning. Whereas before she had been strong in her convictions that she would never mate with him, since their kiss that conviction was wavering. It felt good sleeping with him like this. It felt right and that was terrifying. There was trouble coming their way in the shape of Louis and Pietro. All directed at her and something Liam would do his utmost to counter. The fallout from that was unimaginable.

How could she allow this to happen? She had set her feet on a path that ultimately led to destruction and now it wasn't just her life that was at stake but possible hundreds of others, including Liam. Her decision at the time had made sense to her. Now, in the face of knowing a few of the Varcolac and the pack, it suddenly felt so wrong. Why had she chosen to do this? It was only when Liam spoke that she realised she'd uttered the last words aloud.

"Tell me."

Reasa swallowed hard, denial rocking through her. She had never told anyone of her past, never allowed anyone to have that hold over her. Yet, Liam had allowed her into his memories, into the most shameful parts of his past. He had given her his total trust and she didn't deserve that.

"Tell me, Reasa," he whispered against her temple, his hand stroking down her back slowly. "Who hurt you so badly. Who shaped your views to such extremes?"

Swallowing again, she felt hot tears begin to flow at the gentleness of Liam's tone. There was no condemnation there, only a need to understand. He had never condemned her, this beautiful, strong man, even when she had deserved it.

"My father," she finally answered, the words catching on a breathless sob. As soon as she said them, an image of the man whose seed helped create her entered her mind and she shuddered at the thought, trying hard to push it away. Her body stiffened in Liam's embrace though he kept running a soothing hand down her back.

She couldn't have kept him out if she'd wanted to. Saying the words breached her strongest barriers, crumbled the wall that she'd placed to bury those memories she never wanted to revisit. She could feel Liam's gentle strength at her side; feel his arms keeping her safe. Surrendering to the inevitable, she allowed the walls to crumble completely...

She was young, carefree, a pretty girl living in a secluded wooden cabin in the woods. It was a difficult time with wars and disease prevalent, but her family had found a refuge from it all and she could laugh and dance beneath the canopied trees with no fear.

Their family was wrong in the eyes of society. Her father was from the African continent, her mother a pale white farmer's daughter. They had fallen in love, a love so deep they couldn't be apart. They were soul mates so they ran away together, to share their love and make their beloved daughter Thereasa. They lived off the land and life was good, until the day he came.

Thereasa couldn't remember his face, the man who had found her washing by the lake. She remembered he was very beautiful and had a magical voice. She remembered his bite and her terror. She remembered waking to find herself many miles away from her home. For the first year of her new life she remembered the blood and the screams, the human lives ended so she could thrive.

She missed mama and papa so much that she had to return. She found them where she left them, their sadness obvious in their eyes. Thereasa couldn't bear to be apart from her parents so she did the only thing she could think of...she made them in her own image...she turned them to the life of the vampire.

It should have been perfect. They were together again as a family. However, it wasn't to be as Thereasa's knowledge of the supernatural was lacking. She didn't know that just because people were human soul mates that didn't mean they would be the same in their new life. She didn't know...she didn't know...

"Thereasa, where is your mother?" Her father's angry tone frightened her.

"She said she was going for a walk, Papa." Her father was always angry now. He had been that way ever since he had become a vampire.

"Find her!"

CHAPTER 3

Thereasa was too afraid to say no. Her father was much stronger than she was despite the fact she had lived this life longer. He wasn't afraid to use that strength either, lashing out at herself or her mother when his ire rose too sharply. Gone was the quiet, protective man he had once been. In its place was now an abusive tyrant who frightened them.

Thereasa ran through the trees at supernatural speed, anxious to find her mother to appease his anger. She hadn't run far when she scented a wolf, her feet skidding to a halt as she scented the air. Creeping quietly to the clearing, she clamped a hand over her mouth to prevent a wordless cry escaping. Her mother was wrapped naked in the arms of a man but he was no ordinary man...he was a wolf shifter.

No...it couldn't be true! Her mother couldn't be having an affair with a wolf. They were a family! She belonged with her father!

"No!" The word shrieked out, her mother and the wolf springing to their feet in shock. "Thereasa! Wait! Let me explain!"

"You belong with Papa," she screamed, tears running down her face. She didn't want to hear explanations. She just wanted everything to go back to the way they had been before the man had found her by the lake.

"We're soul mates," her mama wept, a hand reaching out to her daughter. "We can't fight the mating pull, Thereasa. We belong together."

She shook her head in denial, hurt, anger, betrayal infusing her soul. "He's not one of us! He's a Were! You can't be soul mates. You're Papa's soul mate! This is wrong!"

"It's no more wrong than when your Papa and I had you, Thereasa," her mother argued, tears running down her face as she tried to reach her child. "Society told us that was wrong too but it wasn't. Victor is my true mate, my daughter. We must be together. We can't escape it."

"Whore!"

Thereasa screamed as her father appeared at her side. He must have heard her yelling and come to investigate. He looked ten feet tall in his fury and she shrank away from him.

"Francis...I can explain. We couldn't help it. We are soul mates."

"He's a dog!" her father roared, his eyes black, his talons extended. "It's wrong! What you are doing is an abomination!"

"No, Francis...please listen... "

Her mother's pleas cut off as her father sped forward knocking her out of the way as the other man shifted into wolf form and sprang snarling at the enraged vampire. Her father's talons pierced the wolf's sides, his fangs sinking deep into its neck.

Her mother was screaming, loud anguished sobs as the wolf gave one mournful howl before going limp in her father's arms. He tossed the dead carcass aside, its bones snapping as it hit a large tree trunk.

"Whore! You betrayed me and now you must be punished!" her father bellowed again, advancing on her distraught mother. "Go home, Thereasa."

"No, Papa! Please! Don't hurt Mama!"

"Go home!"

But Thereasa couldn't move, couldn't hide her eyes from the horrifying scene unfolding around her. Her father picked her mother's unresisting body from the forest floor by the neck and he ripped his talons down her exposed torso. The pain made her shriek but she did nothing to protect herself. Staring into her mother's eyes, Thereasa could see the light die within, and knew that her soul was lost in the moment the wolf had died.

"Papa, please!" she cried, finally finding her body able to move as she threw herself onto his back, trying to remove his grip from her mother's neck. "Don't, Papa! Don't!"

It was as if she wasn't even there.

"Whore!" he hissed once more before he twisted his hand and his talons sliced her mother's head from her shoulders.

"NO!" Thereasa screamed, agony rocking through her as her mother's body collapsed to the ground, her head still firmly clasped in her father's hand. "NO! Mama! Mama!"

Rage like nothing she had ever experience before rose up deep within. Heart shattering into a million pieces, Thereasa's fangs elongated and her talons punched through her father's back. She shredded his heart in an instant, watching as he dropped her mother's head and sank to the forest floor on his knees.

"I hate you! I hate you! I hate you!" Thereasa shrieked the words repeatedly, blood splattering wildly as she hacked furiously. When reason finally returned she stared down at the mangled remains of her father's body, his head lying beside her mother's.

"Mama? Papa?" Sinking to her knees beside them, Thereasa began rocking as she stared at the carnage. "Please wake up. Please. I don't want to be alone. I'm frightened."

They didn't wake up. She stayed there for three days alternating between pleading to crying to angry words, but her parents never woke up no matter what she did. Finally, she had to accept that they were never coming back. Finally, she had to accept that her father had killed her mother and she, in turn, had killed him.

It was all the wolf's fault. That filthy, disgusting animal had seduced her mother and broken her family. Rising from her cramped position, Thereasa ran at the broken carcass, shrieking as she kicked and hacked at it. "It's all your fault! You're to blame! You murdered my mother the very first time you laid hands on her! It was wrong! You are wrong! I hate you!"

Thereasa fell to the ground sobbing, replaying everything that had happened over in her mind. She screamed as her mother died again, screamed as she took her father's life again, hated as she destroyed the wolf's carcass again.

When she finally rose to dispose of the remains as her Sire had taught her, it was with ice in her soul and a deep hatred in her heart. Never again would she allow anyone to matter to her. Never again would she be weak. While she hated all wolves, she wouldn't go out of her way to hunt them down as that would only get it her way of becoming the strongest, most dangerous vampire on the continent. However, should the day ever come when wolves crossed her path as had just happened, she would hunt them down and destroy the abominations, each and every last one of them.

Liam's heart broke for her as she sobbed uncontrollably in his arms. He had known that there had to be some severe catalyst to inspire Reasa's level of hatred in the Varcolac, but he had no idea it could be anything as tragic as what he'd just witnessed. She felt responsible for her mother's death. She had taken her father's life to avenge her mother's murder. The worst thing was she knew deep within her soul that if she had never turned them to the life of a vampire that they would most likely have lived out their lives together in happiness.

No wonder she hated the mixed matings and the Varcolac. They were evidence that what her mother had shared even briefly with her wolf was real and couldn't have been fought. They lent truth to her mother's words and that would only increase Reasa's feelings of guilt that her reaction had brought her father down on the lovers. Thereasa hated and blamed the wolves, because it was the only way she could live with her overwhelming guilt without going insane.

"You were only young girl, Reasa," he whispered against her temple, holding her as tightly as he could without hurting her. "You didn't ask to become a vampire and it is understandable that you would feel alone and afraid, and want your parents with you."

He kissed her temple as she sobbed without speaking. "What happened is tragic and I can't tell you to forget it as it will always be a part of you, but you have to forgive yourself, Thereasa. You didn't intend for any of that to happen. You had no control over the events that unfolded. You were just a young girl who was happy with her parents and didn't want to lose that love and security."

"I killed my papa," she wept clinging onto Liam tightly. "He was a good man before...before I made him a vampire. If I hadn't done that..."

"Forgive yourself. Remember who your father was before he changed. What would he wish for you, Thereasa? What would your mother wish for you?"

A loud hiccup escaped her as she took a shuddering breath. "They only ever wanted me to be happy and safe," she answered, her voice sounding like that of the young carefree girl she had once been.

"Then be happy, my heart. Be safe here with me. You cannot change the past but you can change your future. You just need to start by letting go of what was and concentrate on what can be. The Varcolac are not abominations, Reasa. The mixed matings are not abominations. You have nothing to hate us for."

Reasa suddenly felt claustrophobic. She was being overwhelmed by emotions she'd kept buried so long and her flight instincts were kicking in. Struggling in Liam's embrace, she wriggled until he let her go. Leaping from the bed, she headed towards the door, stopping before she reached it. Where could she go? There was nowhere to run to, no way of escaping the memories crashing over her.

"Thereasa, it's okay, you're safe here."

Ignoring him, she grabbed her bag from where it rested against the wall, one of the vampires must have placed it there yesterday when they were working within Brandon's mind. "I need to shower," she mumbled, refusing to look at him. She didn't want to see the same pity she heard in his voice reflected in his eyes. She didn't deserve it and she didn't want it.

Liam sighed deeply as she closed the bathroom door with what could only be termed as finality. His mate was shutting him out after having let him into her darkest secrets. He understood that she was overwhelmed but that didn't stop him wishing she would see that she had nothing to fear from him. He wanted to help, he needed to help. Why couldn't she see that?

Sighing again, he got up and grabbed his pack, heading out of the room in search of another available bathroom. He knew when he returned, he would find Reasa's barriers back up but that was okay. He would just break them down again and keep breaking them down until she realised that no matter what her past was, he wasn't going anywhere.

Brandon yawned, uttering a groan as every muscle in his body protested the long stretch, he was giving it. What the hell was wrong with him? He felt as if he'd been in bed for a week. He'd also been having some pretty weird dreams too. Lily had been talking at him for what felt like hours. He couldn't make out what she was saying but he could hear her voice as if from a far-off distance.

Liam had been in them, too, and the assassin who had infiltrated the Praetorian Compound. They had kept calling him, playing what felt like a game of hide and seek with him. Every time he'd thought he'd tracked them down they vanished and he had to start again. It truly had been the weirdest of dreams and one he was glad to be waking up from.

"Brandon? Open your eyes, Bran...please!"

"Lily?" He struggled to open his eyes, groaning again as they felt as if they had been stuck together with glue.

"I'm here! I'm right here, Brandon."

Why did Lily sound like she was crying? His determination to find out was the deciding factor in forcing his eyes open. Squinting against the morning sunlight coming from the nearby window, he looked up to see his friend hovering over him, tears flowing freely down her face.

"Oh Brandon, you're back! I knew they could do it! I just knew it!" "Back?" he croaked out, realising his mouth was dry and he was famished. His hunger was so strong it made his stomach cramp. "I haven't been anywhere." His confusion continued as his stomach churned again. "I'm starving. Does anyone have a cute human nearby?"

Lily started to laugh as a Were tried to make her move aside.

"Lily, let us check him out. Maybe you could find him something to eat so he doesn't try to bite us?" the female Were said, and his friend gasped and disappeared from view.

Brandon wouldn't have minded biting the woman now looming over him. She was very attractive and the need for blood wasn't the only hunger that was surfacing. Not that he would. He was aware his bite would kill the Were if he did.

"How are you feeling?" she was asking him as she shone an annoying light in his eyes before running professional feeling hands over his body.

"Hungry, horny and confused," he answered truthfully, delighting in the slight rounding of the Were's eyes at his bluntness. The doctor, because that's what she appeared to be, didn't respond to his words, she merely continued her examination.

"How do your limbs feel...sluggish, hard?"

"I can tell you what is hard... "

"Brandon, stop playing with the doctor," Lily admonished, appearing back at the bed with a bottle in one hand and the heavenly aroma of chilled blood wafting from the filled glass in her other hand.

His attention was immediately diverted, a sharp pain gnawing at his gut. Grabbing the glass, he slugged the contents quickly, reaching for the bottle to replenish it. He drained the bottle before the nagging pains decreased enough for him to focus once more on his surroundings.

"What's going on, Lily? Why am I in what appears to be a hospital room?" His gaze shifted to the other beds, his brow drawing down as he saw his fellow Praetorians lying there. "What's wrong with them?"

Lily sat down on the chair beside the bed, moving a book from there to the bedside table. Brandon glanced at it briefly, reading the title. "Moby Dick? " Lily hated that book though it was one of his favourites. They'd had countless debates over whether Captain Ahab was brave or a self-absorbed monomaniac. Lily voted for the latter every time.

"I was reading it to you," she answered, a mock-grimace on her face. "Thankfully you woke up so I won't have to torture myself any further."

"Woke up?"

Lily turned to the doctor who gave her a reassuring smile. "He appears to be none the worse for his ordeal. I'll leave you two to catch up."

As she walked away, his friend turned back to him. "What's the last thing you remember, Bran?"

He frowned at the question but cast his mind back to before the strange dreams. Everything felt a bit blurry though his cognitive skills were sharpening as the blood he'd consumed surged through his body. "Everyone was in the living room. The assassin was being brought to justice and there was some kind of strange magic going on. Things were pretty fraught and I wasn't sure what side of the line we were on. I can remember Liam shouting, screaming at Annie for some reason. Then there was this blinding pain in my head and it felt as if Liam was physically inside me, screaming in anguish. I don't remember what happened after that."

Lily nodded giving his hand a reassuring squeeze. "That was days ago, Brandon. Liam was inside your head, and the heads of the others in this room. He didn't know what he was doing but in his distress over what was happening to Thereasa he projected his emotions outwards and some of the Praetorians were injured in the backlash. You were one of them. You've been trapped within your mind ever since."

He gaped at her, trying to understand what she was saying. "You mean he damaged our minds somehow?"

Lily nodded. "It wasn't intentional, Brandon, and he is so overcome with guilt by what happened. He's learned to shield his empathy better and he and Reasa are the reason you're awake right now. They spent all day yesterday in your mind, searching for your shattered psyche so they could help bring you back."

Brandon's thoughts were in turmoil at the news. His mind had been shattered and days had passed? He was staggered by what he was hearing but the more he thought about it, the easier it was to put two and two together. The dream of Lily talking at him was clearly when she was reading to him. The hide and seek game with Liam and Reasa was them luring him back to reality. That had to make Liam one of the most dangerous people he had ever come across, and now he appeared to be working in conjunction with the would- be assassin.

"Please don't hate him, Brandon. Liam worked himself to the point of exhaustion last night trying to fix his mistake."

Blinking slowly, he regarded his friend, only half listening to what she was saying as he processed what had happened. It took a moment for her words to seep through but when they did, he shook his head in denial. "Of course I don't hate Liam. He is Varcolac, as are you, Lily."

He squeezed her hand, wanting to relieve the distress he saw on her face. "I signed up to lay down my life for the Varcolac no matter what the circumstances. I could never hate any of you and most certainly not Liam. It's my job to protect him."

"And we are so lucky to have you," Lily smiled, leaning over to give her friend a warm hug. She had been afraid that the Praetorians would fear Liam after what had happened. It was a relief to know that Brandon, at least, didn't harbour any ill will because of what happened.

"Okay, that's enough of the hugging," Mac growled with a glint of humour in his eyes as he entered the room. "Just because you've been in a coma for days doesn't mean you can take liberties with my mate, Brandon."

It was obvious he was only teasing so Brandon did a little of his own, ensuring his grip tightened around his friend so she couldn't pull away. "Lily gives great hugs," he winked, drawing a bark of laughter from Karn who appeared at Mac's side.

"Do you want to go back into another coma, boy? Keep that up and you may well just do that."

"How are you feeling, Brandon?" Mac asked, extracting his mate from the other male's arms and sitting down in her chair. He pulled her onto his lap, grinning widely at her exuberant expression. He shared her relief, not just because he liked the younger male, but also because it made his Lily happy to have her friend back.

"A little sluggish and disorientated," Brandon answered, turning serious as he reported to his leader. "I have a strong thirst for food still even though I've had a full bottle already. Might be wise to have a large stock for when the others wake up as they're going to be famished."

The Praetorian leader nodded trying not to be overly hopeful. Just because Liam and Reasa were able to bring Brandon back, it didn't mean they would automatically be able to save the others. It was possible that Brandon's connection with Lily and Liam was a deciding factor in the younger male wanting to return.

The sound of the door opening once more had everyone turning to the newcomers. Reasa appeared first, followed closely by Liam. The Varcolac's eyes widened as he saw Brandon sitting up in bed. "It worked," he whispered, relief glowing in his eyes.

"Intriguing," the human woman said, curiosity on her face. "I did not think we would be able to do it. It would appear I am wrong once again." She hung back as Liam crossed over to his friend.

"I am so sorry, Brandon. I never meant to cause you or anyone else any harm." Liam's relief had changed to guilt, his expression sombre as he regarded his friend. He couldn't put into words how happy he was to see Brandon sitting up and talking to everyone. He hoped that his successive actions had gone some way to mitigating the damage he'd caused.

"You're forgiven," the vampire grinned, running a hand through his long dark hair. "I needed the rest anyway. You do know what a slave driver Karn is." He deliberately kept his tone light and teasing to ease some of Liam's guilt. Shit happened and sometimes people got hurt along the way. It wasn't in Brandon's nature to hold a grudge...not unless someone tried to hurt someone he cared about.

"It was an accident, Liam. Nothing for you to beat yourself up about. I'm fine, and I'm sure the others will be too once you've had a chance to annoy the hell out of them by playing hide and go seek in their minds."

Liam's smiled, a slow smile full of gratitude to his friend. His curiosity was piqued too by his words. "You were aware of us in your mind?"

"Sort of," Brandon answered with an answering smile. "It was like a hazy dream. You and Reasa were calling to me but every time I thought I'd found one of you, I would have to start all over again going in a different direction. I can remember feeling exhausted by the time you stopped calling me. I was glad you both went away so I could sit down a rest."

The doctor arrived back at the bed. "Okay, now you've all satisfied yourselves that he's fine, Brandon needs some more food and then some rest."

"I'll get you something more to eat," Lily said wriggling out of Mac's tight embrace.

Her mate rose too. "I'll ensure we have an adequate stock of chilled blood." He gathered his mate close and shepherded her out of the room.

"Are you up to trying with the next patient or do you need more rest?" Karn asked.

Liam glanced at Reasa who nodded her head. "I'm fine to try again."

"Good. I'll round up Elina while you get yourselves comfortable. Just move the chairs beside Brandon's bed to the next one." Karn left the room leaving Liam and Reasa to get themselves set up for the next dream walking.

"Reasa...?" Liam wanted to see beneath the cool mask that was back in place. He wanted to know that his mate was okay after her emotional outpouring earlier. He knew this wasn't really the time and place, but he needed some kind of reassurance.

"Let's just concentrate on what we came here to do, Liam. That's our highest priority and we need all our energy for that."

Conceding defeat for now, Liam sat down beside the next bed, relaxing his body and trying to clear his mind of all external stimuli. It was hard with his mate so close, but it was necessary to bring back the remaining Praetorians.

Gard shot Rayne a questioning look as he sighted a banner emblazoned with Sarayne. A tall athletic male held it up, his shoulder length blond hair partially obscured by a black fedora hat. His mate met his gaze and shrugged, a frown creasing her forehead. "I've never seen him before."

Gard's protective instincts automatically kicked in, as no one out of their inner circle knew Rayne's birth name. "Stay here." He strode towards the other male without waiting to see if his mate would obey. He knew she wouldn't so he was determined to get to the male before she did. He could scent the vampire as he neared; the blond was a healthy age for one of the European covens.

The other male smiled a lopsided grin as the Ancient approached him. His demeanour appeared relaxed though Gard could detect the subtle alertness in his stance. The vampire was no fool; he was prepared for trouble though he was probably reasonably certain there wouldn't be any. They were in the middle of an airport surrounded by thousands of humans.

"You don't look much like a Sarayne," he grinned. "Before you're tempted to forget where we are, Caleb gave me the name. He said if that didn't settle you down then to tell you

Callain and Anakatrine would be most displeased if you felt inclined to detach my head." He spoke low enough that only Gard and Rayne, who had caught up with her mate, could hear.

"I'm Sarayne, though most people just call me Rayne. And you are?"

"Joshua. I am at your service and kind of relieved to see you didn't bring Demetri with you...not that this impressive gentleman isn't enough to send a shiver down most vampires' spines."

His acknowledgement of Gard's dominance level was enough to soothe some of the Ancient's suspicion. His mentioning of Callain and Anakatrine did the rest of the trick. Gard relaxed, running quickly through his mind what Caleb had told him of his frien d. Though not commonly known in Europe, Joshua was in fact a coven leader and one of Caleb's oldest friends. The Ancient trusted him implicitly and had urged Gard to do the same. Joshua had also helped save Pietro's life so that was another mark in his favour. The crowning point was Demetri had vouched for the vampire...that was nothing short of a miracle.

"Can you take us to where Pietro was found?" he asked with little preamble. The sooner they found out what they could, the sooner they could get home to their son.

Rayne rolled her eyes though there was a smile on her face. "This is Gard, my mate. You'll have to excuse his manners, travelling makes him a tad surly."

"Spoken by the woman who slept the entire flight," Gard chuckled, dropping a quick kiss on the top of her head. "You do know you won't sleep tonight with the time difference."

"Then I guess you'll just have to entertain me then," she retorted, turning her gaze back to their escort. "Would it be better if we found accommodation first, Joshua?"

"I figured you would want to be under the radar as much as possible so I've cleared out one of my safe houses for your use. Whoever you're looking for appears to be employing some younglings as lookouts. We spotted three newly created vampires hanging around the terminals here. I sent some of my people off to lead them a merry dance. I presume there will be more hanging around the main hotel district and various bed and breakfast establishments."

"We came in on a private jet. If someone is keeping watch, it won't be hard for them to get the flight list," Gard growled, unsettled by the news.

Joshua nodded his agreement. "This is why we need to hustle and get you stashed into the safe house before that happens. By the time they access the flight list you'll be ghosts and it will make it harder for them to pick up your trail." He turned and headed out of the airport, crossing a road to lead them into the parking garage. When he stopped at a beat- up van with peeling paintwork and plenty of rust on display, Gard quirked an eyebrow at him in question.

"If you think vamps on your side of the pond are arrogant, you haven't seen anything yet," Joshua chuckled. "It is beyond their comprehension that Ancients would lower themselves to travel in a rust bucket like this. Believe me; any other potential eyes we haven't spotted won't look twice at this vehicle."

"And if they do?" Gard was already stowing their cases in the back and ushering his mate into the back seat.

"There's a McLaren engine under the bonnet, though I suppose you call it a hood." Joshua walked to the driver's side, pointing to the left hand side of the vehicle. It had been awhile since Gard had been in Europe so he'd automatically presumed the front passenger seat was on the right.

"If we end up in a road race, we'll most likely come out the winner," Joshua continued as they put on their seatbelts. "If we are rolled, the inside has been retrofitted with a steel roll cage, to minimise any injuries. I fully expect you two are more than capable of healing faster than I am and will be able to neutralise anyone stupid enough to mess with you."

It satisfied Gard who relaxed in his seat, turning his head to look back at Rayne. "I guess we're all set then. Let's get to the safe house and then to the location Pietro was found."

"We sanitised the area, Gard. I don't know what you expect to find there." Joshua was concentrating on the road as he pulled out the parking garage, his eyes darting in all directions.

"We'll know it when we find it," the Ancient answered, satisfied that their escort was up to the task. "Keep him on of trouble, Rayne. I'm going to take a nap."

When Gard opened his eyes again, they were pulling up to the charred remains of a stone cottage. He'd been aware when they'd arrived at a similar styled cottage earlier, but had remained in the van while Joshua and Rayne transported their belongings inside. His mate was more than capable of checking the place over without his interference. While he did chafe at allowing her out of his sight, he knew he'd get no end of grief if he tried wrapping his panther up in cotton wool. Now they were at the location of Pietro's imprisonment and his eyes were lazily tracking their surroundings.

"Do you want to check the right hand side and I'll do the left?" he asked his mate, opening the door to get out of the vehicle.

"Demetri and I swept the area before we entered the building," Joshua supplied, not making any effort to get out. It was more than obvious that Gard viewed him as little more than a glorified chauffeur. It rankled considering they were on his patch but Caleb had asked him to give them what they wanted so he would overlook the slight.

"Knowing Demetri I'm sure you did an excellent job taking into consideration the time constraints you had," Rayne answered, giving him a brief smile before narrowing her eyes at her mate. "With Pietro's life no longer hanging in the balance we'll be able to perform a longer, more leisurely sweep."

Gard returned her gaze, unconcerned, though she could see in his eyes that he'd detected the subtle rebuke she was giving him. It was just like her mate to ignore the pleasantries when he was in full Guardian mode. In his mind, he wasn't here to make friends. He was here to find out who was a threat to his family and friends. Still, a little bit of common courtesy wouldn't go amiss.

Joshua, for the most part, didn't appear to be offended by Gard's abruptness so that was a mark in his favour. Rayne found herself liking the vampire the more time they spent in his company. She gave him another smile as she climbed out of the van. "If you see anything untoward, let us know immediately. Even if you think it's something innocuous. We have no idea of whom or what we're dealing with here so it's better to err on the side of caution."

"I had planned to," Joshua grinned back, his laconic demeanour filling Rayne with confidence. There was something infinitely trustworthy about him and it took her a moment to realise what it was. Her eyes widened a fraction as she nodded her head at him. "Nicely played, Joshua."

Gard was immediately alert, crossing back to her side and shooting a hard look at the vampire. "What?"

"He shares Liam and Reasa's talent. He's an empath."

It was Joshua's turn to look startled, his body language shifting imperceptibly. His shrewd gaze met Rayne's for a slow heartbeat and then he relaxed once more, a rueful smile crossing his handsome face. "How did you know?"

"I'm not that trusting, for one," she answered, still smiling. "And Demetri would spit you out faster than trust an outsider. I always did wonder how he worked so easily with you when he was here. Now I know."

Gard's eyes were still hard as he stared the other man down. "Whatever you're doing, stop now." His glare turned to his mate. "And just how was he able to breach your defences?

You know what's at stake here, Sarayne. You can't be this complacent."

It was her turn to be rebuked and she took her chastisement in the spirit it was given, her mate being concerned for her welfare. "You're right, Gard. I wasn't shielding as strongly because I was relying on Caleb's judgement of his friend. In my defence, he is very strong, probably on a par with Thereasa. I do find it curious that our European counterparts appear to have retained stronger mental skills than we have."

"Self-preservation can be very focusing," Joshua replied with a small shrug. "If I had known Reasa shared my gift, she wouldn't have gotten past me so easily." He shrugged again. "But then, I had donated a substantial amount of blood to Pietro at the time so my reserves were weakened."

He smiled again and then rested back against his seat. "Trust no one here...not even me. No one is quite what they seem and believe me, I have come across a few others who have some skill level in empathy. Let's just consider this as a lesson well learned."

For a moment it appeared Gard was about to press the issue but Rayne placed a hand on his arm. "Joshua is right. Now we have fair warning we will know what to expect. Let's see if we can find anything that could help track down our adversary." She shifted into her panther form, pressing her inky black body against his legs and emitting a low purr when he automatically reached down to stroke a hand down her back.

"I've placed a safeguard at the front of my mental defences," Rayne communication telepathically. "I suggest you do the same, something only we would know. That way we will be able to detect if anyone tries to tamper with our minds."

"Hmmm I knew there was a reason I chose you for my mate," Gard's voice rumbled through her mind, approval lacing every word as he continued to stroke her. He searched and found her safeguard instantly, a smile crossing his face as he did. It was a tall tree standing innocuously in front of a barred wooden door; the very same tree they had played in all those years ago. He mirrored her safeguard in his own mind and then stood up straight.

"Remember, Joshua. No mind games, and alert us if you see anything out of the ordinary." He turned and began a slow walk to the left of the burnt-out building, leaving his panther to begin her sweep of the right.

Dante pulled out his phone and checked his messages. It had vibrated in his pocket while he'd been talking with another other vampire in Louis coven, signalling he had a text. it had taken him a moment to extricate himself and slip outside but now he was reading the message, his lips tightening...'They're here.'

'Update when you can,' he tapped, and then shoved the phone back into his pocket. The pieces were all beginning to fall into place. There was still too much he was in the dark about, however the things he did know were enfolding just as he expected. With a quick glance at his watch he knew he had a little time in hand to make a quick side trip before Louis noticed his absence.

Dante took off at supernatural speed, running the relatively short distance to the hidden cave tucked away behind a thick copse of brambles. He ignored the scrapes he received as he made his way inside. The cave burrowed into the hillside with a narrow entrance that branched into a more cavernous area. Rock walls neatly divided it into three separate chambers.

The main chamber had a hot rock pool for bathing in and a rug on the floor, with cushions thrown down for seating. It was currently empty though the sound of his arrival brought its inhabitant from the left hand chamber.

"Hey, beautiful," Dante smiled, moving forward to engulf the petite woman in a tight bear hug. Long ebony waves tumbled down her back as she returned his embrace, her silver eyes unfocused as she rested her head against his chest.

"You shouldn't be here," Mila sighed, though it was evident from her tone that she was glad he was.

"I know, but I wanted to check in to make sure you were okay." Dante had been irrevocably drawn to the woman in his arms since the first moment he had met her. His friend Abraham had introduced them, a bare month before he had met his death at the hands of a rival coven. It was as if providence had conspired to place a new protector in her path before she lost the old one. It was a calling Dante had never chafed at being assigned.

"I'm more than capable of taking care of myself, Dante." Mila pulled away, walking unwaveringly towards the cushioned area to sink gracefully onto them.

It always amazed him to watch her interact with her surroundings. No one on the outside looking in would ever know that this frail, beautiful woman was blind in the conventional sense. Abraham had saved her from certain death, when disease had ravished her weakened body, turning her to the life of a vampire after her father had begged for her life. Mila had survived, however, her normal sight hadn't returned after the change. Instead, she had developed a new way of seeing, an ability to sense her surroundings by sound and vibrations.

If she encountered a moving object, that object transmitted itself to her mind in the form of a picture, her vision as clear in that 'snapped' moment as if she still had her sight. Her blindness had also morphed into something else, the ability to See future moments, though they had to be quite catastrophic before a Vision came to her.

Of all the people he had come across in his long life, Mila's abilities were the most unique and fascinating of them. They had spent many long hours discussing what she could do, trying to decipher how her talents had come about, but had never been able to come up with any kind of answers. Mila was simply Mila, the one person he treasured most in his world.

Dante loved her though he had never spoken of his feelings. He had no right to love or happy-ever-afters, not after the life he had led before being turned to a vampire. His history was strewn with blood and carnage, his self-righteous piousness being the cause of untold deaths. No, he didn't deserve forgiveness or happiness, but he would bask in the beauty of his love for however long she allowed him to accompany her.

Smiling sadly, he followed Mila down to the cushions, bracing an arm behind her so she could rest her head on his shoulders. "I know you don't need my protection," he belatedly answered her. "But I give it none the less."

"I know, and I am grateful for that, more than I can ever say." Mila sighed, closing her eyes to enjoy the companionable silence that often surrounded them. It was so soothing to sit quietly, savouring each other's company as they mulled over their own thoughts.

For a long moment, the only sound in the cave was their shared breathing, and then Mila shivered and sat up straight, concern shadowing her exquisite features. "Something bad is coming," she whispered, her voice shaking as the words breathed out. "Something terrible is on the horizon, blinded by the sunlight so I can't see what it is."

CHAPTER 4

Dante shivered at the words, wrapping his arms around Mila protectively. His hand stroked soothing down her arm. "Can you see anything else?" He couldn't keep the concern out of his voice.

"It's so dark, so cold. Death...head to tail in black." A sob escaped Mila as her shivering increased. "The world will swim in blood as the Justice Seeker wreaks havoc. There will be nowhere to hide, nowhere to run."

"Who is it, Mila? Try to see their face."

"Burning orbs...fire in their depths. Madness...depravity...a soul lost to grief. One so young, so lost, so full of unimaginable pain." Mila swallowed another loud sob, her shivering beginning to lessen as her sightless eyes stared off into the distance. "There is hope though; there is one who can reach the Justice Seeker. We must find her, Dante, and quickly, before everything we know is coated in blood."

As quickly as the Vision happened, it vanished and Mila sagged against him. Dante held her secure in his arms, kissing the top of her head as she took a few moments to come back to herself. "It's over, sweetness. You're safe here with me."

"Such rage, Dante," she whispered. "So much pain. I don't know if we'll be able to withstand his fury when he comes. If we can find the girl in time, we may have a chance."

Her words filled him with dread but he tried to hide his disquiet. This was the strongest Vision Mila had ever had, the most detailed one he could remember. It meant that whatever was coming their way was something they had never encountered before. Something so dangerous it could be the end of all of them.

"Who is the girl? Did you see her clearly?" It was important to get as much detail as possible after a Vision.

Mila nodded though her expression turned puzzled. "She is a waif, a human stray, young...just turned to womanhood. She is pretty, but hides behind thick glasses. Oh, she has such beautiful hair, long to her waist, the deepest brown with flecks of blonde highlights. The girl is graceless despite her beauty, awkward. She obscures her body in jeans and a T-shirt, using one of those hoodie things to hide her face.

Mila stiffened again, her eyes going wide with surprise. "She lives with wolves, Dante, though she is not of their pack."

"Shit!" he groaned at the news, his concern increasing. "We can't get close to any of the wolf packs here, Mila. How are we supposed to get to the girl if she's protected by Weres?"

"We can't," she answered after a long moment. "However, we can guide him to her once we discover where she is. I will start tracking the local packs to see if I can pick up any sign of her. We still have a little time."

Dante turned her around to face him, his eyes searching her features. He could see the stubborn set of her mouth and knew she had made up her mind already. That didn't stop him from speaking. "You know I don't like it when you go out on your own. I will do the investigating."

"We don't have time for you to divide your efforts...or to be so overprotective," Mila smiled reaching up to stroke his cheek. "You need to be focused on what's going on in the covens, Dante. Let me take care of the wolves."

He wanted to argue more, but knew it would be useless. When his Mila got that set look on her face...well that was one of the reasons he loved her so much. She refused to be a victim; she refused to accept that her lack of conventional vision limited her in any way. She was frail in appearance but so strong in will. She was his beautiful lady and always would be.

"Very well," he sighed, resting his forehead against hers. "Just don't do anything foolhardy, okay?"

"You're the risk taker out of us, dear Dante; I am but the trusted sidekick." She winked as she laughed, the soft tinkling sound making him yearn to taste that laughter in his mouth.

The urge to yield to temptation was strong but he held himself in check, maintaining his role of friend and guardian. Mila deserved so much better than him, and he knew one day that someone would come along and take her from his life. He knew his heart would break on that day but he would let his love go with no hesitation. Her happiness was paramount to him, it usurped all else and always would.

"I'd better get back before I'm missed," he said with a resigned sigh, standing and drawing Mila up with him. "I've heard some news. The Council have sent their investigators and they've arrived already. I need to be close to Louis to try to steer him in the right direction when he learns of this." "I'll let you know what, if anything, I find out," she answered, leaning against him as he wrapped her in his arms. "Be safe, dear Dante."

"I promise," he whispered into her hair. "No foolhardiness...remember."

"Be gone with you," Mila laughed, shaking her head at his protectiveness, though her tone was warm with affection.

Dante memorized that image of her standing there, before he turned and made his way out of the cave. Things were about to get busy and that image would have to last him for a while, until he could sneak away and come back to her.

"Ugh, he smells so wrong!"

"I'll be right there!" Gard moved at supernatural speed through the woodland, using his mate bond to track Rayne's location. It didn't take him long to find her though he was surprised how far she had travelled from the cottage.

"What made you look this far out?" His puzzlement was clear as he waited for his mate to shift back to her human form.

"I was wondering what Andrei or Alexei would do in the same circumstance," Rayne answered, rising to her feet and brushing her long hair over her shoulder. "I figured they would have used the trees initially, vampires are very sneaky that way." She shot him a smile, letting him know she classed him in that statement.

It brought an answering smile to his lips. "I had the same idea but scented nothing where I was."

"Michael travelled in this direction, using the trees for quite a while before he finally dropped down to the ground. He probably went on foot from here because he was nearing that road a mile or so that way." Rayne pointed off to the north and Gard heard the quiet hum of passing vehicles in that direction.

His attention turned back to his mate and he frowned, remembering her words. "What do you mean he smells wrong?"

Her expression changed, a distasteful pout crossing her face. "It's hard to explain it. My panther just didn't like his scent at all. The only way she could communicate it to me was wrong."

Gard had no choice but to accept what she said. He could pick up a mild vampiric scent but he had to concede that her Were ability when it came to scent was that bit more enhanced. Was this wrongness Rayne picked up insanity? He had heard before of some Weres being able to detect madness as a distinct scent. Opting to mull it over he pulled his mate into his arms and kissed her soundly. Whatever it was, they had picked up Michael's scent and now they needed to let Joshua know that they would be parting company with him to follow that scent.

"You wait here," he finally said when he'd finished ravishing her lips. "I'll let Joshua know we're heading off on our own."

Pietro sighed and squared his shoulders before pulling open the apartment door. It had taken him a while to work up the courage to head downstairs to the bar, longer than he had expected it to. He tried to convince himself it was because he wanted to put off being in public as long as possible but he had to admit that his conflicted emotions to do with Cassia were the main problem.

Despite Andrei's insistence that he work the previous night, Pietro had taken the time to settle into the upstairs apartment and try to deal with his anger at the blonde wolf who refused to get out of his head. Everywhere he looked he expected to see her, every sound he heard made him think of Cassia. He could scent her on his skin. He could still here the mournful wolf howl that had shattered his heart.

Was she okay? His concern wouldn't abate no matter how hard he tried to put her out of his mind. He had asked Andrei and been told to fuck off in no uncertain terms. His friend's expression had been so cold that for a moment Pietro had thought Andrei might possibly lash out, however he had merely turned away and disappeared into his basement office without a further word. Pietro couldn't really blame him, Cassia was his niece after all. Still, his friend could have at least let him know she was okay.

Sighing again, Pietro headed downstairs. There was little point in putting off the inevitable. He was about to be the main attraction in a freak show and nothing was going to prevent that. Striding into the bar area, he felt a sense of homecoming as he watched the wait staff finishing off the last minute cleaning projects before the doors opened for the night's revelry. He hadn't held court at the Dive in over twenty-five years and yet, this was his domain, this was what he knew.

One of the Youngling vampires stopped to stare at the scars on his face and he growled low in his throat. "Something I can help you with?"

She scurried off without a word and for a moment he felt some satisfaction but that quickly waned. He might still be able to scare Younglings but he was sure once word got out, he'd be subject to the scrutiny of every Elder vampire who wanted to view the freak show. He guessed he would have to deal with that as and when it happened.

Moving over to the bar, he settled himself behind it as the doors opened. It was time to see if he could still cut it among his peers.

Pietro blinked in surprise as his first customer of the night arrived at the bar and sat herself down on one of the barstools. He looked around for her companion but he was nowhere in sight.

"Annie?"

"Pietro?"

She smiled at him and it was obvious that she wasn't going to answer his unasked question. Her exquisite features were a carefully constructed mask of innocence though he had to look away from the intensity of her questioning stare. He didn't even know if it was Annie sitting there or the vampire queen. He had yet to meet Anakatrine though he had heard plenty about her.

Deciding that it was most probably Annie given their surroundings, Pietro opted not to push for answers. No one ever knew what the beautiful redhead was truly up to, he doubted even Caleb did some times. "What can I get you?" he finally asked, shooting her a quick smile.

"Red wine please." Rhianna brushed her red curls over her shoulder and turned to survey the early patrons already beginning to fill up the bar. "Looks like there's going to be a large crowd tonight. I wonder why that is. I didn't think this place pulled in crowds like Karpathia's."

"Word has probably spread that there's a freak show in town," Pietro answered setting her drink down in front of her. He couldn't hide the bitterness from his tone.

She sighed, turning back to him. "You're probably right. Sometimes I despair of our kind."

He had expected a lecture and was surprised not to receive one. He didn't know Rhianna as well as most of their inner circle did but he was aware of her high empathy level. It was on the tip of his tongue to ask but then he realised that she was setting him up to do just that. That sparked his irritation and he held his tongue out of pure stubbornness.

"So, where's Caleb? I didn't expect he would let you out of his sight any time soon."

It was Rhianna's turn to watch him speculatively for a moment before she smiled and sipped at her wine. "Ancient Council business, he will be along later."

Pietro wanted to laugh at her feigned innocence. He was well aware that anything Rhianna Armand did...well there usually was some reason behind it. He decided to call her bluff. "Exactly what is it I can do for you, Annie?"

Her smile turned enigmatic and there was a twinkle in her lavender eyes as she beamed at him. "Perhaps the question should be what can I do for you, Pietro?"

It was hard not to smile back and he conceded defeat with a rueful shake of his head. "Okay, what can you do for me?"

"Well I can let you know that Cassia is going to be okay, for one, and I can sit here with you while you become accustomed to the inevitable scrutiny you're about to be subjected to."

The relief at her words was palpable. He didn't give a rat's ass about being stared at, but having some positive confirmation that Cassia would recover from his absence felt like a burden being lifted from his shoulders. Pietro couldn't put a finger on why he was so concerned about the wolf, after all, it wasn't as if he was her mate. No, they had just scratched an itch, and while the sex between them had been nothing more than that...it had been amazing. It was natural to be concerned about her; he had always been considerate to the women who'd graced his bed. Add in the fact she was Alexei's daughter, and his concern was totally justified.

"I'm glad to hear that, Annie, about Cassia. I don't need my hand being held though."

Rhianna laughed, causing a few heads to turn in their direction. "Oh, Pietro, you are so very male. As if you would have the first inkling of what you truly need." She sipped at her wine again and when her gaze connected with his there was something very old hidden in their lavender depths. "I believe I will wait for Caleb here, none the less."

A vampire sidled up to the bar before Pietro could answer, the male sitting on a stool beside Rhianna. He was an elder; beautiful as most of their kind was, but clearly so new to the area that he couldn't detect danger when it was staring him in the face.

"Whatever this little beauty is having and mine will be a beer." He slid money onto the counter, dismissing the bartender and focusing on the petite redhead. "I knew I made the right decision coming to this godforsaken place. If I'd known the scenery was so exquisite I would have come sooner."

Rhianna let her gaze roam lazily over him, acknowledging that some women would find him quite a catch. Silvery blond hair and clear crystal blue eyes painted a pretty picture but he couldn't hold a candle to Caleb. "That seat is taken, my friend."

"Really? I don't see anyone but old scarface here." The vampire's lip curled in distaste as he spoke, though he didn't spare a glance at Pietro. "Surely you don't find those blemishes attractive?"

A chill seemed to fill the air as Rhianna's eyes narrowed and the smile that had been on her face melted away. "On the contrary there is nothing more beautiful than the mark of true courage. Every line that speaks of pain and suffering, every tear that tells the world one has suffered but conquered despite that...to me that is something to be revered and respected above all else." Her gaze turned from the man at her side and she smiled at Pietro. "This seat is still taken."

"You know, you're very snooty for a Youngling. I think someone needs to teach you some manners." The amorous note had vanished from the vampire's voice to be replaced by a hard edge.

If he thought his words would concern her, he was sadly mistaken. Instead of cowing Rhianna, she laughed softly. "And you truly think you are the one to do so? Believe me, friend, many much better than you have tried. I suggest you go enjoy your evening elsewhere before you regret your decision to sit here."

"Who's going to make me, Youngling? You? I hardly think so."

Pietro moved without thinking. The entire time he had listened to Rhianna's conversation with the other male his protective instincts had kicked into gear, his ire rising with each passing word. This fuckwit thought it was acceptable to hit on Caleb's mate? He thought it was safe to ignore Pietro's presence because he had some visible scars on show?

Pietro vaulted over the bar at supernatural speed, slashing his talons across the other vampire's face as he did. In less time it took a heart to beat, he was squarely between Rhianna and the vampire now lying on his back on the floor. "Get out!"

The vampire was too stupid to pay any heed. He sprang to his feet, throwing a punch and kicking out at the same time. Pietro deftly avoided both, landing his own punch in the vampire's face, the force of his blow propelling the other male across the room to land in the midst of a crowed table.

People scattered in all directions as the bartender stalked to the stunned vampire and lifted him from the floor by his neck. "If you want to keep your head I strongly suggest you get the fuck out of here now and don't ever come back," he hissed through clenched teeth, giving the vampire a rough shake for good measure.

Pietro tossed him towards the door and glared at the rest of the room as the wounded vampire beat a hasty exit. "And that goes for anyone else who thinks to challenge scarface. Spread the word. Pietro de la Rios is back and this bar is his. Anyone who thinks differently will answer to me!"

Stunned silence filled the room for a long moment and then everyone went back to what they were doing. The wait staff hurried over to clear up the mess, Pietro's gaze cataloguing the entire room until he was satisfied that he'd made his point. With a shake of his head, he turned back to Rhianna to find her smiling as she watched him.

"Can I have another glass of wine, please? On the house I think...seeing as you spilled my first glass when you vaulted over the bar."

It took a moment for her words to sink in, for his brain to catch up with what had just happened. Pietro kept his expression as neutral as possible though he knew he wasn't fooling the redhead. He had vaulted over the bar and taken down the vampire as if he were a Youngling and not an elder. Technically, the other male should have kicked his ass however Pietro felt stronger than he'd ever felt before.

How was this possible? He should still be recovering from Europe but if it hadn't been for the scars he bore, he could almost believe Europe had never happened. Something had healed him faster than should have been possible and he was starting to have an inkling to what that might be. There was only one thing he'd done since he'd returned that could account for the faster healing. He had taken Cassia's blood as nourishment...

The six vampires filed silently into the imposing redbrick mansion nestled behind a twelve-foot high wall in one of the exclusive residential areas at the edge of the city. The female who opened the door waited for the last one to pass and then closed it quietly behind them. Her eyes alighted on Michael and acknowledged him as the leader of the group.

"Organise your men and then meet me in the library. It's the mahogany door just there." She pointed to a door to the left of the ornate staircase in the main hallway, turning in that direction without waiting for a response.

Michael felt the urge to break her neck because of the way she ordered him about. Not that it would have killed her as she was a vampire like them, but it would have hurt and shown her who was boss. However, he wasn't allowed to do that despite how much he would have liked to. He had ordered him to obey the female, telling him that she was his eyes and ears on this continent.

With a flick of his hand, he motioned the others to head upstairs and find rooms to make themselves comfortable. He headed towards the back of the house to where the female waited. Opening the door, his gaze focused first on the female and then the room. It was a library like any other he had seen, full of towering bookcases filled with books, and the customary desk and seating areas. The female was sitting behind the desk, watching him with a neutral expression.

She looked young but something told him that appearance was deceptive. Everything about the woman was deceptive. There was no way in hell her hair was short and blonde. He could just make out where the wig began and he could see the barest hint of a ring around her irises that told him the pale blue of her eyes was a lie too. Whoever she was, she had gone out of her way to alter her appearance.

"What do I call you?"

"Candrea will suffice, and you are Michael," she answered coolly, motioning him to sit down. "How many of your team work for The Master?"

He hissed as he was lowering himself into his seat, fire in his eyes as he glared at her. "Do not mention Him out aloud!"

She was undaunted by his response, a half-smile gracing her beautiful face. "Yes, he did say you were a bit of zealot, but I hadn't expected you to be this far gone. There is nothing wrong with speaking of him. Naturally, he should only be mentioned to those who perform his tasks, and as we are both his willing disciples, I will continue to speak however I like in your presence. If you have an issue with that I suggest you raise it with him and he will educate you accordingly."

Michael gritted his teeth, forcing himself to remain in the chair facing her as the urge to take her head built at a steady rate. He wouldn't like it if he hurt the female. Michael kept that mantra running through his mind as he continued to glare at Candrea.

"What are your orders?"

"Answer my question!" The words grated out, raw command in Candrea's tone as her hand slapped the desk hard.

Michael jumped at the unexpected sound, his eyes narrowing in fury. What question did she want answered? He couldn't remember her asking one.

"How many in your team work for The Master?"

It was only as she repeated it that he realised he had spoken the words out aloud. "None. Only me."

His answer appeared to set her thinking for a moment because she didn't respond immediately. Finally, she nodded and leaned on the desk. "Any that are not killed during the assault on the pack will need to be taken care of then. Are you up to that task?"

Killing brought him the most happiness, not including speaking with his Master. Nothing transcended that. The smile he gave her was nothing short of chilling. "It will be my pleasure."

"Good." Candrea rose, smoothing down her figure hugging skirt as she did. "I will leave this phase in your capable hands then. You will not contact me or attempt to discover who or where I am. If you have need of me for any reason leave the library curtains open at night with that table lamp on." She pointed to a small lamp near the window. "I will be informed and come as soon as I can."

Michael stayed rooted to his chair as she left, his homicidal impulses still driving him. He felt out of control and that wasn't a good thing with the task ahead of him. "Master..."

"You arrived safely, Michael?"

The instant his voice filled his mind, the vampire felt the first tendrils of peace begin to wash over him. His voice was so beautiful...it wrap around him, enveloped him, lifted him to a level of serenity so blissful he could live in the moment forever. "Yes, Master. I have met with the woman as you instructed. I am finding her...challenging. She speaks of you out aloud, Master!" He couldn't keep his loathing from his tone.

"You must do as she says, Michael. I have already instructed you on her importance to me. She is my voice there and you must heed her words."

The Master's voice was cold and hard, menace creeping into it as he spoke that sent a shiver of fear down the vampire's spine. "I obey, Master. Please don't be angry with me. Please!"

"As long as you heed my words there will be no need to incite my wrath. Carry out the task Louis has assigned to you, however, perform your main task too. Find the weakness I seek and return with that knowledge as soon as possible. Do not fail me, Michael."

The Master withdrew from his thoughts, but not before he sent a shaft of reassurance down their bond. It was enough to make Michael sit up straighter, his mind clearing a little of its zeal so he could perform the duties assigned to him.

Rising, he headed out of the library and upstairs to find a room where he could rest. Candrea was lucky she'd put the idea into his head to contact him, otherwise she may not have seen many more days. He must treat her as he would the Master...until such times he allowed him to kill her. Smiling, Michael lay on the bed fully clothed, closing his eyes to rest after their long journey.

PART 6

CHAPTER 1

"Well that was unexpected." Rhianna grinned up at Caleb, who returned her rapt gaze though there was a hint of thoughtfulness in his golden brown eyes.

They were gathered downstairs in Andrei's office at the Dive, the Romanov twins lounging on the sofa with speculative expressions on their faces. Rhianna had told Caleb of the earlier altercation when he'd arrived to pick her up. He had immediately summoned the twins to the club and ordered Pietro to have someone tend the bar and meet them downstairs.

Pietro wasn't looking too happy at being scrutinised so closely, his body language tense and a deep scowl pulling at the scar on his cheek.

"Yes, it is a very interesting development," Caleb agreed, his gaze peering off into the distance for a moment as he considered the implications of what had happened.

"If you're going to discuss me don't you think you should clue me in," Pietro grumbled, his irritation ratcheting up a notch. He didn't want to be the centre of attention and he especially didn't like some of the glances Alexei was shooting in his direction. His friend was clearly unhappy with what had happened between him and his daughter. Pietro was sure Alexei would have something to say about that very soon.

It came sooner than he anticipated though, as it was the blond vampire who answered him. "You've taken my daughter's blood," Alexei growled, an undefined emotion in his eyes. "There has been some speculation that Varcolac blood could heal your scars, however that doesn't appear to be the case."

"Alexei..." Pietro wasn't quite sure what he was going to say to his friend, he just knew he would have to come up with something good. He was surprised when he was cut off.

"That conversation is for another place and time." Alexei's tone held a note of finality that his friend was wise enough not to challenge. He was right anyway. They would have that conversation at a later date.

Pietro turned back to Rhianna and Caleb, raising an eyebrow in query.

"It would appear that while Varcolac blood can't heal your scars, it has significantly boosted your recovery time from the aftereffects of your ordeal," Rhianna explained. "From that little display, I would hazard a guess that you're back to full strength."

As her words sank in, Pietro replayed the fight, remembering the table where the vampire had landed. He'd thrown the other male clear across the room and with such force it had shattered the thick wood into splinters! No wonder the room had responded instantly when he had warned them. Before Europe, he had been strong but now...he was stronger than he had once been.

He had wondered at why he had felt so strong...if it could have had something to do with Cassia's blood, but the realisation still stunned him. He could feel the raw power of his increased strength flowing through his veins. It made his heart pound hard and a feeling of dizziness assault him, but he dampened the weakness down, his beast preening at the enhanced abilities he now had.

Cassia's blood had not only nourished him, it had made him stronger. He was staggered at the knowledge and didn't know what it could mean for him. He just knew that right now, he didn't feel half the failure he once had. He would analyse what else he was feeling later.

"I'm stronger." It didn't cross his mind to withhold the information. These were his oldest friends; this was his Queen and King. They had a right to know because it could help combat the threat from Europe.

"Did Cassia bite you?"

"Caleb!" Alexei's growl was fierce.

"I'm sorry, Alexei, we're not trying to make this more difficult for you than it already is, but we need to know." Annie's expression was sympathetic as she reached across and placed a hand gently on the Ancient's arm. "Caleb's question is a good one though possibly could have been broached with a little more tact."

Her mate grinned, his expression unrepentant, and it was hard not to laugh at his smugness. He was enjoying watching Alexei's discomfort, as was Andrei.

"Karma's a bitch, isn't it?" Andrei laughed, mischief dancing in his eyes as he teased his twin.

"Keep it up," his brother answered, cold, hard menace in each word.

"No she didn't," Pietro interjected, before the Romanov twins could devolve into one of their rare, but vicious fights. It was bad enough dealing with Andrei after his dalliance with Cassia, but Alexei too? He could understand his friend's need to protect his daughter. Alexei didn't need his nose rubbed in the fact his best friend had slept with her.

"So the infected vampire just needs to drink Varcolac blood to enhance healing," Caleb said, tapping a long finger against his lips. "Do you think there would be some merit in testing their blood against the live sample of the toxin? Possibly we could discover the antidote or an inoculation that would protect vampires from being infected?"

Andrei and Alexei both bristled, disbelief crossing their faces. "You want to experiment with our children's blood?" Andrei drawled softly, the small smile playing at his lips a blatant warning sign.

Rhianna placed a hand on her mate's arm when he went to speak, her gaze firmly fixed on Andrei. It halted whatever response he was about to give, his eyes searching her expression for a moment before he inclined his head.

She gave him a warm smile, glancing quickly at him before turning back to the others. "Andrei, you know in your heart that the Varcolac, Rayne included, would be the first to offer samples of their blood to try to protect those they love. It would be no imposition to them and they would come to no harm from it. We would never allow any harm to come to them."

"It still doesn't mean we have to be happy about our children being used as guinea pigs, Annie," Alexei retorted, making it clear he shared his brother's views. "Pietro's recovery occurred naturally. Cassia chose to nourish him with her blood. This...this...experimentation isn't natural."

Lavender eyes flared brightly, the air around them burning hot for the briefest of moments before it cooled down again. The male vampires mopped at their brows with the exception of Caleb, who stood behind his mate with his hands resting on her shoulders.

"We use the tools that fit the job," Anakatrine, Queen of Vampires, announced, leaning into the strong body behind her. "We have not suffered for countless millennia to get to this point just to have petty egos and overprotective fathers get in the way. Your love for your families do you credit, however our people are in danger. Your children are our future. No harm will come to them from any actions we may take this day."

"I hate it when she does that," Alexei grumbled, his anger waning as he watched Rhianna blink slowly once, and then turn her head to look up at Caleb.

"It is rather disconcerting when you're not expecting it," she smiled ruefully.

"This is something we need to talk to Rafe and Mallen about, possibly Cassia too," Caleb announced, his hard stare focusing on the Romanov twins ensuring they weren't going to continue to be stupid. When he saw they were thinking with their heads as opposed to their hearts, he relaxed his tense stance, gathering Rhianna close. "We'll head over there right now. Rayne and Gard are due to check in soon too if they haven't already. It might be best if you two stay here."

"Fuck that, it's my daughter that's involved. Andrei can keep an eye on things here. I'm heading back to the pack with you." Alexei didn't wait for approval from them, he spun on his heel and headed out the office, using the back entrance to leave the club.

"Can I watch when you and my brother have your chat?" Andrei laughed, merriment dancing in his eyes as Pietro watched his friend depart.

"Bite me!" the bartender growled, nodding to Caleb and Annie, and heading back upstairs to his bar. He'd had enough of talk about healing and Cassia. He was roiling inside, a fury so dark that he hoped that no one decided to test him again until he had it firmly under control.

Something about the thought of Cassia's blood being given to others infuriated him. It made no sense, seeing as he'd cut off all ties with the wolf. It didn't stop his loathing though or dampen the need to rip something or someone apart with his bare hands...

* * * * *

Caleb pulled up outside their home and turned off the car engine. For a moment he just sat there, listening to the silence, and then he turned his head to look at the woman at his side.

Rhianna's eyes were closed, her face relaxed in sleep. It had been a particularly long day for both of them though he oddly felt wide-awake. Staring at his beautiful mate, he was loath to wake her up, so he slid soundlessly from the car, moving around to the passenger side. She stirred a little when he scooped her out of the car, and then she settled against his wide chest.

He was often staggered by the trust she had in him. She always had, even when there had been times he'd given her reason to doubt him. He had always thought he had appreciated just what she brought to his life, but it had only been when they were apart that he had realised just how lost he would be without her.

His Annie was all that was good about him. She was the lighter side of his soul that often tempered the darkness. He couldn't love her any more than he did. She was the reason his heart beat, the single most important thing in his life.

"You think too much," she murmured sleepily, rubbing her cheek against his chest as he carried her into the house.

"Have you taken up mind reading, oh wise one," he chuckled, kicking the door closed behind them and heading up the ornate staircase to their room.

"Don't need to. Your heart picks up a beat when you're thinking deeply about something. I can hear it thudding in my ear."

Caleb dropped a kiss on top of her head, gently laying her down on their bed. "I can't keep any secrets from you, can I?" he laughed, his golden brown eyes glowing with love as he stared down at her.

"Would you want to?" Her lavender eyes fluttered open sleepily, a hint of curiousness shining in their depths.

His hand reached out to brush her tangled curls from her cheek, lingering there to touch the softness of her skin. "No, I do not wish to have any secrets from you, my love."

For a long moment she peered up at him and then she smiled, tangling her fingers in his hair. "Right answer," she laughed, pulling his head down until their lips were mere inches apart. "That deserves some kind of reward. What do you think would be a suitable one?"

"You are such a wench at times, my heart. There is only ever one reward that I ever want from you." It was hard not to laugh at the smug expression on her exquisite face, and he settled on kissing her soundly to forestall any further conversation.

Kissing his woman was always like the very first time. It didn't matter how many times he sipped at the sweetness of her lips, he drank as if he were starved. Love, lust, and passion, collided in an instant spark between them, need clawing at his gut to be satisfied.

Everything about his Annie filled him with an unquenchable thirst and he knew he would never tire of laying with her like this. "I love you," he breathed into her mouth, kissing her answering words as they escaped her lips. "You are my reason for being, my sweet Annie. You are the very air that I breathe. Tell me it will always be this way. Being apart from you almost crushed me. I was so afraid you wouldn't come home."

She moved quickly, pushing him back as she sat up, climbing astride him, and wrapping her arms around his neck. Resting her forehead against his, her serious lavender eyes demanded his full attention. "There is nowhere else I would rather be, Caleb. Home is wherever you are and I will always come home to you. Please don't ever doubt that. Nothing will ever take my love from you."

"Annie..." The wealth of love that travelled their mate bond enhanced her words; filling his heart with so much affection that the very last of his concern that he would lose her melted away in an instant. Capturing her mouth once more, he kissed her hard and bore her back against the bed, his hands peeling her clothes adeptly from her body.

He wanted to be gentle, he wanted to take his time, but his need to join with his beautiful mate was more than he could stand. Sliding deep inside her velvet warmth, Caleb rocked his hips slowly, sliding in and out of her body to the slow thudding of their heartbeats.

"Loving you like this is a moment of perfection, Annie. Nothing transcends being with you, nothing is more perfect than making love to you."

A soft moan escaped her, her hips rising to meet his downward thrusts. "I don't ever want you to stop loving me like this, Caleb. I want to spend eternity with you; joined together, feeling our hearts beat in tandem. I love you, my beautiful vampire, now and forever."

They danced together in the ancient rhythm of love, Caleb's lips travelled every inch of her soft skin with a feather light touch. He tempted and teased his love with long, slow caresses, inciting her passion, slowly building her up to that perfect moment of union that was just outside her reach.

How he loved every moment with her. He teased her mercilessly until she demanded more, and then he picked up the tempo, taking her with long, hard, deep strokes until her body arched up and she cried out her pleasure. Her body rippled around his, and it was enough to shatter his self-control and send him tumbling over the edge.

"Annie!" Her name was ripped from his throat as his own pleasure peaked, and he was soaring on a wave of ecstasy so intense his entire body shook with the effort it took to hold himself up.

His Annie was trembling when he finally came down from the heady heights they had soared, and he soothed her brow with tiny kisses. With a final tasting of her trembling lips, Caleb lay on his side behind her, spooning her body against his, stroking a hand over the curve of her hip as their breathing began to calm down.

"I love you, Annie." Snuggling his face into the side of her neck, Caleb closed his eyes and allowed sleep to claim him.

Rhianna lay in the protection of her mate's embrace, listening to the gentle rhythm of his heartbeat that told her he had fallen asleep. She was sleepy too, but something was keeping her awake; something that teased at her subconscious mind.

Being careful not to wake Caleb, she raised herself up on one elbow, letting her eyes wander around the bedroom slowly; trying to find what it was that was nagging at her brain. Her gaze flitted over her dressing table, alighting on the old leather-bound book that was resting where she had left it.

Masking Lavender, the second book Anakatrine had selected from her library, a book that hadn't been examined as thoroughly as the other because it hadn't appeared to be as crucial. She had read some of it, and been stunned at what it contained. The knowledge within belonged only to those of royal blood, and Rhianna hadn't translated it to English just in case it fell into the wrong hands.

Caleb hadn't asked to read the book, he appeared to have completely forgotten about it. The only other person who could have read the text was Gard and she had no idea if he had even seen it let alone read it. Was she the only one to know what it contained? Should she mention it to her mate?

Caleb had said he would never keep a secret from her. If she didn't tell him what she'd learned would that mean she was keeping a secret from him? The knowledge within the book couldn't truly relate to them, could it? They weren't really Anakatrine and Callain, they were but vessels for their spirits.

No, now was not the time to be diverted by things that would likely never come to pass. There was so much else at stake at the moment, and they needed all their attention to be focused squarely on Europe where the real danger lay.

Lying back down, Rhianna snuggled into Caleb's chest, sighing with pleasure as he gathered her close in his sleep. "I love you, Caleb," she whispered, closing her eyes and allowing her tired mind to finally drift off to sleep.

* * * * *

"Mallen...oh my goodness...it works." The words whispered out of Cassia's mouth but everyone in the lab heard her, all heads turning to look at the blond wolf who was staring down a microscope.

"Let me see." Mallen strode across the lab, his expression hopeful as she stepped aside to let him view the results. "Your lymphocytes are working." The words breathed out quietly, hushed awe filling the room. "Your B-cells are creating antibodies to the toxin."

Mallen looked up again, a wide grin crossing his face as excitement filled him. "I don't know why you thought of using a sample of your bone marrow as opposed to just your blood, Cassia, but it's worked."

Relief like nothing she'd ever experienced before flooded through Cassia. The first attempt at just using her blood hadn't achieved the desired results and they'd all been bitterly disappointed. She'd had Mallen extract a little bone marrow and retested. That was where antibodies were made, and it seemed the logical choice. To find it had worked...Cassia was so overcome that tears flowed freely down her cheeks.

She couldn't account for how Pietro had become stronger though. He had only taken blood from her, not any bone marrow. Was it a mate thing? Would she ever know the answer to that? For the moment, she didn't care. They had finally found something that could counteract the toxin in Amort. It would take a while to harvest enough bone marrow from the Varcolac to make sufficient antidote, but they would soon be able to inoculate every vampire against the poison.

"We have to tell Rafe," Cassia announced, laughing through the tears still streaming down her face.

The doctor smiled at her, his grin as big as Cassia's. "You do it, honey. It was your idea and you've worked your butt off to get here. We'll start working on a suspension to deliver the antidote."

Giving him a quick hug, Cassia ran out of the lab, slamming through the front door of the Alpha's home and nearly knocking Lacey over as she was coming downstairs.

"Oh, I'm sorry, Lacey!" Cassia was immediately contrite, placing steadying arms out to ensure her Alpha didn't crash to floor. "Is Rafe awake? I need to speak to him urgently."

"He's eating breakfast, I believe." Lacey laughed at the exuberant expression on the younger woman's face. She didn't ask any questions, merely escorted her into the dining room where her mate was tucking into bacon and eggs.

Rafe glanced up with a raised eyebrow as they entered, quietly placing his fork and knife down beside his plate.

"We did it," Cassia announced with the biggest smile. "We have an antidote, Rafe!"

"You're certain?" Rafe rose from his seat to stride over to them.

Cassia nodded, trying to regain her composure and not giggle like a schoolgirl. "The Varcolac have antibodies in their bone marrow. We harvested a little of mine and tested it against the toxin. My B-cells immediately began multiplying to attack the poison. The process was still ongoing when I left, but Mallen agrees that it is a viable antidote. If any other vampires become infected as badly as Pietro, we can use our antibodies directly to cure them."

"Cassia, that's fantastic news!" Rafe gathered her up in a warm hug, grinning at Lacey who had started to cry. "Come here," he growled softly, pulling his mate into a group hug.

"Oh Rafe...Annie and Caleb will be so happy." Lacey fought to stop crying, relief in every word.

"Mallen is currently synthesising a suspension we can use to create a vaccination too, so that we can effectively inoculate the entire vampire race here," Cassia continued, stepping back and smiling as she looked at her Alphas. "In theory...that will mean that even if they are infected by Amort, their own bodies should be able to fight the poison."

"You have made us so proud, Cassia," Rafe said, a burst of love and pride flowing down his Alpha bond with the blond wolf, bringing happy tears to her eyes.

"It was a group effort," she answered and felt another burst of deep pride, this time from both the Alphas.

Lacey extricated herself from Rafe's arms, gathering the younger woman close. "You are an amazing young woman, Cassia Romanov, and we are so blessed to have you in our pack. You have given up much to help, not only the vampires, but also to protect your pack. It is time you now did something for yourself. Go and claim your mate, honey. Don't take No for an answer either. It's your time now. We can handle everything else."

"I agree." Rafe smiled down at her, reaching out a hand to ruffle her curls affectionately. "If you need any pointers, I suggest you ask your Aunt Loretta. She had the most difficult time convincing your Uncle Andrei that he was her mate."

Now that she had finally done what she'd set out to do, Cassia could now look to her own future. Getting through to Pietro probably wasn't going to be that easy, but she had the blessing of her Alphas as well as her parents.

"That might be a good idea," she answered with a half-smile tugging at her lips.

Heading back out into the compound, Cassia turned in the direction of her own house first. She wanted to pack a light travelling bag before she had a chat with Loretta. Her aunt had said she could talk to her if she needed to, and this seemed like as good a time as ever. Pietro de la Rios was about to be in for a big shock if he thought he could get rid of her that easily. Cassia wasn't coming back to the pack until she had her vampire in tow.

Her parents were out when she got home and there was no sign of her sister. Cassia threw some clothes into a backpack, as she waited for her call to her mother to connect.

"Hi, sweetheart, is everything okay?"

She smiled at the distracted quality in her mother's voice. Whatever she was doing, it had most of her attention.

"We found an antidote, Mom. We can cure any more vampires who are infected as long as we get to them in time."

"Cassia, that's fantastic! Oh honey, your father and I are so proud of you. I presume Rafe knows?"

There was so much love and pride in her mother's voice that it brought happy tears to her eyes. "Yes, I'm just back from speaking to him and Lacey. I wanted to let you know not to worry when you came home and find me out. I'm going to go see Pietro and I may stay with him for a little while."

There was a long pause before her mother exhaled softly. "I'll let your father know and I will make sure he stays out of your hair until you and Pietro have had time to sort things out. Cass...there won't be a repeat of the last time, will there?"

Although she tried to hide her worry, Cassia could hear it in every word her mother said. She wished she were with her mom so she could give her a reassuring hug. "Mom, I will be fine, really I will. I was just caught off-guard the last time. Now I know how difficult it will be to convince Pietro he's my mate, I'm prepared for him to put up a bit of a fight."

"If you need us, you know where we are, honey. We will always be here for you, no matter what. Now, go get that mate of yours and shake some sense into him. You should stop by your Aunt Loretta's before you head over there. She could give you some helpful tips on how to get through Pietro's thick skull."

Cassia burst out laughing, shaking her head. "You're the second person to suggest that. I was intending to anyway. Okay, I'd better get going so I'll give you a call later tonight, Mom."

"Take care, honey."

She was still smiling as she threw her backpack over her shoulder and headed downstairs, locking up behind her, and heading over to her aunt's house...

* * * * *

"Are you sure?" Cassia stared at Loretta with a doubtful expression, trying not to smile at the pure devilment shining in her aunt's eyes.

"Believe me, honey, Pietro was way too helpful back then when I had the same problem with your uncle. Oh, he feigned innocence and stuck to it, but I have no doubt whatsoever that he was completely aware of what he was doing at the time. The phrase poetic justice comes to mind."

"What mischief are you getting up to now, woman?" Andrei entered the kitchen and swooped down for a quick kiss from his mate before turning to his bemused-looking niece.

"I was just giving Cass some advice on how to get Pietro's attention."

He turned to look back at Loretta before throwing his head back and laughing. "Yes, that would be poetic justice," he echoed his mate's statement that he'd walked in on. "You have my wholehearted approval, niece."

Cassia wasn't so sure she liked how eager her aunt and uncle were for her to publicly humiliate her mate. One part of her could see the humorous side of possibly doing so, but the other part was concerned that Pietro had been through more than enough already. His ego may not be able to withstand any more humiliation.

"I'll bear it in mind," she sighed giving them a quick hug. "I'm going to head over to the Dive just now to try to speak to him."

"Do you want me to go with you?" Andrei asked, his earlier amusement vanishing in an instant, and his expression turning serious.

"No offence, Andrei, but that would be like taking my dad with me. Actually, now I come to think about it, it would probably be worse." Cassia hugged him again to take any perceived insult from her comment. Not that her uncle was the least insulted. Instead, he gave her one of his warm smiles that he reserved for those family members that he treasured.

"You have a point, sweetheart," he conceded.

"You shouldn't look so damned proud of that fact," his mate interjected, though she was laughing as she said it.

"Thanks for the advice," Cassia called over her shoulder as she headed out of the house. Now that she had made up her mind that she was going to beard the lion in his den, she wanted to get over to the Dive before her courage failed her. Her wolf was anxious to be with their mate and so was the woman. Climbing into one of the pack Jeeps, Cassia fired up the engine and headed into town.

* * * * *

Fox hit the disconnect button on his phone and slid it into his back pocket. His Alpha wanted him home on the next flight available, and he wasn't best pleased about that. His wolf had been antsy for days now, ever since he had bumped into the blonde wolf and her vampire companion.

Cassia; yes that was her name. Cassia what? Who was she and why had his wolf sat up and been so interested in the woman? He didn't think it was the mating instinct kicking in though he could be wrong. What he'd learned about the wolves here was that their mating instinct was an instantaneous thing as opposed to a more gradual thing among his kind in Europe. Surely if it was the mating pull Cassia would have known instantly and tried to claim him?

It was disconcerting how he couldn't get her off his mind though, and he didn't like it. He had been sent over here by his Alpha to track down the non-aligned Weres that had been crossing the Atlantic Ocean. His mission was to try to determine what they were up to, and what, if anything, their actions may mean for the European packs.

There was far too much uncertainty among the supernatural races in Europe at the moment. The vampires were up to something. This was evident in the way their attention had turned away from trying to exterminate the Were population there. Something was focusing them stateside, and there were rumours of Ancient vampires being on European soil for the first time in centuries. Add in the strange behaviour of the lone wolves crossing the Ocean, and there was enough strangeness happening to concern most of the covens as well as the few integrated packs that still managed to reside as a unit.

He didn't have time to be diverted by a wolf, no matter how beautiful she was. He didn't have any of the answers that he'd hoped to find either, so he wasn't happy about being summoned home. He couldn't refuse his Alpha though. If she said they had to come home then they had to. Muttering a curse, he spun on his heel and threaded his way back towards the motel they taken up residence at.

He'd barely taken a handful of steps when a scent wafted towards him on the breeze and he froze on the spot. He had only scented it once before, but his wolf new instantly who it was. His head turned to the left, catching a glimpse of blonde curls vanishing into one of the nearby nightclubs - Cassia. His feet were moving before he could register what he was doing, moving towards a place called The Dive and the woman that he couldn't get out of his head...

* * * * *

"We're closed!" Pietro barked out, as the front door opened, not deigning to turn from stocking the shelves with bottles of alcohol.

"I said we're closed!" He roared again, spinning around when it became apparent whoever it was wasn't leaving. His mouth dropped open, and he blinked in surprise when he saw who his visitor was. How the hell could he not have scented her? It was only as he thought it that he realised that she must have masked her scent as she entered.

Closing his mouth and swallowing hard, he greedy gaze roamed over Cassia's exquisite face, drinking in each feature like a starving man. Had it really only been a day or so since he had last seen her? It felt like a lifetime, and he didn't like the way his hands felt so clammy and his heart raced just at the sight of her. She looked good...better than good. She looked perfect. There were some tell-tale signs of strain around her mouth, but apart from that she looked well.

"What are you doing here, Cassia?" The words barked out more aggressively than he intended, and he had to force himself not to cross over to her when she flinched noticeably. He truly didn't want to hurt her, not even when he couldn't shake the feelings of betrayal seeing her brought back to the surface.

"We found an antidote to the poison. I wanted to let you know that, so you wouldn't be worried about being infected again."

Pietro inhaled deeply, a shiver of relief coursing through his body. She had done it? His beautiful wolf had finally found a cure to Amort? Pride as well as relief threatened to overwhelm him, and it was all he could do to remain standing where he was. He wanted to hold her close, to tell her how proud he was of her, and yet, he couldn't bring himself to take that first step.

"Congratulations, Cassia. I know how hard you worked to find the cure. I didn't lose faith that you would succeed eventually." He swallowed again, turning away because he couldn't bear to see the uncertainty in her eyes. "You didn't have to come all the way out here to tell me. Andrei or Alexei could have let me know."

"I wanted to see you." Cassia hesitated, took a deep breath and continued." I needed to see you, Pietro...I know you're angry with me. I understand why you feel betrayed that I sided with the pack against you. It wasn't like that, not the way you think it was."

"It doesn't matter... "

"It does and you know it." The vehemence in her voice was surprising considering she had barely been speaking above a loud whisper before.

He could feel Cassia moving towards him, and he kept his back to her, continuing to restock the bar. He didn't want her to be here. He didn't want to see the evidence of what his rejection was doing to her. Why couldn't she just leave? Then she wouldn't hurt so much and neither would he.

Pietro held himself tense, afraid she would touch him, and he would lose all control. To do so now would only hurt them both all the more later. He couldn't forgive Thereasa. He couldn't return to the pack, and Cassia couldn't be apart from her people. That day had proven that more than anything else ever could.

"Hurting Thereasa...knowing that you had hurt Liam and all those you love in the pack, that would have killed you, Pietro. You say you don't understand what a pack is and yet you run with your own. Alexei, Andrei, Demetri, Caleb, Mac...Annie, Mara, Loretta, Cedar...the list goes on and on. They are your pack. You may not be a wolf, but what you feel for them is just as intense as what I feel for my pack. Can't you see that?"

Spinning around, he pinned her with his mismatched gaze, denial blazing from their depths. "It's different and you know it. Cassia...don't do this. I cannot be part of your world any longer. I have only hatred in my heart and the desire for revenge. That won't change, not until Thereasa is dead. This is who I am. This is what I am. You have to see that and understand that there is nothing but heartache for you if you continue down this path."

His words brought tears to Cassia's eyes, which poured down her cheeks. Inhaling sharply Pietro wanted to scream at the universe. It wasn't fair that he'd been placed in such a position. He should never have touched Cassia. He had known at the time that it was wrong, and yet, he had taken what he wanted. Now he was hurting the one person who had done the most to help him since the fiasco of Europe.

"I'm sorry, Nina. I never meant for you to be hurt by our time together. One day you will find your mate and what we shared will be but a distant memory...hold onto that fact."

Was he listening to what he was saying? Trying to hold back sobs, Cassia stared at her vampire as if he'd just grown two heads. The idiot had no idea! He had no inkling that the reason she was fighting so hard for him was because he was her mate. Of all the stubborn, idiotic males she could have fallen for she had to pick the one with a skull as thick as a brick wall. She opened her mouth to tell him when a new scent suddenly appeared, causing both their heads to turn in the direction of the doorway.

Fox's wolf growled the instant Cassia turned around to face them. Her cheeks were wet with tears, her expression so full of anguish his beast reared up, glaring at the vampire behind her. What had he done to her? Why was she crying?

"Fox?"

"Who the fuck are you?"

They both spoke at the same time, Cassia clearly remembering him from before, the vampire adopting an aggressive stance.

"What did you do to her?" His response came out directed at the vampire, his body automatically adopting a fighting stance. Where he was from vampires had only one use for wolves, and that was to see them dead on the spot. They were only two wolves and this vampire was older than most he'd come across, but that didn't mean they couldn't go down fighting. It didn't cross his mind to wonder at why he was willing to die to defend Cassia. It was purely instinctual. It was his job to protect his people and he would do so against this vampire no matter what the cost.

Cassia saw the other wolf about to spring a split second before he did. Her shocked brain couldn't understand what was happening, but she moved as Fox did, placing herself in front of Pietro.

"Stop!"

"Get out of the way, Cassia!" She was suddenly spinning away in the opposite direction, picked up and thrown over the bar by Pietro as his talons came out and he surged forward towards the threat.

"No! Stop! What are you doing?!"

Fox shifted, a huge black wolf replacing his human body as he barrelled into the feral vampire. They crashed backwards, spinning into tables with a resounding thud.

Pietro kicked out as he rolled, his feet tossing the wolf clear across the room as he sprang agilely upwards, flowing like a black shadow towards his prey.

"Pietro! Fox! Stop it this instant!" Cassia had no idea what the hell was happening. She just knew that the two males were fighting for no good reason. She had to stop it before it escalated any further, and she didn't know how to. What they hell was wrong with them? They didn't even know each other. Why the hell were they fighting?

They couldn't be fighting over her...could they? The instant the thought materialised she knew it was the truth. Fox must have seen her come inside and come to investigate. She could only guess at what he had envisioned was happening when he entered. He was a wolf and a European one at that. To him, all vampires were the enemy. He must have thought Pietro was hurting her in some way, and he was trying to protect her.

Oh, for the love of all that was holy! How could she be surrounded by such idiotic males? Fox's wolf was circling Pietro, trying to find a weak area to attack. Her vampire was matching his movements, seeking his own best point of attack. There was so much hate and pain in Pietro's soul, Cassia wasn't sure if he would be able to see that this was just a misunderstanding. If he bit Fox...he would kill the wolf instantly.

Fox sprang; his wide jaw sinking into Pietro's left shoulder as they crashed to the ground. He howled and released the other male as sharp talons sliced into his sides. He knew he had made a fatal mistake the instant he did. His throat was now bared to the dripping incisors of the vampire. All it would take was one bite...the bite the vampire was moving forward to inflict...

CHAPTER 2

Ice! Freezing cold sugared water and ice...it drenched them both, shocking them out of the feral grip they were caught up in. Fox shifted back to human form, groaning and spluttering as he rolled away from the vampire, clutching at his injured side. His infuriated gaze swung upwards to see the blonde wolf standing above them, an ice bucket in hand.

Pietro coughed and pulled himself upright, wiping the sticky substance from his face. His eyes met Cassia's and for a moment he could only stare at her in surprise. Oh no...she did not just pull Loretta's shit on him! Did she really think she would get away with her aunt's antics? His name wasn't Andrei, and this fight wasn't about a wolf claiming her mate. If she thought he was going to put up with this kind of humiliation, especially in front of a strange wolf...

"Now that I have both of your attention would one of you kindly like to explain to me why you're in the process of not only trying to wreck this bar but also kill each other?"

"Cassia..." Pietro growled, and she held up a hand to halt him.

"On second thoughts, I don't want to hear what you have to say right at this moment, Pietro de la Rios. You've caused enough trouble today." Cassia knelt down beside Fox to check his injured side.

The wolf batted at her hands, his gaze still fixated on Pietro. "I am fine."

"You're bleeding onto the floor and I'm a medic. So be quiet and let me look at your injury." She waved towards her pack, which she had left close to the door when she'd arrived earlier. "Pietro, bring me my pack. I have a medicine case in it."

The vampire opened his mouth to say something, and then closed it again, stomping over to the pack and placing it gently beside her. He was clearly still incensed, but made an effort not to break any of the delicate things tucked inside.

"Hold still...this may hurt." Cassia cleaned out Fox's wound, relieved to see that it wasn't too bad. His enhanced healing abilities would have it mending within a couple of days. She could have given him some of her blood to speed up the healing time, but she wanted him to have a reminder of what an idiot he was.

"I thought he was hurting you," Fox said through gritted teeth, as he allowed her to minister to him.

"Pietro would never hurt me," she answered intent on cleaning him up. "My dad and uncle are his two best friends. He may have a bit of a thick skull and say stupid things, but I don't hold that against him."

"I am still here," Pietro growled.

"Oh, I know. I can feel you breathing down my neck," she replied with a weary sigh. "Why don't you start clearing up some of the mess you made? I don't need your assistance here."

"He's the wolf from before, isn't he? What's he doing here? Why the fuck did he come into my place and attack me? What the fuck is there between you two?" Pietro knew he sounded petulant, but he couldn't stand to see Cassia's hands touching the other male. Now that the cloud of rage was lifting, he was as perplexed as she was about what the hell had just happened, and why the European wolf had felt the need to protect Cassia.

"Is he your mate?" The words whispered out, a dull ache filling him as he watched her hands still and her body stiffen. Dear God, was he right? Had he almost just killed Cassia's mate? The thought of another's hand touching her sent a black rage throughout his soul, and yet, he was the one pushing her away, telling her to find her mate.

"You are the stupidest, most obstinate, mule-headed male I have ever come across, Pietro de la Rios," Cassia spluttered, rising so quickly he stepped back in surprise. With her hands planted on her hips, she looked utterly adorable as her eyes spit fire at him.

"No, Fox is not my mate, you silly vampire! YOU are!"

His chest hurt and his head spun. Had she just said...? Surely he had misheard her. It couldn't be true...she couldn't have just said that he was her mate. Could she? The pain in his chest was like being on fire, and it took him a moment to realise why. He couldn't breathe! Cassia was glaring at him, totally convinced that they were mates, and the thought took all the breath from his body.

"Breathe, Pietro."

"No," he hissed out, shaking his head in denial. "I'm not your mate. I can't be." Pain flickered across her face but he was caught up in the memory of the last day in the pack compound, of how he had rejected her, of the mournful howl of the wolf..."No!" Spinning on his heels, Pietro fled, running as far and as fast as he could from the truth.

"Well...that wasn't quite the reaction I was hoping for," Cassia sighed, trying to swallow down the deep misery that overwhelmed her as Pietro rejected her once again.

Rising to his feet, Fox stared after the departed vampire, his thoughts in chaos. The wolf was the mate of a vampire? He'd heard all about the mixed matings and Varcolac, but seeing it up close and personal was mind-blowing.

"You don't seem very surprised despite your words," he remarked, turning to look back at her.

"Oh, I'm not. This is the second time that he's run from me, but I'm nothing if not dogmatic. He'll have to come back sooner or later, and I will be waiting for him when he does." Cassia busied her shaking hands by cleaning as much of the mess Fox had made bleeding onto the floor. "I don't need your protection, Fox, though I do understand that it's in your genes, and you couldn't help yourself trying to rescue me."

He watched her for a long moment, and then turned towards the door once more. "I can see that now," he said with a rueful smile. "There is something about you Cassia...I can't quite put my finger on it, but from my wolf's interest, I thought for a moment that possibly you might have been my mate. I can see now that I was wrong."

His bemused tone earned him a small smile as she straightened up wiping her hands with a sterile cloth. Cassia ran her eyes slowly up and down him before her smile widened. "Well, you are a fine specimen, Fox. I'm sure you must have a bevy of beauties eager to share your bed, even more so now."

His head tilted to the left, confusion dancing across his handsome face. "How so?"

"When you get home you can tell them all about how you fought with one of the most deadly vampires, and lived to tell the tale...because you did. Only the Ancients and Mac are more deadly than Pietro. You're lucky to survive the encounter."

Her words sent a shiver down his spine, as he realised just how close he'd come to dying. He couldn't afford to place himself in jeopardy when his Alpha needed him so badly. He had to get out of there before the vampire came back to finish the job. He was needed back home.

"Best of luck to you, Cassia. I hope you win your mate."

Her smile was both hopeful and sad. "Me too." She watched him head towards the door before she called out, "Uhm...Fox!" When he turned to give her a quizzical glance, she nodded her head downwards. "You might draw a few stares if you leave like that."

He looked down and groaned out aloud. "Fuck!" He'd shifted to wolf form and now he was buck naked. That Cassia wasn't bothered told him that she must be used to it with her pack.

"Wait there, I'll see if something of Pietro's will fit you. You look about the same size." She disappeared upstairs, returning quickly with a black pair of jogging bottoms and T-shirt.

"Won't the vampire mind?"

"He can live with it," she snorted, humour dancing in her eyes as she watched him pull the clothes on. "Serves him right for being an idiot."

Walking to the door with him, she paused at the entrance as he walked outside. ""What are you really doing here, Fox? What brings wolves like you to our shores?"

He stiffened, turning his head to look back at her. "Wolves like what?" Her arched eyebrow told him she wasn't fooled by his mock-innocence, and he made a mental note to never underestimate this feisty wolf should their paths ever cross again.

"You know what I mean. I can tell a soldier when I see one; I've trained in that position myself to protect my pack."

He was struck by the urge to tell her everything, but knew that he couldn't do that. He would be betraying his Alpha if he said too much, and he would die before he ever did that. "It's not me you should be watching out for, Cassia. It's the wolves you don't see."

"Fox! What do you mean by that?"

He kept walking, resisting the urge to look back at the woman who so intrigued him even though he wasn't her mate. Something told him that he would meet Cassia again one day, and that when he did, his life would never be the same.

Cassia watched Fox leave, wondering at his cryptic comment. She would have to tell Rafe about it. The secretive wolf had clearly wanted to alert her to something, but for whatever reason, couldn't tell her outright what it was. The wolves she didn't see...intriguing.

Heading back inside she stared at the wrecked bar and then grabbed her backpack. She would wait for Pietro in his apartment upstairs. If he thought she would just give up on her mate he was in for a very rude shock. Smiling, she headed upstairs into her vampire's lair to await his return.

Reasa stared into the open fridge, frustration threatening to spark her temper. She was tired and cranky from the long hours spent in the injured vampires' minds, and to top everything off, her stomach was making the most ridiculous of sounds.

"Hungry much?"

The unexpected male voice startled her in the darkened kitchen, and she shrieked and spun around, the light from the refrigerator revealing Karn, the second in command at the Praetorian Compound.

"Didn't mean to scare you," the blond vampire continued, reaching inside to grab a quart of milk. "Do you still have enhanced sight?" He gestured to the lack of light in the kitchen. "Only with your hearing now muted I would have thought your eyesight would be too.

"It is," she answered looking away from his all-seeing eyes. "I didn't want to disturb anyone by turning on a light."

He watched her for a second and then crossed the room and turned on the light. "We can't be having you bumping into things and doing yourself an injury. We don't want Liam to put everyone back into a coma again, do we?"

She hadn't really thought about it, but then, she tried her hardest to concentrate on the task at hand and not think about the redheaded Varcolac who was starting to be able to read her every thought and emotion the more time they spent inside each other's heads.

"Why don't you have a seat at the table?" Karn commented when she didn't speak. "I suggest you snack on something light like cereal as it's the middle of the night. It should blunt your hunger enough to get back to sleep but not be too heavy to keep you awake. I'll have a word with Mac in the morning to ensure both you and Liam get enough rest and food breaks. Both of you look exhausted all the time."

She watched him pour out some cereal into a bowl and add some milk. Then he placed it in front of her with a spoon and sat down at the table beside her. She couldn't fathom out why he was being so nice to her. He had nothing to gain from it.

When she just sat there looking at him he smiled and waved a hand at the plate. "It won't eat itself, girlie."

She recognised that tone. It was the one she heard him use regularly around the others; it conveyed both admonishment and humour. She had particularly noticed it became especially noticeable around Elina. He appeared to delight in pushing at Liam's cousin to try to get a reaction. Most of the time the other woman treated him with haughty distain, but every so often there would be a flash of irritation in her eyes that only served to make the blond vampire grin from ear to ear. She could tell it was the reaction he was hoping for. It was also apparent that Elina was clueless to the fact that she was rising to his bait.

Swirling her spoon around the bowl a couple of times, Reasa finally gave into her hunger pangs and took a spoonful of cereal. As she ate she watched Karn, and his gaze never left her face. "Why are you being so nice to me? Everyone else pretty much pretends I'm not here, with the exception of Liam, Elina, Mac, Lily and Brandon."

He appeared to consider her question before he gave her a small smile. "You frighten the others."

Reasa spluttered over her next spoonful of cereal, almost choking as it went down the wrong way. "I frighten them?!" She wiped at her mouth with the napkin Karn hastily produced. "How can I possibly frighten them? I'm human. It's not as if I can do them any harm."

"You forget that a handful of weeks ago you were them, Reasa. That is what frightens them. The fact that there is a possibility that they could have their immortality removed and become as human as you now are. I didn't say there was any merit to the way they feel, just that they do feel that way."

When he put it like that she could see why the other vampires could fear her. She was an object lesson to all of them. If they screwed up there was a chance they could become just like her. It must be a very sobering thought for all of them. "So, because they pretend I don't exist this makes you want to be friendly towards me?"

Karn chuckled though he kept his voice low so as not to disturb the sleeping house. "No, girlie, I want to be friendly towards you because I see how exhausted you are and yet every morning at dawn you get up and spend hours at a time inside fractured minds to help those lost souls find a way home. I see your skin tear from whatever it is that is happening mentally to you and yet you keep going in. Oh, I know Elina heals you as it happens but that doesn't mean you don't feel the pain. I didn't know you as a vampire, Reasa, but what I see of you as a human woman is pretty awe-inspiring."

Staring into his eyes she was stunned to see that he actually meant every word he said. He truly did like her for who she was now and it had nothing to do with who she had once been. For some reason ,that made her feel even more ashamed of her past than anything had before. "You place your faith in the wrong person, Karn," she said bitterly. "This woman before you is not the woman I used to be. I have done countless terrible things in my past, things that would shock you."

To her chagrin he merely chuckled again, shaking his head in amusement. "Oh Thereasa, every single vampire in this compound can say the exact same thing, especially the older ones. We are all a product of our time, and where we come from. It's only been the last century or so that we have started coming even close to being civilised. I dare say I could tell you tales that would make your hair curl."

"I know that but..."

"No buts, girlie. You know I speak the truth." Karn appeared to be thinking of something before he spoke again. He let out a low sigh and rested his elbows on the table.

"When Mac found me over a thousand years ago I was nothing more than a wild animal. I had been on my own for so long I was almost feral. I had taken to hiding up in the Carpathian Mountains in Romania, only coming down when the need to feed drove me out in agony. I tried to sustain myself on animal blood so I could stop myself killing humans but it was to no avail."

His expression drifted off as he spoke, as if he were lost within a memory that was replaying itself. "Mac crossed my path on one of my trips down to the villages. I was almost insane with hunger at the time, so much so, that when I scented him in the area I was ready to fight to the death to protect my hunting ground. He knocked me on my ass so hard I swear I was seeing stars. Then I realised that I really was as I lay on my back looking into the night sky with Mac's talons around my neck."

"What happened then?" Reasa couldn't stop herself from asking when he stopped talking and didn't appear as if he would continue.

"He could have killed me. I was too weak from hunger to defend myself but instead I heard him talking softly to someone else and then I could taste the sweet hot blood of a human dripping into my open mouth. I tried to fight him to get to the blood but he was too strong for me. In the end I just had to lay there and accept the small hand-outs he gave to me. By the time I was sated enough, he let me up and I was astounded to see four villagers sitting beside the trees, all still alive."

The expression in Karn's eyes sent a chill down Reasa's spine when he looked at her. There was so much self-loathing on his face it was painful to witness. "You see, until that very moment I had always killed to satisfy my hunger. I didn't know there was any other way. In one night Mac taught me how to feed without the need for unnecessary loss of life. He taught me to feed often and in small amounts to ensure I would never lose control and reach that feral state again."

"He saved you," she whispered and he nodded his head. "This is why you follow him now, because he believed in you and gave you a future."

"Yes he did and I will follow wherever he chooses to lead me. However, that isn't the point to this story, Reasa. The point is we have all done unspeakable things in the past that we are ashamed to admit to. It's what we do now that matters though. We can be enslaved by our pasts or we can learn from our mistakes and work to make not only ourselves, but those around us into better people. I don't care what the old Thereasa did. I can only look to the woman I know now and am impressed by her strength of will and unfailing dedication to helping those lost souls upstairs."

Reasa looked down at her bowl, the now soggy cereal appearing to swim before her eyes. A lone tear splashed into the milk, followed by a second and then another. Karn liked her. He was the first person that wasn't protecting her for Liam's sake or grateful for being brought out of a coma. He actually saw her as a person and found something to like about her.

Scrubbing at her face and fighting down the strong emotions that threatened to overwhelm her, she stood up keeping her gaze averted from the blond vampire. "Thank you."

"You have a hard road to walk, Thereasa. Yes, there will be those who may only ever see the old Reasa, but there are countless others who will see the new one. You don't have to walk that road alone. You have friends who are willing to give you a chance and share your burden with you. All you have to do is let them in."

Karn placed a hand underneath her chin to tilt her head up to meet her eyes. "I am one of those friends. If anyone gives you a hard time here, you let me know and I will have words with them. And if you ever need to talk...about anything...you can come to me, okay?"

"Okay," she whispered, giving him a watery smile. She couldn't believe it but she actually had a friend. For the first time in a long time there was something good in her life and she was afraid she would do something to ruin it as she had everything else. Something told her Karn didn't offer his friendship lightly. She prayed that she didn't do anything to let him down.

"Good, now off to bed with you, girlie, before Liam comes looking for you and decides to kick my ass for having you up at stupid o'clock in the morning."

With a gentle prod he sent her heading back upstairs and she went feeling dazed by what had just happened.

"Reasa?"

Liam's sleepy voice muttered in the darkness as she closed the bedroom door behind her. She stumbled in the dark making her way towards the bed and let out a small gasp when strong arms circled her body and she was lifted onto the bed.

"Where were you?" There was nothing but curiosity in his voice and for the first time she stopped to really listen to what Liam wasn't saying in so many words. There was no concern that she had run off. There was no accusation that she might have been doing something underhand. He completely trusted in her and that fact was only now starting to sink in.

"I was hungry. Karn sat with me while I ate some cereal. He was keeping me company."

"You should have woken me. I would have made you something to eat." Again there was no judgement in his tone, only a desire to look after her.

"Freya is right. I do need to learn how to cook. Perhaps this is something we can do when we have finished with our task here? That's if you can cook."

Liam went so still that for a moment she wondered if she had done something wrong, then he lay down, pulling her into his embrace as he had done every night since they had been at the Praetorian Compound. "I would like that very much, Reasa," he said quietly, his voice thick with emotion.

It was so easy to relax into his embrace, to feel his breath against her neck as she closed her eyes to go back to sleep. She had become accustomed to his gentle touch, to the feel of his strength surrounding her. He didn't press for anything else. He was content to have her close. She had to concede that she had never felt more protected than she did by his side. "I would too, Liam," she answered with a sleepy yawn, snuggling down and allowing sleep to claim her.

* * * * *

"They need a break, Mac. They've been at this constantly for days now. They need to work their physical muscles as well as their mental ones. I found Reasa exhausted in the kitchen last night so hungry it was a wonder her stomach rumbling didn't wake up the entire house. She was too tired to prepare herself anything but her body was demanding it. This isn't a request...I'm telling you they need a day off."

Mackenzie stared hard at Karn as he mulled over his words. The dream walkers had been spending days at a time inside the wounded vampires mind, slowly bringing them back to the here and now. So far, four of them were awake, Brandon included. It was hard not to push for the final two to come back. There was a sense of urgency, like they were running out of time. The longer the vampires were in their coma-like state the harder it appeared to be to bring them back.

"We could lose the last two, Karn. You know that."

"We could lose Liam and Reasa, Mac. Those men lying up there pledged their lives to keeping the Varcolac safe. If they had a choice in the matter they would tell you to put Liam first, and you know that."

When Karn was so vociferous about something he wasn't about to back down on it. He clearly was concerned for Liam and Reasa's health. Mac sighed and rubbed a hand over his face, finally nodding his agreement. "Fine...but you tell Liam. You know he's not going to like it."

A smile crossed his number two's face and it was all Mac could do not to burst out laughing. There was a saying that an expression said a thousand words, and there was no mistaking the expression on Karn's face. If Liam kicked up a fuss about this decision, he would be butting heads with one of the most intractable men Mac had ever come across.

"Liam will just need to do as he's told," Karn said, turning on his heel to head out of the study.

Lily uncurled herself from the large armchair she was sitting in and crossed the room to slide into her mate's open arms. "I might like to be a fly on the wall for that conversation."

Mac chuckled and kissed the top of her head, inhaling in her wonderful scent. "You'll forgive me if I prefer that you stay away from that one. Anyway, I wanted your help with something else."

She glanced up at him, curiosity shining in the depth of her eyes. "Oh?"

Mackenzie's lips tightened in a disapproving line. "Kothari." "Ohhhhh." Lily sighed and rested her head back against his chest. "What has he been up to now?"

"He's deliberately freaking out some of the Praetorians. He keeps telling them things they have done or said in the past. How the hell he knows these things is beyond me, but it's starting to make some of my people go out of their way to avoid him. He's deliberately taunting them, Lily, and if he doesn't stop it's going to cause problems."

"That doesn't sound like our Kothi," she laughed, but there was a weary sigh contained in the words. "Have you spoken to Kal about it? He can usually get through to Kothi when he's being particularly difficult."

Mac sighed too, brushing his cheek against her hair to soothe some of his growing irritation. "Kal's out with the wolves most of the time. He appears to be fixated on keeping the compound safe after Reasa's attack."

That made sense when it came to her brother. He always felt so responsible for everything, even when it was something outwith his control. Lily fought down another sigh and then a thought popped into her head that had her pulling out of his arms.

"I know what we can do to solve both Liam's and Kothi's problems. Come on." Grabbing his hand, she pulled her mate from the study, heading towards the kitchen where there was the sound of a disagreement taking place.

"Kothi, be quiet. This has nothing to do with you," she announced as they entered to see a red-faced Liam squaring up to Karn who appeared just as irritated. "Liam, calm down and sit down." It was so unlike her to be that bossy that both her fellow Varcolac closed their mouths, and Liam actually sat down.

The room was full of Praetorians who had come to watch Karn lay down the law. It was always gratifying to see him lay into someone other than themselves. Reasa was standing quietly to one side, resting her back against one of the countertops.

Lily let her gaze travel over the vampires present and then she smiled. "Guys, just so you know, Kothari isn't able to read minds. He spotted the Praetorians protecting us long before I ever did. He has been shadowing you since he was a child, listening to everything you've ever said and done. None of the Varcolac can read minds no matter what they try to have you believe. You will stop teasing them, Kothi, right now."

"Spoilsport," Kothi muttered under his breath as he saw his targets looking at him with less than pleased expressions. He had been enjoying playing with them, fascinated by the increasing level of panic that had been starting to escalate in some of the vampires' eyes. Now Lily had spoilt everything and he would have to find some other way to entertain himself.

"And as for you..." Lily flowed so quickly towards Liam that it took a moment for anyone to react. By the time they did, the large male was lying flat on his back, a dazed expression in his eyes. "You're so slow these days even a girl can put you on your ass. Mental muscle is great, Liam, but it's pointless if you forget to take care of your physical muscle."

"That was just what I was saying," Karn growled, coming to stand beside her. "This dream walking stuff is cannibalising your bodies, Liam. It appears to need a large amount of fuel and what you and Reasa are eating isn't enough for the amount of time you're in other peoples' heads."

Liam's stunned gaze swung towards his mate, shock rippling through him as he noticed for the first time just how exhausted she was. They had slept later than usual today. She should have looked more rested. "I didn't realise... "

"No, because you're too pig-headed trying to save the world to the detriment of yourself and Reasa," Lily berated, her hands on her hips. "If Mac and Karn say no more dream walking today you will damned well listen to them, Liam Eriksson, or I'm phoning your mother and you can explain to her why you're trying to kill yourself. Am I completely clear on both matters?"

Silence filled the kitchen as her gaze swept from Kothari to Liam and back again. Finally the dark-haired Varcolac smiled one of his rare smiles, amusement lacing his tone when he nodded his head in her direction. "Yes, Mother."

"Yes, Lily," Liam said, his gaze still fixated on his mate, contrition in every word.

"That's settled then," she smiled, turning her exultant gaze up to her mate who was wearing a smile that contained all of the pride he felt for her.

"You're going to make a wonderful mom," he laughed, gathering her close for a hug.

"If our children turn out anywhere near as difficult as these two, you can sort them out," she teased back.

"Okay, sparring time everyone," Karn announced heading to the backdoor. "We'll start with you two troublemakers. Front and centre!" "Have you ever seen the Varcolac spar?" Brandon asked, slipping into step with Reasa as she followed everyone outside.

She turned her head enough to look at the vampire, taking a careful catalogue of his features. He was handsome as vampires were wont to be, but she wasn't looking for that. Her keen gaze took in the continuing signs of recovery. In a few days' time no one would ever know that he had once been so lost, there had been little hope of him ever waking up.

Following on from her conversation with Karn, she could now detect the vampire's open offer of friendship. She hadn't noticed it before because she had put his attentive behaviour down to gratitude. Now it appeared Brandon genuinely liked her and wanted to spend time in her company. His relaxed demeanour and incorrigible personality was endearing, and she found herself more receptive to the idea of being friends with him that she would have expected.

"Elina did kick my ass when I first arrived here," she answered drolly. "I am aware of their prowess."

The goofy grin he shot her way almost made her laugh aloud. "Oh, that was nothing. Wait until you see them spar. That's something completely different. Lily sparred with Mac when she first came here and she was magnificent. Then she sparred with Kal and it was so clear how much she had been holding back with Mac. They are so amazing they're mind-blowing. I can't wait to see what Kothari is capable of."

His enthusiasm and interest in Kothari made her feel uneasy. She hadn't seen much of the younger Varcolac since he had arrived, but she could sense just how dangerous the boy was. One look at him and she knew that there was something very wrong with Kothari. The fact that he made Louis appear like a choirboy was a good indicator of that...and he was about to spar with Liam.

She was unaccountably afraid, so much so that she called out, "Liam!"

His expression was quizzical when he turned to face her, but he halted his progress into the main sparring circle to allow her to hurry over to him. "What is it?"

"Remember what you learned when we dream walked in your mind. You are a multifaceted being, Liam. Do not favour one aspect of your personality over the other."

His brown eyes became more confused, and he reached out a hand to gently place it again her cheek. His expression lightened a little when she didn't automatically pull away. "What are you trying to tell me, Reasa?" "Do not trust him," she hissed out, her eyes never leaving his. "He is dangerous, Liam. Do not let your guard down."

"Kothari is my friend. He would never deliberately hurt me," Liam countered, totally confused by the fear on her face.

"Listen to me, Liam and hear what I am saying. That boy is the most dangerous being I have ever come across and I have come across many scary things in Europe. He may be your friend, and he may not mean to hurt you, but he is walking a very fine line, I can see it in his eyes. Bring your vampire forward, and don't rely on your wolf. Now is the time to meet fire with fire. Now is the time that you must be whole."

There was so much foreboding in her voice that for a moment Liam considered cancelling the sparring match. She was truly afraid that something bad was going to happen and the only way to dissuade that fear would be not to fight with Kothi. He couldn't understand why she was so worried though. He couldn't understand what it was she was seeing when she was looking at his friend. The only way to prove to her that there was nothing to worry about was to show her.

"Okay, I will do as you ask, but there really isn't anything to be concerned about, Reasa. It's just a friendly sparring match."

'Just a friendly sparring match,' he'd told her barely five minutes ago and now he was lying panting on his back as Kothari circled in a slow, wide movement. What the hell was wrong with him? His friend had come at him like a demon possessed, kicking, talons slashing, fangs biting every which way he turned. Liam had been so unprepared for the ferocity of Kothi's attack that he'd taken blow after blow until he was knocked down and fighting for breath.

"The bigger they are, the harder they fall," Kothi laughed, but there was no humour in his words, instead, there was a trace of malice.

Liam groaned and pulled himself up to his knees, his eyes narrowing as he glared at his friend. "I thought this was supposed to be a mock fight," he growled.

"I am fighting, and I am also mocking you, so I would say it was," was the sarcastic reply he received, and it only served to send a spike of anger flooding through him.

"He's a cocky little shit," his vampire whispered in his mind. "I think you need me, Liam my boy."

There was something very disconcerting about having his other half address him as if it was a separate being. Liam wondered if this was what insane people experienced as the norm. Shaking his head, he rose to his feet and took a deep breath. "If you want a fight then I guess it's time to give you one, Kothari."

As soon as he'd finished speaking, he quickly coaxed his wolf into a more submissive stance, ignoring the frustrated growl he received from it. Strength surged through his muscles as his vampiric side rose up sharply, and his fingernails turned to wickedly, sharp talons.

"Oh, Liam has a vamp does he?" Kothari laughed again, moving at supernatural speed before he had stopped speaking. He cursed loudly, spinning away as quickly as he'd attacked, holding his side as blood seeped through his fingers.

"Yes, he does, Kothi, and he very much wants to play with you." Holding up two fingers, Liam made a come-hither gesture, his grin turning to one of pure malice. "Let's dance, little boy."

"Maybe this wasn't such a good idea." Lily swallowed hard as Liam and Kothari crashed into each other, talons flashing wildly as they barrelled into the treeline. Reasa was sitting forward, her gaze intent on the two sparring males.

"Glorious," she muttered under her breath, causing Lily to turn her gaze from her friends to watch her expressive face.

Thereasa was riveted to the ongoing contest, her expression rapt as she tried to follow the speed at which Kothi and Liam were moving. For a moment, Lily thought she was watching them both, but after a few seconds she could see that Reasa was tracking Liam more than Kothi.

Realisation dawned, and Lily felt a sense of hope building up inside. This was what Reasa knew, what she was most comfortable with. Liam's display of his more vampiric side had caught the former vampire's attention and she was liking what she saw very much. Her friends may come out of the sparring match feeling like they'd been run over by a truck, but Liam was giving his mate the one thing that she needed to finally connect with him; his vampire.

Reasa cried out when Liam swiped his talons across Kothari's face, forcing the younger man to stumble backwards and run a hand across his eyes to clear them of blood. Their wounds healed instantly but their blood got in the way at times. Liam followed up his swipe with a kick to the midriff, catching Kothari off-guard and sending him crashing to the ground.

"Yes!" Reasa jumped up, throwing her fist up high. "Go, Liam!"

Her cry distracted him and Kothi was back on his feet, cutting the legs from the larger man as his head turned to look at his mate. Liam rolled agilely and leapt back up, managing to avoid the fist that was aimed at his neck.

Kothari was wild, attacking him in a flurry of movements so fast it was hard to avoid them. Liam managed to, but it took all of his concentration so he tuned out all external sounds around them. He was panting heavily; feeling the effects of the long days spent sitting by the hospital beds. Kothari didn't have that level of fatigue to slow him down, and he appeared intent on taking Liam's head.

"Kothari!" Liam called to his friend, but he didn't appear to hear him. Talons found purchase in his body and he groaned as they sank into his side. "Kothi! Stop!" He tried again, as he felt his knees buckle under another attack. This time his friend had snapped his left leg and there was nothing to hold him up.

* * * * *

Annoying sounds...buzzing around his head and fuelling his rage.

"Go away!"

His prey was weakened...he was almost there. Another moment longer, a quick slice to the femoral artery, and his prey would bleed out so quickly it would be enough to divert his attention. Then his head would be his. Then he would be victorious!

Kothari's talons whipped downward, scythed through flesh to find the artery he required. The sounds were buzzing louder, the noise unbearable as he closed in for the kill. All breath left his body, as he was suddenly catapulted backward, landing hard in the dirt, the largest deep brown wolf he could remember seeing landing squarely on his chest.

A huge jaw wrapped around his neck in an instant, and he froze where he was, waiting for the inevitable moment to come.

"Kothari!"

The name resounded in his head and he tried to shake it away.

"Kothari, you better fucking answer me because I don't want to have to explain to your parents why I had to take your head. Speak to me! NOW!"

"Kallum...?"

The cold haze of fury that had enveloped him began to clear, and he realised that it was his friend with his powerful jaws around his neck. What the fuck had happened? One minute he'd been teasing Liam and the next he was a hairsbreadth away from death. It was only as the fog continued to clear from his mind that he noticed he was pinned down on all sides by wolves, and Karn and Mac were crushing his legs.

"Kallum?" This time the words croaked out of dry lips, and the large wolf moved away, shifting form back into his friend.

"He's back," Kallum announced, his expression grave as he rose up to tower over Kothari.

It took another moment for the others to release their hold and move away, their expressions distrustful as they watched him keenly.

"What happened?" Kothi asked, though inside he was quivering with fear. Deep down he was only too aware of what had happened. He had lost control. "Liam..." Panic filled him, fear clawing at his gut as he sat up to find his friend.

Liam was sitting up gently disentangling Lily and Reasa from his large body. "I'm fine. No harm done," he grinned, though his clothes were drenched in blood that could only indicate that he'd had a severe arterial bleed.

"You almost killed him," Kallum ground out, fury dancing across his face as well as concern. "What the hell were you thinking? Does anyone matter to you at all? Is there even one person here that you give a shit about? You've crossed the line this time, Kothari. Rafe is going to have to be informed about this."

"I didn't...I didn't mean to hurt Liam. Kallum, you know how I feel about everyone, about the pack. You're my family." Always before he could count on the Varcolac to keep him in check. They always had his back no matter what. Now Kallum and his other pack members were looking at him with such distrust. If he lost them...if he didn't have them as his anchor...

"I remember a time not too long ago when we once sparred together, Kal. It got a little out of hand that time too." Lily's quiet words were the only sound for what felt like forever and then her brother let out a long sigh.

"Touche," he muttered, though he still didn't look very pleased.

"There is no harm done," Liam repeated, coming over and reaching a hand out to Kothari. "We're good."

Kothi hesitated for a moment and then tentatively accepted Liam's hand, allowing him to pull him up. "Kal is right. Rafe needs to be informed of what happened. I think it's best if I head back to the pack."

Lily gave him a reassuring smile, laying a hand gently on his arm. "That sounds like a good idea. Why don't you catch up with Dara while you're there. Have her keep you company for a little while. Don't spend too much time on your own, Kothi."

The thought of possibly losing control again and in front of Dara wasn't one he was willing to risk. No, he would speak with Rafe and see what advice his Alpha had to offer. Then he would go home, lock the doors, and stay there until his parents came home. When they did...he would tell them everything. Maybe they would be able to help him. Maybe he didn't have to fight this thing alone...

Turning away, he took off running, flying as fast as he could away from the tragedy that had only barely been averted. He wasn't safe around his friends any longer. He wasn't safe around anyone any more.

* * * * *

"I told you not to trust him."

Liam blinked slowly, watching Reasa pace up and down their room. He couldn't deny that it had been a close call with Kothi but that wasn't what had his full attention. Reasa was concerned about him. Oh, she was berating him and telling him what a fool he was but he didn't mind in the least, because with every word that escaped her lips it was clear that she cared.

"He didn't mean it, Reasa. Things just got a little out of hand."

"A little out of hand?" She stopped pacing to glare at him, her voice deceptively soft. "Just when I was starting to think that maybe, just maybe, my fear of the Varcolac was unjustified I see that boy almost rip your stupid head off. And all you can do is sit there and say things got a little out of hand?"

"Reasa, I'm fine. You can stop worrying now," Liam sighed, rising and crossing the room. "I'm not concerned about Kothari in the least. Yes, he walks a very fine line and nobody knows that more than I. I have been shadowing his mood swings all our lives. Kothi teeters on the edge but the one thing that always pulls him back is his love for the pack. The fact that Kal got through to him so easily is a testament to that."

She still looked doubtful but that didn't stop a wide grin crossing his face. "You're very vociferous in my favour," he commented, amusement dancing in his eyes.

Startled eyes met his and her tongue snaked out to wet her lips. It was the wrong thing she could have done as it fixated him on her mouth and recalled the memory of kissing her. Liam had relived that moment so many times in his dreams but had been careful about keeping his distance. Oh, he hadn't given any quarter when it had come to sleeping with him. No, he had been quite determined that they would not be separated after spending all day helping the Praetorians.

He had wanted Reasa to be comfortable in his presence, to know and come to expect his touch without fear that it would come to mean some form of sexual advance from him. He had wanted her to get to know him, to see him as a person first and come to trust him. From her reaction to his fight with Kothi, it would appear it had worked. She was concerned about his well-being. She cared.

"Don't try to change the subject, Liam Eriksson. We are discussing your lapse in judgement here."

She looked totally adorable as she tried to remain stern when all the while she was slowly backing away from him, her hands twisting nervously together. His wolf growled softly and he could have sworn he heard his vampire laughing with glee. They were both enjoying their prey backing herself into a corner.

"Were we?" he asked, a smile teasing at his lips. "I'm more interested in why you feel the need to tell me off. Were you worried about me, Thereasa? Were you really that concerned that Kothi might genuinely hurt me?"

CHAPTER 3

"In case you haven't noticed it does take both of us to help bring back the Praetorians," she countered, emitting a gasp when her back hit the wall. They had been here once before in her room at Freya's home, and that hadn't gone too well in her favour.

"If I recall correctly, weren't you shouting 'Go, Liam.' when I was fighting? Did you like seeing my more vampiric side? I remember he liked you very much when we were talking to him."

"Liam..." She swallowed hard, her eyes darting away from his.

"Yes, Reasa?"

"Liam... "

He couldn't have stopped himself from kissing her if he tried. She was so beautiful, so intoxicating. Liam claimed her lips in a soft kiss, lightly running his tongue along her bottom lip. Her mouth quivered under his and then she sighed and her lips parted, allowing him entry into the sweetness within.

She tasted heavenly, all hot and spicy, and sweet, sweet Reasa. His hand came up to the nape of her neck, holding her in place so he could plunder her mouth in a kiss so full of passion it felt as if an inferno had ignited between them. His heart kicked up a beat, and his body hardened in an instant as he lost himself in the heady intoxication of his mate.

Reasa tried not to respond to him but it was impossible not to wind her arms around his thick neck and pull his mouth onto hers. Her emotions had been chaotic ever since she had watched

Liam fight with Kothi. She had gone from exultation to abject fear in a fraction of a second and her head was still spinning from it.

That had nothing to do with the way Liam's lips teased against hers, the way his tongue flicked inside her mouth and she felt she was being devoured from the inside out. No, her spinning head was from fatigue and too many extreme emotions in such a short period of time...it was.

"Liam." Oh Lord, had she just moaned his name like a besotted woman lost in the throes of passion? Surely that hadn't been her. Surely she wasn't luxuriating in the feel of his hard, well-muscled physique pressing her back against the wall. It was her and she couldn't deny it any longer. She was attracted to Liam; she was more than attracted to him. He had somehow managed to creep past all her defences until there was nowhere she could hide from him.

He knew secrets about her she hadn't shared with anyone else. He was aware of the ugly truth that haunted her days and he still cared, he still treated her with respect and what she now had to concede was the inescapable truth...love.

Liam, in return, had revealed his own secrets. He had trusted her with what he considered his deepest shame. He was so unlike anyone she had ever known, so free with his thoughts and feelings, hiding nothing behind defensive walls. He stood before her, a gentle giant with so much empathy he had lived his entire pack's pain and joy his entire life. Still that hadn't dissuaded him from opening up to her, from revealing everything and trusting she wouldn't hurt him.

Why was she still fighting him? Why wasn't she just letting him in? She had thrown her lot in with his pack and the vampires here. She had to rely on them for protection as she was human now. It was just the tiniest of steps to accepting Liam's claim on her, and the way he made her feel was proof that it wouldn't be such a bad thing. So, why couldn't she just take that final step...

"Liam." This time his name came out completely different and he responded instantly to the feel of her withdrawal.

Raising his head up, he captured her gaze in his, a query shining in his deep brown eyes. "I know you feel what's between us, Thereasa. Why do you fight it so much?" There was no condemnation in his tone, only open curiosity.

"You know why...you just don't want to deal with it," she replied, pressing her hands against his wide chest, feeling the drumming of his heart against her fingertips. The temptation to curl her fingers against his flesh, to feel his skin against her palms was strong...instead she pushed gently and sighed with relief when he backed away, giving her the space she needed.

"I can't deny that I am attracted to you, Liam. If nothing else, I will always tell you the truth from this point forward. I can't deny that the Varcolac are not what I first imagined them to be...Kothari notwithstanding. But we cannot forget Pietro in all of this, no matter how much you may wish to believe that it will all work out in the end. Things will come to a head with him and when it does...one of us will most likely die."

"I will not let him hurt you." Liam hissed out the words, fury replacing the sleepy passion that he'd still be lingering under.

"You cannot hurt him, Liam," she countered, walking over to the bed, and sitting down, waiting for him to take a seat beside her. "If you do you will most probably send Cassia rogue and you can't live with that. You will never be able to bear the burden of hurting her, of possibly being the cause of her death by your actions. You know that. You just don't want to face it."

"Then we'll go to Europe and live there. It is your home, what you know."

She wanted to shake him and hug him at the same time. He was so obstinate and clearly not thinking straight. "I'm human, Liam. I would be dead within a week of setting foot on European soil. I have made too many enemies there and you're completely ignoring the fact that Louis will be sending someone here to kill me, if they're not already here."

He was silent for a long time, staring down at the hardwood floor with unseeing eyes. "Then what do we do, Reasa, because I can't be without you?" he finally asked, turning haunted eyes to her. "You are my mate, the only woman on this planet that owns the other half of my soul."

He was so convinced of that, and the longer she was with him the more she was coming to believe it too. Liam had been so gentle with her, so caring and loving that she had slowly been falling under his spell even as she had fought him with every fibre of her being.

"I don't know," she whispered, sorrow filling her soul as she gazed back at him. "I don't think there is anything we can do, Liam. All I know is that if we take things any further, the fallout of that will be a thousand times worse than it will be if we don't."

Reasa reached out and took his hand, staring as their fingers tangled together. "You are a good man, one of the best I have ever known. I don't want to be the instrument of your destruction anymore, Liam. Not as I was once convinced that I had to be." It was a huge admission for her and she knew he would be aware of that.

"We'll talk to Rafe and maybe Annie and Caleb," he answered, his tone subdued. "Perhaps they will have better answers for us. Just know this, Reasa...I will not give up on you. I will not give up on us. We are mates and we will find a way to be together."

His stubbornness was endearing but Reasa knew in her heart that there were no easy answers to their dilemma. She had told him she would tell him the truth, and she would do her best to keep that promise...but her thoughts were already turning to ways to leave the pack, to ways to leave Liam Eriksson before a deeper tragedy could befall the Armand-Hanlon Pack, one that was worse than her arrival.

* * * * *

"Can I help you with something?" Dante eyed the couple who were just crossing over the border to Louis territory, his pale eyes intent as they swept quickly over them. In a fraction of a second he could tell that they were both Ancient, the male being the older of the two.

The female was very beautiful, her long black hair secured in a high ponytail. Her scent told him that she was a were shifter but not of the wolf variety...she was a cat. He'd come across very few cat-shifters in his time, so he was intrigued to see one, especially one that old. The male was pure vampire, his deep auburn hair loose about his shoulder, his surprising lavender eyes narrowed with suspicion.

"We want Michael." It was the vampire who answered, expectation in each word. It was clear he was used to instant obedience, and his companion glanced at him with a small half smile playing across her lips before she turned back to Dante.

"What my mate is trying to say is we're looking for a vampire called Michael. We believe he can be found in this area. This is Louis' territory?"

Dante nodded, there was little point in denying it as they clearly were aware of just where they were. "I think you should most likely speak to Louis personally," he answered, "though I would advise a little more of a cordial tone. He tends to get a little waspish if he isn't accorded the respect he feels he deserves."

"Louis had better have the answers I want otherwise feeling disrespected will be the least of his problems," the vampire retorted, his expression remaining bland despite the open threat in his words.

"Gard," the cat sighed, weary amusement lacing her tone. "You do know that you catch more flies with honey, don't you?" Shaking her head, she smiled at Dante. "He doesn't like being away from his sister for too long. He gets a little tetchy. I'm Rayne, and this is Gard...and you are...?"

"Dante, I am acting as Louis' second in command at the moment. We have been expecting you ever since the troubles in Edinburgh."

Both of them stilled for a moment, their expressions turning carefully neutral. "Best not to mention that," Rayne finally said quietly. "That's a very sore point with us so the least said about it the better. Can you please take us to Louis?"

He hesitated, wondering if it would be wise for them to see Louis and then he turned and headed towards the coven hideout. "Follow me..." Events had to play out as they were destined. Dante had learnt that the hard way.

They were at the smallholding deep within the forest in under half an hour. Dante had taken them the long route to ensure that Louis' spies would have enough time to alert the coven leader to their presence. By the time they arrived inside the large house that was currently the coven's main base, the seats around the makeshift throne were lined with coven members and Louis sat atop the dais, one leg thrown casually over the ornate arm of the throne.

"What have you brought me, Dante...trespassers?"

"This is Gard and Rayne. They have come looking for Michael."

"And what would you have with my coven member?" Louis' casual body language was a carefully constructed artifice. None of his coven were fooled by his stance and neither were his visitors.

"We would have his head for almost killing one of ours," Gard answered, "and we want to know what he has told you about a certain individual who is now in our care."

There was hushed muttering around the room as Louis sat forward, fire dancing in his eyes. "How I punish my coven members is of no concern of those from across the ocean. You have my regrets about what happened to your vampire, but you also have the cause of that issue within your ranks. Neutralise her and I will resolve the Michael problem for you."

Lavender eyes glowed with displeasure, a low growl coming from Gard's lips. "You appear to be under the misapprehension that we are having a dialogue, Louis. This is not up for discussion or bargaining. Give us Michael and we will leave your coven alive."

"There are upwards of thirty-five vampires here, old one, and only two of you. Do not think your age evens the score. My coven hasn't survived this long and become this strong because we like each other. We are the most feared coven in Europe and you would be best to heed that fact." Venom dripped from each word, Louis' eyes darkening to almost feral as he spoke.

"I only need one to take down this coven though my mate gets a bit cross with me when I have all the fun," Gard countered, his voice so cold that some of the younger vampires present shifted nervously as the tension thickened in the room.

"Well yes I do, honey, but we're not getting very far with this train of discussion. Can I try?" Rayne gave him a sunny smile and that appeared to worry the younger vampires more than her mate's fury. It was clear that they were used to some truly dominant females in their coven.

When he nodded, she turned to Louis, her smile appearing innocent. "We have a message for you, Louis, from Freya Eriksson. She asked us to make you aware that Thereasa is her nephew's mate and therefore now a part of her family. Her exact words were, 'Tell Louis St Geraint, that if so much as one hair on Thereasa's head is harmed because of his actions, or inactions, that I will take a personal trip to Europe to have a little chat with him.' I believe that was verbatim, wasn't it, Gard?"

The silence in the room was deafening. For a long time no one moved or spoke, and then Louis let out a long, deep growl and his face darkened with fury.

"EVERYBODY OUT!"

The vampires scattered at his roar, panic and fear filling the room as they filed out of every exit possible leaving only

Dante remaining. Louis' enraged gaze connected with Dante and he pointed one long taloned finger at him. "Call Michael. Find out where he is and then give them his location."

Gard shot Rayne a puzzled expression, raising an eyebrow in query. "I definitely need to spend more time with Freya to find out just what all the fuss is about. I don't like knowing that she's scarier than I am."

Louis walked down the steps of the dais, coming to stand before them, his eyes never leaving Gard's face. "I fear no one, old one, but I do respect those who have helped build this coven into what it now is. Freya Eriksson has earned my trust and the right to ask me for a boon. You haven't."

"Then what do we need to do to earn that right, Louis?" Rayne asked, drawing his attention from her mate. "Freya is part of our pack. Your packs may be different over here but where we come from pack is family. Doesn't that count for something?"

Again, silence reigned and then Louis smiled, the first genuine glimmer of humour crossing his face. "Oh, I like you," he laughed, some of the tension leaving his big frame. He thumbed a gesture at Gard, appearing unable to stop taunting the Ancient. "He's lucky to have a mate such as you."

"Can I kill him?"

Rayne laughed, relieved at the more relaxed tone from her mate. "No, dear, we still have some questions that need answered. It would go some way towards better relations if Louis were to agree to answer them with no direct threat of impending death. Try to play nice."

"What questions?" Louis' interest appeared piqued, or perhaps he really did react better to females than males. Some people did relate better to the opposite sex and there was enough age in the coven leader that he could be one of them.

"I'm particularly interested in why there is so much interest in what's going on Stateside. The European covens haven't been the least interested in us before. Why now?"

"That's something I've been pondering for a long time," Dante commented, entering the conversation for the first time. His gaze was fixed on Louis as if waiting for permission to continue.

The coven leader finally relaxed more, nodding his head at his second in command. "Dante isn't a permanent member of my coven. If you're looking for answers he is likely the best person to speak to." The coven leader walked over to one of the tables that had chairs in a grouping of four. The others followed him and sat, Gard and Rayne's gaze now on Dante.

Dante was a little concerned about the level of scrutiny he was under and unclear on how much he should divulge in front of Louis. So far, the coven leader appeared receptive to at least Rayne's charms. The message from this Freya woman had wrought an interesting change in his friend's demeanour towards their visitors too.

He took a deep breath and decided to play it by ear. "As Louis has mentioned, I am not aligned with any one coven here. As such, I have been free to travel all over Europe for the last quarter of a century. As I've travelled, I noticed a strange anomaly among the covens, something so unusual that it piqued my interest. The covens were suddenly speaking with a common tongue. They were all turning their gaze across the ocean; they were all muttering about the mixed matings, and how dangerous the hybrid births were."

He paused for effect, letting the words sink in. "Now, that may not appear strange to you but believe me, for us, it's a loud warning bell being rung. I searched everywhere, listened intently to what was being said, but could detect no sign of where this interest originated. The only thing I could determine was the covens were starting to work together."

"You believe there is a central point to this change in behaviour?" It was Louis who asked the question, his gaze intent as he stared at his second in command.

"Louis, you know our people as well as I do. If there is a central or originating point..."

"Then whoever is at that centre is stronger than all of the covens here put together," Louis completed the sentence.

Gard and Rayne shared a glance as Louis growled in displeasure. "Why didn't you tell me this earlier, Dante?"

The nomadic vampire met his angry gaze without flinching. "Until now I wasn't certain that you weren't that central point. You said it yourself, Louis. Yours is the strongest coven in Europe. You were the one who sent Thereasa after de la Rios in Edinburgh. You were the one who was heavy handed with the Amort toxin."

The coven leader jumped up, his chair crashing to the ground as he leaned on the table, fury dancing across his face. "It was supposed to be a simple information gathering exercise. The vampire wasn't supposed to be nearly killed. I didn't anticipate that members of my coven that I had trained personally would suddenly start acting so recklessly and out of character."

"Then why give them the poison, St Geraint?" Gard thundered, rising to tower over the irate vampire. "Why did you even formulate a toxin that could kill your own kind if not to gain dominance stateside as well as here?"

For a moment Rayne thought the coven leader was going to be foolish enough to attack her mate, but whatever murderous thoughts were crossing his mind, Louis held himself in check, the muscle jumping in the side of his jaw the only outward indication of the strength of will that took.

He ignored Gard's questions, turning to look back at Dante. "Where did you start hearing the first whispers of commonality, Dante? Wherever that was, that is likely going to be closest to the nest of whatever viper we have among us."

"Romania."

Gard stiffened, his expression turning thoughtful as he gazed off into the distance. "You're sure?" he finally asked.

"Yes," Dante answered, watching the redheaded vampire extend a hand towards his mate.

Rayne took it without question, allowing him to pull her up to her feet. "You suspect something?" she queried, her expression expectant.

"I think it's time we went home," her mate replied, giving her a pensive smile.

"But...we haven't learnt anything, Gard." Rayne's confusion was clear for everyone to see.

"Not that home, Sarayne..." He left the rest of the words unsaid, knowing she would work out what he meant

Realisation slowly dawned across her face and a shiver ran through her slender frame as her gaze locked with his. "I haven't been there since I was still a child. Are you sure about this?"

"I'm sure. It's the only logical place to look. If the first whispers came from Romania, then we have to go there and find out just who is behind all this."

"Do you want to clue the rest of us in on this?" Dante asked, a feeling of foreboding beginning to build as the couple continued to have eyes only for each other.

"There are some things it is best not to know," Gard answered, though he was staring at Louis as he spoke. There was more than distrust in his eyes. He was making it abundantly clear that he didn't want to divulge any more information to the coven leader.

"You look at me as if I am somehow the cause of all of this. I am just as much a pawn in this game that is being orchestrated by whoever is in charge."

"Tell that to Pietro de la Rios," Gard growled, his eyes narrowing with displeasure. "Tell that to all the other vampires who may have fallen victim to your poison." Looping an arm over Rayne's shoulder, Gard turned away, heading out of the coven's headquarters.

"How enlightening to see that with age comes narrow-mindedness," Louis spat out, fury lacing every word. "Amort isn't my poison, Gard. It isn't even the making of vampires. It was invented by our Were population here. They made it to exterminate our race..."

Pietro closed and locked the main doors to the Dive, knowing he couldn't put off the inevitable any longer. Cassia was upstairs in his apartment, where she had been all night since he'd returned to the nightclub.

He'd stayed away for as long as he could, finally returning when he received a particularly blunt voicemail message from Andrei telling him to get his ass back to work. Now he had to go upstairs and talk to his wolf, even though he had no idea what he was going to say.

What could he say? She had announced that he was her mate and for Cassia, that was the end of any discussion. She was more wolf than vampire, and she followed her animal genealogy. That was what made her so pack orientated. That was why she'd had no choice but to protect Reasa that day. He was finally beginning to understand that a wolf pack wasn't that different from a vampire coven, and his wolf had claimed him as hers.

Sighing, he headed upstairs, still stunned by Cassia's revelation but he supposed that explained many things. Like why he had been ready to rip Fox apart for daring to think he had any kind of claim over Cassia; why he had been so unaccountably drawn to the blonde wolf from the moment he had first laid eyes on her. He had been willing to risk Alexei's wrath to be with her, not to mention Andrei's, and that wasn't something he did lightly.

Cassia was his mate.

He ran the words through his mind, testing them out, examining the emotional appeal to them. They brought forth such strong feelings of belonging, and of ownership, only that wasn't the correct word. No, he didn't own Cassia; he belonged to her, as she belonged to him.

She belonged to him.

Pietro let himself into his apartment, his gaze travelling over the living area and finding it empty. He knew she was still there...he could scent her in the apartment. A quick check inside the small kitchenette showed it was empty too though there were clean dishes on the draining board.

Crossing to the refrigerator, he opened it, not really surprised to see the food inside it. Cassia must have gone out at some point. She must have taken the back stairs down to the basement exit, which meant Andrei had given her the code to let herself back in. For a moment he wanted to throttle his friend. Andrei was having too much fun at his expense with this one, but then, he had enjoyed himself when Loretta claimed his friend so he supposed he couldn't really complain.

That only left one place she could be and he inhaled deeply before he silently opened the bedroom door. Cassia was curled up on top of the bed, the bedspread half covering her lower body. She was still dressed though it appeared that she'd been asleep for a while.

Her curls were tumbled across her face, one arm supporting her head as she slept. She looked so adorable he wanted to cross the room and climb in beside her. He wanted to lose himself in her arms and pretend that they didn't have to deal with all the issues complicating everything.

He couldn't though, he knew that. They had to talk and that meant waking her. Crossing the room quietly, he sat down on the side of the bed, unable to resist the urge to brush her silky curls away from her face. Cassia murmured in her sleep, rolling onto her back as her eyes fluttered opened. "Pietro."

"You shouldn't be here, Cassia. You should be home safe at the compound." He watched the sleepiness leave her face, a small frown marring her forehead.

"I should be wherever you are," she answered, moving to sit up until they were bare inches apart. "I meant what I said earlier, Pietro. You are my mate."

He hadn't expected anything less than the total conviction in her expression. If only it were that simple, though. Pietro couldn't deny the way his heart sped up at the thought of being mated with her, at how much he longed to know that sense of belonging that only true mates experienced. Yet, how could he make her understand just how difficult this was for him? Yes, she was empathic enough to understand, but she didn't appear to see that the issues they faced weren't that easy to overcome.

"Cass...even if that's true; you have to know how impossible this situation is."

"I know there are issues we need to overcome, Pietro, believe me, I completely understand that. What I don't understand is why you're not willing to try. You are so convinced that you will fail at any attempt to compromise that you just don't appear to want to even contemplate it. Don't you feel the mating pull? Am I not worth the attempt?"

If ever there was a woman who was worth just that and so much more, it was definitely Cassia Romanov, but still he hesitated, still he wasn't sure he could be the man that she believed him to be.

"This isn't about you," he argued, rising from the bed to pace in agitation. "This is about me, Nina. I am not the forgiving kind. I have spent centuries alone, dealing out justice as and when required. Even before Europe I was this man and I don't know how to be anything else." He stopped to look at her, his expression haunted. "I am flawed, Cassia and it has nothing to do with these scars I wear now. I can't forgive, Reasa, not even for you."

Cassia stared at him, hearing the subtle plea in his words. He truly believed everything he said and it was hurting him as much as the feelings of continued rejection were hurting her. She wasn't willing to give up trying, though. She wasn't willing to concede that he couldn't learn to compromise for the good of the pack. He wanted her as much as she wanted him, of that she was certain. Well, she would fight for him; she would be his strength even as he doubted himself.

"I'm not willing to accept that," she finally replied, rising slowly from the bed, her hands placed on her hips. An idea was slowly forming in her mind, something so outside the box it would probably call to the vampire within him.

"I challenge you... "

Pietro frowned, confusion dancing across his face at her sudden change in tactics. "To what?"

"A sparring match, the best of three. If you win, we mate and I live here with you outside the pack. If I win, we mate and you live with me at the compound."

His expression turned incredulous. "I'm not fighting you."

Cassia's head cocked to the side, a small smile teasing her lips. "Scared I will beat you?" "You're Varcolac...of course you'll beat me."

She hadn't considered that and her brow puckered as she thought it through. "Okay, that's a valid point. I will promise only to use one part of me, the vampiric side. That way we will be evenly matched; vampire to vampire."

This had his expression turning thoughtful, and she could see that him wavering. He had never seen her vampiric side. That surely had to tempt his own vampire...the urge to see just what she was when she embraced the other half of her nature.

"Your wolf is your stronger side," he pointed out.

"Exactly, this way it will be fairer to you and I give you my word not to use any magical abilities as well. We will be an even match, Pietro."

His eyes flashed with excitement and for a moment she thought she had him, and then he shook his head. "I'm still not fighting you. I can't, Cassia. It goes against everything I believe in. I'm supposed to protect you whether or not you actually need my protection."

CHAPTER 4

Lord, he was stubborn and utterly frustrating at times. It was all she could do not to let her irritation show. "You're not fighting me. We're sparring. I spar all the time when we're training at the pack. You'll be honing my self-preservation skills."

Cassia could see he was going to continue being stubborn so she opted to take the decision out of his hands. Without waiting for his response, she coaxed her wolf down within herself and slowly gave over more control to her vampire. It was an odd sensation given she didn't typically interact with that half of her psyche on a conscious level. She was surprised to find that doing so was actually quite exciting.

"Cassia, I..." Whatever Pietro was going to say cut off when she leapt towards his, talons extended. He reacted instinctually, spinning out of her way by dropping low and pivoting to the right.

Wow, he was so fast, faster than she had anticipated he would be. This sparring match may not be as simple as she had first imagined. Still, she would keep to her word. If he won...she would leave the pack, however she didn't have any intention of losing so she would have to beat him fair and square.

"Fine," Pietro growled, anticipation crossing his face, as he watched her closely. "If you're intent on playing, then let's play, Nina." He was countering her attack even before he finished speaking, landing a glancing blow to her arm that she didn't have time to fully deflect. It hurt a bit but didn't inflict any real damage.

She countered with a kick to his side, dancing out of reach before he could counter-strike. He was moving so fast he blurred out of her line of sight before she realised what he intended, and she uttered a shriek of dismay as her legs were kicked from under her and she landed with a dull thud on the carpet.

Pietro landed on her chest, one hand encompassing her throat, pinning her in a submissive position. "One - nil," he laughed, delight shining in his eyes.

He looked so gorgeous as he held her immobile she was almost ready to give up and concede defeat, but her pride wouldn't let her. It wasn't even just about her pride either. Pietro needed the pack more than he knew. He would never completely heal until he had confronted and defeated all his demons from his time in Europe. That meant finding some way to come to terms with Reasa. That meant she couldn't afford to lose to him.

"Best of three remember," she answered, trying to ignore the feel of his hard body pressing so intimately with hers. She wanted to wrap her arms and legs around him until there wasn't even a fraction of an inch between them.

"Yes you did say that," he grinned, jumping up and holding out his hand to help her to her feet.

He looked so confident, so completely sure of himself that she was tempted to smack his hand away but she didn't. Instead, she accepted his hand and made sure to accidentally rub her body against his. The way his eyes dilated and the sharp intake of breath was all that she needed to tell her he was sufficiently distracted.

Cassia spun to the left, twisting Pietro's arm up his back as she kicked him behind his right knee causing it to buckle from the hard blow. As he gasped and sank to his knees, she brought her right hand around his neck. "One all," she whispered, laughing at his outraged snort.

"I was helping you up! We hadn't started the second round..."

"An enemy does not wait for you to be prepared for his or her attack. They strike in a moment of weakness."

For a moment she thought he would continue to protest and then a wicked smile crossed his face as she stepped back to allow him up. His expression sent a chill down her spine when he turned to face her. "Touche, Nina. I will not make that mistake again."

Oh Lord, she was in for a world of hurt. His eyes told her that she pricked his male ego and any reluctance he'd had about fighting her was a thing of the past. Whoever won the next fight decided their fate. Pietro was determined that he was going to win this one, as determined as she was.

Pietro came straight towards her, so fast that she barely had time to move out of the way. The slight tensing of his right leg was all she needed to tell her he was going to leap, so she dropped low, diving forward into a roll as she did. He jumped and she rolled under through his legs, coming back to her feet facing him at the same time he turned.

Only he didn't pause as he turned, he was flowing back at her in the same movement, and the only thing that saved her was the small armchair to her left that she hit him with.

"Fuck!" Pietro yelled as he took the chair full on to his face, but she didn't stop to see what his reaction was. Cassia sailed over the bed in one leap, grabbing the bedside cabinet and cracking him again as he followed her movement.

"Oh, Nina, you are so going to pay for that." This time Pietro took a moment to pause, scrubbing blood from his forehead to clear his vision.

The healer in Cassia noted that the cut on his brow had healed instantly but she didn't let her sigh of relief come out. If he noted that she was even slightly concerned about any damage she may inflict, he would use that weakness against her. He was crafty like that, and she had been around her father and uncle way too long to underestimate a vampire of his cunning.

"You would have to actually lay hands on me to make me pay, Pietro. You appear to be having a little trouble in that department. Would you like me to tie one hand behind my back? I mean, I did think I had hampered myself enough with the 'no wolf, no magic' offer but it appears my vamp is a little too much for you too."

Oh, that bit him deep, so much so, he hissed at her, his hazel eye darkening to almost black. It probably wasn't wise to taunt him but she was feeling particularly reckless...or to be more exact her vampiric side was. Cassia had no idea her vampire was so wild. She filed that thought away for later perusal; she needed to be totally focused on the male before her.

"I would have thought Alexei and Andrei would have taught you not to poke a sleeping tiger, Nina. Apparently, they were very remiss in your upbringing. Allow me to educate you...
"

"Shit!" Cassia feinted left and then left again as Pietro came at her in a flurry of movements that were so fast she was acting more on instinct than any real evasion skills. She ignored the pain in her side where his talons bit deep, and scrambled backwards as they veered towards her face.

He was cornering her...backing her towards the farthest wall where there was nothing she could use in her defence. If she didn't stop reacting and start acting, he was going to have her boxed in with nowhere to go.

"Dad! No! Wait!"

Pietro spun around at her shriek, cursing as she jumped onto his back, wrapping her legs around his waist and an arm around his neck.

"You little... " He pitched forward, digging talons into her thighs and yanking hard.

Cassia shrieked again but this time it was because she was sailing over his head, heading straight towards the large mirrored wardrobe face first. Oh, crap that was going to hurt. Pietro snaked an arm around her waist and spun her backwards before she hit the glass, the move driving the wind from her body.

He was following her down onto the bed as her back hit the mattress hard, and she knew that if he completed the move, he would win their contest. So she did the one thing that her father had drilled into her since the moment she hit puberty. Cassia brought up her knee and gasped as pain shot through her leg.

The pain was nothing compared to the roar that issued from her vampire as his groin area connected with her knee, his full body weight behind the blow. She didn't hesitate though. She rolled at supernatural speed, her talons wrapped around Pietro's throat, pinning him to the bed as his eyes watered.

"Two - one."

Still sucking air into her sore lungs, Cassia slid from his body and lay panting on her back beside him. For a long time there was only the sound of their laboured breathing, and then Pietro turned his head to look at her. "Alexei or Andrei?"

"Both."

"That figures."

When he didn't say anything further, she glanced in his direction to find him staring up at the ceiling, his expression giving nothing away.

"I'm sorry. That was a bit of a low blow."

His lips twitched a little, and then his head turned and she could see amusement dancing in his eyes. "No pun intended?"

Now the match was over, she was starting to feel guilty at the underhand tactics she'd used, even if he did appear to find it funny. Dear Lord, she'd broken furniture across his body, not to mention...

"I didn't mean to hurt you." "No, you meant to win and you used everything in your arsenal to achieve that. Don't ever apologise for doing what is necessary, Nina. You do what you must to win. No holds barred. Though I must confess being bested by what is technically a Youngling is quite ego bruising, but your vampire...she is spectacular."

Cassia laughed, her heart still thudding in her chest. "She scared the crap out of me," she admitted. "I didn't know I could be that sneaky."

Pietro half sat up, his head supported by his hand as he looked down at her. "Yes, the Alexei distraction worked excellently. I can't believe I fell for one of the oldest tricks in the book. I almost had you up until that point." Her sheepish grin teased another laugh from him.

"I didn't know if that would work but it was the only thing I could think of in the spur of the moment."

Pietro's expression turned serious, his finger lightly brushing her cheek before twirling around a golden curl, his gaze intent on the way it clung to his skin. "You're completely certain?"

Cassia knew what he was asking her. "At first I wasn't," she admitted, because he deserved nothing but the truth from her. "My wolf appeared undecided and that confused me for a while but now she has claimed you. You are my mate."

Her wolf didn't know. He didn't think that was possible, not from what he'd learned about Weres over the centuries. Cassia's honesty was refreshing, but there was something she was holding back.

"When did you know for sure?" He asked the question but deep in his heart he already knew the answer. He could still hear the mournful howl of the wolf that day, when he had rejected the woman lying beside him...when he had accused her of betraying him.

"Does that really matter, Pietro? We belong to each other. That's the only thing that matters."

She was letting him off the hook, granting him forgiveness for the harsh words he'd said that day. It would have been so easy to accept her generosity but he had never been one to take the easy route. "It matters, Cass...to me. That last day at the compound, I was so consumed with the need for revenge. I was more than aware of what the pack meant to you, and yet, I still said those things to you, accused you of betrayal."

Sitting up, Cassia pushed him backwards, until their positions were reversed and she was the one leaning over him. "I understood. It just took my wolf a little longer to and as you know I tend to follow my animal as opposed to my vampiric side. For a short time I needed to allow my wolf to come to terms with your rejection but I was never in any danger of going rogue. I don't think the Varcolac can go rogue, not in the same sense that a Were can. I was hurt but I was never in any danger, Pietro. I need you to believe that."

His beautiful wolf was reassuring him when he was the one who had caused her so much anguish. Everything she had ever done since the first moment they'd met was to think of his needs, to put him first and he had selfishly lashed out and hurt her. She deserved someone so much better than him, someone with far less emotional scars.

"You did not just say that," Cassia laughed, her curls tumbling around her face as she shook her head. "My dad and uncle are two of your best friends."

He hadn't realised he'd said the words out aloud until she started laughing. Yeah right, who was he trying to kid? She'd grown up surrounded by two of the most emotionally challenged vampires he'd ever known and she'd still turned out pretty amazing. Taking him on would be a piece of cake after that.

"You're not going to be dissuaded, are you?" The fierceness that blazed from her eyes was the only answer he needed, her possessiveness making his heart stutter. She was claiming him, and he couldn't deny that he wanted that as much as she did. Cassia had such faith in him, such belief that they could conquer anything as long as they were together. He'd be a fool to walk away from the love she was offering him, and though he may have acted foolish in Europe, he had no intention of continuing that streak.

"I love you, Cassia Romanov." Just saying the words out aloud felt surreal, but he knew they were true, and had been for a long time. When had she crept into his heart? He didn't know.

He was just aware that she was firmly embedded there and always would be. Cassia was his heart and soul. She completed him in every way possible, and he would do whatever it took to have a future with her. He would even try to forgive Reasa, because if he couldn't at least try, he may lose his feisty wolf, and he couldn't imagine not having her in his life.

Cassia's breath caught as he uttered the words she'd longed to hear, his mismatched eyes glowing with such fierceness it took her breath away. Her beautiful vampire was surrendering; he was willing to compromise for her. It brought tears to her eyes that he could lay himself vulnerable to her after all he'd been through. She knew it wasn't easy for him and that he was willing to try to be with her.

"I love you, Pietro de la Rios," she whispered back leaning down until their lips almost touched, and she could feel his breath teasing her mouth. It set her heart fluttering in a way nothing else ever could. The emotions threatening to overwhelm her in that moment were reserved exclusively for the glorious male lying beneath her. As she exhaled slowly, he sucked her breath into his mouth. When he did the same, she breathed him into her soul.

"One breath...one heartbeat. My soul is yours for eternity. Will you mate with me, Pietro? Will you complete me?" Her voice hitched as she asked and she held her breath as she waited, her wolf peering from the depths of her questing eyes.

"What is it you wolves say when you claim your mates?" The deep rumble of his voice didn't hide the possessiveness of his gaze.

"Mine... "

Pietro snaked a hand around the nape of her neck, stealing that last agonising inch that separated them. His touch was gentle, teasing...a slow rubbing of lips in a kiss so tender, her tears overflowed.

"Mine," Pietro growled into her mouth, licking the salty wetness on her lips. "You were always mine, Nina, from the very first moment I laid eyes on you."

Her wolf howled its glee, rejoicing in their mate's acceptance. He was finally theirs. He was finally hers. It was as if she had lived only for this moment, and she was going to remember every single second of it. She had her mate. She had her beautiful vampire.

"I don't know what to do," he whispered against her lips, his vulnerability so endearing her heart felt as if it would burst with love for him.

"Then let me lead," she answered, pulling back so she could read every emotion flickering across his face. "I promise you will enjoy it."

Pietro started to laugh, excitement shining from his eyes, mixed in with love, and healthy dose of lust. "Oh, I have no doubt that I would, Cassia, though I am not so sure how good I will be in the submissive position. It doesn't come naturally."

The sultry expression that crossed her face sent his blood pressure sky high, the wicked smile curving her lips made his body pulse with the need to be buried inside her. "That's okay, lover. I can hold you down if required. I am Varcolac after all."

Ordinarily the thought of not being the one in control was total anathema to him, however the way his wolf was looking at him right now...hell yes she could do whatever she wanted if it meant she'd pour her luscious body all over his. "I'm all yours, Nina." Was that really his voice? The words practically purred out of his mouth and from the dilation of Cassia pupils, he could tell she liked them.

"Of course."

Cassia's smile turned even more wicked if that were at all possible. He was about to comment on it when his T-shirt ripped down the centre and the cooling air of the bedroom whispered across his bare chest. His heart thudded loudly, his cock flexing in the confines of his jeans. His wolf looked like she wanted to eat him all up, and he wasn't one to deny her base instincts.

Gentle fingers touched his brow, tracing the scar down his face, lingering on his neck where his second scar met with his shoulder. Cassia frowned as she touched the ridged flesh, golden highlights reflecting in her eyes signalling her wolf was very much present.

"Sacrilege," she growled quietly, a hint of fury lacing the word. "This belongs to us. This is where we make our mark. It sends my wolf insane with rage that someone laid hands on you, that someone desecrated what is ours."

"Then claim it back," he commanded, surprised at the wealth of emotion in each word as he raised one hand to place it over her trembling fingers. Until this moment, he had never wanted anything so badly in his life. He wanted to sooth her wolf's fury. He wanted to feel her mark him so that it would eradicate the memories attached to that scar and replace it with something so beautiful, that those memories would never haunt him again. "I am yours, my wolf, now and for eternity."

"Mine!" Cassia slithered down his body, her lips tracing butterfly kisses against the scar on his cheek, down the hard curve of his jaw, along scarred flesh of his collarbone. Her touch was light, teasing and it made his hips flex upwards, his body seeking the ultimate blending of their souls.

"Greedy boy," she laughed against his skin, kissing her way over his chest, her tongue snaking out to lick and taste him.

Each touch was an exquisite torture, each caress a pleasure like none other. It was difficult to lay there and allow her to do as she wanted, but he was determined to let his sultry wolf have her way with him. This was her moment; this was what her wolf needed. When they mated together, he wanted it to be the most magical experience of her life.

Her lips grazed his stomach, forcing him to suck in a deep breath. The evidence of his need was outlined brazenly against the fabric of his jeans, and he jumped when he felt a lone talon measure his length in the slowest of motions he could imagine. "Cassia... "

"Yes, Pietro?"

How the fuck could she sound so sexy and innocent at the same time? The witch was playing with him and loving every moment of it, and he had to admit to himself that it was excruciatingly erotic to be on the opposite side of this kind of foreplay. Perhaps he would allow her to do this again sometime...but not too often.

"You're playing with fire, Nina."

Sensual laughter greeted his words, and his patience and blood pressure reached fever pitch.

"Then I guess you should burn me, my beautiful vampire..."

His jeans shredded under her talons and he uttered a low curse. Before he could move he felt her hot breath tease his flesh and then her tongue licked slowly up his throbbing cock.

"I think I need to kiss you better. I did hurt you here." Her muffled laughter cut off as she swallowed him down, his hips rocking up to meet the glorious heat of her mouth.

"Cassia!" He roared her name out, clutching at the bedspread to stop his hands fisting in her curls and pull her mouth more fully onto him. This was her moment and he had to give it to her. He had to let her see just how much he loved her, what he was willing to do for her.

It was sweet torture though, pleasure, and pain all mingled into one. She kept her touch teasing, always promising more, but never fully delivering. Every nerve ending felt alive, his desire stoking higher and higher with each flick of her tongue, each slow stroke of her mouth over his straining flesh. Was this what it felt like when he loved her, when his hands and mouth danced over her soft skin drawing every nuance of pleasure he could? If it was she was getting payback in the bucket load, and he had to concede that it was highly erotic to experience her brand of vengeance.

Her wicked mouth worshipped every inch of his throbbing cock, sliding smoothly up and down in a slow rhythm that had his heart pounding so wildly he could hear the echo in his ears. Soft hands travelled up his thighs, coming to cup his heavy sacs, squeezing them in tandem with her suckling.

Dear Lord, he was ready to blow, helpless against her dual assault. She took him completely into her mouth, pressing her wet heat down until he slid down her throat and she massaged his balls firmly. Pietro roared loudly, the sinewy muscles in his neck straining as he threw his head back and exploded. She sucked and squeezed, swallowing down his essence greedily, humming with pleasure as he emptied himself into her willing mouth.

It was the most amazing thing he had ever experienced. He had heard tales before of how being in love totally changed lovemaking, how that emotional bond heightened the pleasure, made each orgasm so much more intense. He'd never believed it, always having been satisfied with his previous sexual experiences. Now he knew the truth of it. Now his climax was both a physical and emotional release, and he had eternity to lay with his wolf like this.

Cassia crawled back up his body, one small hand stroking his semi-hard cock back to full hardness as she kissed him deeply. He could taste himself on her lips but he didn't care. It was so erotic to know that the mouth he was devouring had loved him so intimately, that allowing her to pleasure him that way had brought her as much pleasure as it had him. "You're so wicked," he chuckled against her lips.

"I'm about to get a whole load wickeder," she laughed, sitting up and pulling her shirt off in one move, freeing her breasts to his greedy gaze.

His hands rose to cup them and she slapped them away playfully. "You don't get to touch unless I give you permission. Now be a good boy and put those hands behind your head." She was rising as she spoke, snapping the button of her jeans, and slowly lowering the zipper as he obeyed her.

Lust and laughter danced in her eyes as she wiggled the denim down her hips, taking her panties with it. The bed shook precariously but she managed to keep her balance as she undressed. When she was finished, she stood above him, her heart beating a wild tattoo as she watched the naked lust in his eyes roaming over her body.

"Come here," he growled and she wagged her finger at him as she laughed again.

"This is my party, remember. We play my way or not at all." "Seriously?" Pietro let out a pained groan, frustration building up inside. "You're killing me here, Cassia. Let me love you."

Slowly sinking to her knees, she straddled his body, pressing her wet heat against his hard length. They groaned in unison, Cassia's hands coming to rest on his chest as she teased him with her body, slow languid strokes against his cock imitating what was to come.

"I can't stand much more of this," he warned, his nostrils flaring at the heavenly aroma of her arousal. He meant it too. If she didn't slide herself onto his cock right now he would roll her over and take her hard and fast as he craved to do.

Cassia delighted in teasing him, thrilled at seeing the hint of desperation beginning to shine in his eyes. This is what he did to her, how he made her feel when he loved her so dominantly. She knew the torturous build up only heightened the sexual experience, so she continued to grind herself against his cock with deliberate movements.

A scant second before he lost all patience with her, she rose above him that tiny bit higher and slowly slid his cock into her hot core. Oh god, he felt so hard, so thick and strong within her body. It was as if this was the first time they had lain together. The feel of him filling her so completely was the most erotic thing in the world.

Pietro kept his hands behind his head though she could tell from the corded muscles in his neck that she probably didn't have too much time left to enjoy her position of dominance. It didn't matter if he failed her demands. What mattered was that he was willing to give her this moment. That he was willing to acknowledge that though he may control their sexual play, he still respected her as his equal.

Rising slowly up and down, she enjoyed her moment, riding his body in a dance older than time, and more beautiful than the most exotic work of art. Cassia made love to her vampire with her heart, body, and soul, showing him what he meant to her, what would always be his for eternity.

He couldn't take it anymore, he just couldn't. Cassia was sheathing his cock so erotically, her breast swaying with each movement that it was inciting his blood lust to rise. He needed to taste her. He had to touch her soft skin and lick her all over before suckling her life's essence into his eager mouth.

Pietro raised his upper body up, his arms snaking around her back as his lips zeroed in on one hard nipple and he sucked it deep into his mouth, flexing his hips at the same time to drive himself in deep. He couldn't get a good angle in this position so he lifted her off him, moving to rest on his knees.

"This is your seat I believe, my lady." The roguish grin he shot her turned into a muffled groan as he pulled her back astride him, sliding her back onto his throbbing cock.

Cassia's breath gasped out as she wrapped her arms around his neck and accepted him eagerly. "Oh! I believe you are right," she giggled breathily, pressing down to meet his upward movement. "That feels...perfect."

"Hold tight, Nina."

It was all the warning she got before he took full control of their joining, bucking into her body with hard, fast strokes, sending liquid fire racing through her veins. She was soaring through the heavens, pleasure crashing over her with each deep thrust he gave her.

"I can't wait..." he gasped, his fangs already lowered, desperation in his eyes.

She understood what he meant. Her wolf was baying for her to claim him, urging her to mark him as theirs. Cassia licked at his collarbone, licked against his shoulder. She nibbled at the scar that desecrated their territory, a low growl escaping her.

"Be mine forever, Pietro."

"Always."

Cassia felt the heat of her climax building, her body moving faster and harder as she rode her beautiful vampire. She was almost there, almost ready to soar as her passion exploded over her. With another growl she whispered, "Mine." Her teeth sank into his skin, as he slammed into her hard and she shattered, her vision obscured by a kaleidoscope of colours dancing behind her eyes.

Pietro's fangs sank into her neck, his body pulsing thickly as he emptied himself into her. She climax again, shuddering wildly as he clamped her body to his and drank from her neck, completing the mating ritual and nourishing his still healing body.

Pietro continued to rock into her, mindless to anything but the feel of her wet heat fluttering around his cock and her hot blood flowing down his throat. It had always been good between them but this moment transcended everything they had ever experienced and he didn't want it to end.

"Cassia...oh God, Cassia." "I know," she gasped out between panting breaths, holding him against her as he kissed the side of her neck, their bodies still joined. Her wolf was ecstatic, preening itself now that they had claimed their mate. She wanted to laugh at its antics but didn't think Pietro would see the humorous side if she did.

Pietro knocked away the remnants of the broken chair that was on his pillows and gently laid her down on the bed, lying on his side so they were facing each other. "Is it done?" He wasn't sure if he was supposed to feel a wolf inside him or something now she had bitten him. He didn't feel any different so he was worried that maybe it hadn't worked.

"Oh yes," Cassia smiled, her gaze dropping to the spot where she had bitten him. Her smile faltered and a frown furrowed her brow, her hand reaching out to touch his skin. "That's odd."

Her concern made him uneasy. "What is?"

"My mark...it hasn't healed." When he shot her a blank look she sat up and he followed her. "Usually the physical mark disappears though the psychic bond remains. Yours should have too but it's still there."

Rising to look in the mirror, he saw what she meant. Where she had bitten him across his scar, there was a clear impression of her bite mark. When she said it hadn't healed she hadn't been entirely accurate. The bite mark looked as if it had been there for years. It had technically healed...it just hasn't vanished. It had to have something to do with the scarred area of his body. Something about the Amort toxin had altered those areas of his body so that they would never truly heal.

Seeing Cassia's uncertain expression in the mirror tore at his heart. She was probably afraid that he'd view this as he viewed his other imperfections. She couldn't be further from the truth though. Crossing back to the bed, he pulled her into his embrace, capturing her gaze with his and refusing to allow her to look away.

"I'm glad," he said gruffly, emotion making his voice sound huskier than usual. "I want to wear your mark, Cassia Romanov. I am proud to wear it and don't you ever think otherwise."

"You're sure?"

For an answer he kissed her, long and slow, and with so much love that she would never doubt how much she meant to him. When he let her up for air they were both breathless. "I'm sure."

Pulling Cassia down beside him, he covered them with the bedspread and held his mate close. She was his now...for eternity. They were joined together and no one and nothing would ever come between them.

"Sleep, Nina, while you can because I know I'm going to want to sample your sweet body again in the very near future."

"Greedy, vampire," she laughed, cuddling close and wrapping her arms and legs around his hard length. "Let's see who wakes who first."

Pietro burst out laughing, kissing the side of her neck before closing his arms and inhaling her sweet fragrance. "You're on... "

"Thank you, Liam, Reasa. What you've done for the Praetorians will be remembered." Mac's expression was earnest as he shook first Liam and then Reasa's hands.

PART 7

CHAPTER 1

Lily was standing beside him, beaming with happiness. As usual, she threw formality to the wind and smothered them in affectionate hugs. "I am so jealous I can't dream walk," she laughed, ignoring Reasa's stiffness as she hugged her tightly.

The former vampire appeared uncomfortable with the open affection but she didn't pull away.

"I'm still trying to come to terms with the fact I clearly have a weak mind to be affected in the first place," Brandon grumbled from below them where he waited at the Jeep. Despite his words there was open amusement on his face as the couple walked down the steps towards him.

"I'm sorry." Liam apologised for what had to be about the one hundredth time, earning him a glare of reproof from the vampire.

"How many times do we need to tell you to can that shit, Liam? We signed up for this duty and not one of us regrets it. Hell, we got at least a week off from that torture Karn calls training. You did us a favour." Brandon grinned at the blond vampire as he spoke, his irreverence drawing a dark scowl in his direction.

"Glad you enjoyed it, boy, because you've got a week to make up for. I'll see you all around back in half an hour." Karn flashed his own grin at the younger vampire, more than a hint of malice in it.

Brandon groaned and rolled his eyes as the others laughed, Liam included. Karn was going to work their asses off, but to see the last shards of guilt fade from his friend's expression was enough of a reward for what they'd be subjected to. He couldn't leave it at that though...he wouldn't be Brandon if he did.

"So, just to assuage my curiosity...can you explain to us why we even need the Praetorians anymore? I mean, it's not as if the Varcolac need any protection. They could take us out with probably only one or two of them breaking any kind of sweat."

It was a valid question despite the fact it was asked in jest. Karn didn't answer, though he did look to Mac. The Praetorian leader's expression was relaxed, his arm wrapped around his mate.

"We were originally tasked to protect the Varcolac, that is true," he answered. "However, the Varcolac call the pack their home, and as such, that makes the pack ours to protect by default. Until the Triumvirate give us a new task, we continue as we are. We will be vigilant and on call to either the Armand-Hanlon Pack or the Hanlon Pack. We will help to guard them from all intrusions be they local or from Europe. Our job is not done here; it has merely morphed into a new one. So I suggest you get your ass out back and get training, Brandon."

He laughed as he said the last bit, genuinely fond of the young male his mate had chosen to be her closest friend. It was hard for anyone not to like Brandon, and anyone who made his Lily smile was a friend of his.

Brandon mocked saluted, and winked at Lily before he jogged around the house to do as he was bid.

"That boy is nothing but trouble," Karn groused, though he was smiling as he said it.

"That's funny, because he reminds me of you when we first met," Mac countered, drawing an irritated snort from his second in command.

Liam smiled at the banter, a feeling of sadness coming over him that they were leaving the tight knit community. He'd enjoyed his time there and he could see the good effect it had had on Reasa too. She had loosened up a lot, her walls starting to come down as the Praetorians had welcomed her into their home. Perhaps he would talk to Rafe about allowing them to return to the compound when the threat from Europe has been dealt with. He wouldn't mind living with the Praetorians.

"Time for us to head back," he announced, opening the Jeep door so Reasa could climb in. "If you need us for anything, let Rafe know and we'll come back."

"You both have our thanks, Liam," Mac answered, a large smile on his face. "You're welcome here anytime."

Starting the engine, Liam headed back towards the pack compound. Reasa was quiet beside him, the silence deepening the closer they came to pack lands. He could see her shutting down as each mile passed and he wanted to curse out aloud. He couldn't face taking a backward step, not after the way she'd allowed him closer up at the Praetorian Compound.

"Do you want to return to Freya's home when we get back?" He asked the question even though he didn't want to hear the answer. If she retreated from him, he didn't know how he was going to reach her again. When she didn't answer straight away he glanced sideways to see her staring out the side window at the passing trees.

"Thereasa?" Her head turned and he couldn't make out what she was thinking. It set his heart plummeting into his stomach. She had retreated.

"Would your mother be agreeable to me residing in her home once more?"

It was the last thing he'd expected her to say, her response surprising him so much he stepped on the brakes to bring the car to a halt. Unclipping his seatbelt, he turned to face her. "Is that what you want? Think about it before you answer, Reasa. I only want you to say yes if it's what you truly want."

"It is what I want," she answered, her expression remaining neutral. "I find I have become accustomed to spending my days and nights with you, Liam. I do not want that to end."

She wasn't declaring she was ready to mate with him, but it was the most hopeful news he could have expected at this point. Liam would have let her go if she'd asked it of him. He was just glad that he didn't have to. He smiled slowly, his heart feeling suddenly lighter. "I am sure my mother will be agreeable to you staying with us again. I know she hasn't been exactly welcoming, but you have to understand that she's only concerned about me. She's very protective."

"Ashleigh's reaction is one of the things I do understand," she sighed, leaning her head back and closing her eyes. "You have an incredibly amazing mother, Liam Eriksson. She would walk through fire for you, and lay down her life for you. Being truthful, I am in awe of her. If only my mother had been the same then perhaps my life would have turned out differently."

When she didn't say anything further, Liam restarted the engine and continued on, a huge smile on his face. Things would get better, he just knew it. His mom was an amazing woman and it filled him with joy that his mate could see that too. Now, he just needed to convince his mother to see how amazing his mate was. He was convinced he could do that, even if it might take a little time.

Reasa remained silent with her eyes closed until they pulled up in front of his home. Her gaze turned apprehensive for a moment, her body stiffening when the door opened and his parents came outside.

"Liam, you're home." Ashleigh gathered her son close, laughing as he picked her up and gave her a huge bear hug. "You did it. You brought them back. I'm so proud of you, honey." "Yes, you both did." Nors smiled as he held the car door open for Reasa to step out. "You've done an amazing thing, Thereasa. Thank you."

She appeared startled by his warmth, a blush crossing her cheeks as she looked away. "Liam did all the hard work. I merely helped him to finesse his phenomenal strength."

"Nonsense, you worked just as tirelessly as I did," Liam countered, moving to her side. "And you didn't have the luxury of healing from the physical wounds our bodies took while we were dream walking. Not once did you complain about it. In fact, you never mentioned it once to me. Elina had to tell me that she was healing you while we were working to bring the Praetorians back."

"Your bodies took physical damage?" Ashleigh gasped, concern spreading across her face. She was aware that Liam wouldn't have been in danger but Thereasa was human now. "Are you okay? Should we call Mallen over?" Her concerned gaze was directed at the former vampire who appeared to shrink even further into herself.

"I am unharmed," she muttered, looking everywhere but at the woman in front of her.

"Come on, let's get you inside before the rest of the pack come out to be nosey. They're still talking about your departure last week, and some of the younger heads still need to cool off a bit. Nors, grab their packs. Have you eaten yet? I can put on some breakfast." Ashleigh ushered the couple inside as her mate did as she bade.

Reasa turned perplexed eyes to Liam, unsure of how to react to suddenly being mothered by the woman who would have quite happily have seen her rot the week before. He shrugged but grinned happily.

"Just go with the flow, Reasa. There's no stopping her when she gets in one of her 'mothering' moods."

"I heard that, Liam Eriksson!"

He laughed loudly. "You were meant to, Mom."

Liam retrieved their packs from his father. "I'm going to head up to my room with our stuff. I take it there's no problem with Reasa staying with us again?" He threw the question out light-heartedly though his gaze was fixated on his mother's reaction.

His parent shared a brief look and then his father smiled. "I'll give you a hand, son."

There was no mistaking the fact that he meant for them to leave the women alone for a while to have a 'talk'. Liam wasn't so sure if Reasa was up for that but his father's expression told him that he didn't really have a say in it. With a resigned sigh, he followed him out of the kitchen.

Reasa didn't know what to do when Liam left her alone with Ashleigh. For want of anything better to do she sat down at the breakfast table, tensing a bit when Ashleigh sat down across from her. The blonde Were eyed her speculatively for a moment before she gave her a half smile.

"There's no need to look so concerned, Thereasa. Wiser heads than mine have prevailed." Ashleigh paused, looking down at her joined hands resting on the tabletop before she looked back at the former vampire.

"I love Liam with all my heart," she began, that love blazing from her eyes. "His happiness is the most important thing to me and for a time, I wasn't able to see that too clearly. I was too busy being a mother reacting to her child being in harm's way that I didn't want to see in you what he saw. The only thing that registered with me was that you tried to kill him."

She paused, letting the words sink in. "I'm not going to lie to you, Thereasa. I am still working on that and it may take me a while to fully forgive you for hurting my son. However, I am willing to try to see past it."

Reasa knew it had to be hard for her to say that, and it was probably more than she deserved. She nodded her acceptance of Ashleigh's position. "If it is of any assistance, I do regret that action now, Ashleigh."

Brown eyes searched her face for a long moment, and then there was a softening to Were's expression. "I can see that," she conceded. "I think I even believed it before you headed to the Praetorian compound. I just wasn't ready to have this conversation with you. I needed some more time to work through the emotions I was going through."

"You were a mother protecting your child," Reasa answered, her body still tense indicating how uncomfortable she was with the situation. "I respect and understand your position. If our circumstances were reversed, I would have reacted exactly as you did. You are a good mother to Liam."

Ashleigh laughed, but there was no humour in it. "No, I was a selfish mother, afraid of losing her son. The relief at knowing the Varcolac were immune to your poison was quickly tempered by Liam claiming you as his mate. In my mind, you had failed to take my son away from me in one way, but were instead going to take him from me in another. No one knows the mating call of a Were better than I do. There is no stronger pull in the universe and Liam follows his wolf. That I rejected his claim and made your time living here untenable is not the act of a loving mother."

Reasa had expected her time at the Eriksson house to be more of the same when it came to Liam's mother, but this unexpected admission left her in confusion. There was a bitterness to Ashleigh's tone but it wasn't directed at her. Instead, it was directed inward and that wasn't what she'd expected to encounter at all.

Hesitantly, she reached out, placing her hand over Ashleigh's. She had done so instinctively and was further confused when the Were didn't pull away but instead turned her hands around to capture her's in a tight grasp.

"I do not find you at fault for your treatment of me, Ashleigh. I am aware of how much importance you hold in Liam's heart. It is hard not to as I have walked in his memories and seen the love his family have given him throughout his life."

Reasa blinked slowly, trying to find the words she was looking for. "I am not good at this kind of thing," she admitted, "but what I do know is Liam has a huge heart, full of so much love and forgiveness. I believe he receives that from you, his mother. Do not hold onto a past action that is but a mere fraction of a second in comparison to the wealth of moments where you have excelled yourself. You do yourself a disservice if you do."

She had never known she had such eloquence or such inclination towards forgiveness. Clearly, Liam was rubbing off on her because she was astounded to find that she meant everything that she said and that she truly did want to assuage the self-loathing she was seeing in the other woman's expression.

"I am ashamed, Thereasa," Ashleigh whispered, a lone tear falling as her grasp tightened. "Yes, you came here with ill intent but I allowed myself to be blinded by that fact and I failed to see how much you have grown in your time with us. I let hate dominate my heart and I have hurt my family by doing so. It has taken me a while but I am starting to accept that Liam can never be happy without you in his life."

Something twisted in Ashleigh's heart as she said the words; the knowledge that she was part way to forgiving and that it didn't make her a bad mother if she did. Liam had chosen this woman to be his life's mate, and now she was really seeing her for the first time, perhaps that wasn't as bad a choice as she'd once believed. "You are welcome in my home, Thereasa. For however long you wish to remain here."

Did miracles happen? Reasa had never believed in them before but sitting here with Liam's mother was a revelation that astounded her. Ashleigh was willing to welcome her into her home and into her family. Though she hadn't said the latter words, the implication was there. She swallowed hard to dislodge the lump that was suddenly clogging her throat. "I am grateful for your generosity, Ashleigh." She couldn't think of anything else to say.

The blonde Were scrubbed at her wet cheeks, rising from her seat as she did. "How about we start again and see how we get on? Make a fresh start for both of us? We both love Liam so we have a strong foundation of commonality."

Reasa nodded her agreement a split second before what Ashleigh had said fully penetrated her brain. Her heart sank, shock rocking through her body as the full import of what she'd just done registered. She had just admitted to Ashleigh that she was in love with Liam! Now that the thought was out there, she wasn't able to take it back and deny it. She couldn't avoid it, couldn't pretend it wasn't there. Somehow she had fallen in love with Liam Eriksson and she didn't know what to do about it.

How could she leave him now? Leaving was the only solution to the problem she had been able to come up with and she'd had to go and make it so much worse by falling in love with Liam? She had done nothing but bring irrevocable harm to the pack and their vampire friends. Louis was out to kill her, of that she had no doubt, which meant she would continue to bring harm to the very people who were now welcoming her into their lives.

She couldn't be responsible for that, she just couldn't. Liam would have to understand. He had to let her go and not come looking for her. It was the only way the pack would ever be truly safe.

The sound of Liam and his father coming downstairs shook her out of her reverie and she absent-mindedly answered a question about food that Ashleigh had just asked her. By the time the two males entered the kitchen, Reasa's expression was carefully neutral, no indication of that had just occurred visible to see.

She remained quiet as the family interacted, accepting the food placed in front of her and playing with it rather than eating. She felt sick to her stomach and nothing could have convinced her to eat anything. For the most part, they didn't appear to notice, and she almost let out a sigh of relief when the plates were cleared and Liam and his parents rose from the table.

"Just how bad are things with the younger pack members?" Liam was asking his father as they stood.

"Aaron has them out patrolling the south side of the compound. He's been tiring them out so they don't have too much time on their hands to think. The signs are that it's working already. Quite a few of them have calmed down." Nors held his son's gaze. "Cassia has mated though. She's returning to the pack later today with Pietro."

Liam frowned, concerned brown eyes turning to Reasa. The last time they had all been in the pack together Pietro had tried to kill her. Hopefully now the vampire has mated, some of Cassia's pack orientation may have transferred to Pietro.

"I have to go meet with Rafe now to let him know how we got on at the Praetorian compound," he finally said with a half-smile gracing his lips. "As it's pretty quiet right now around here, why don't you stretch your legs a little and go for a walk around the compound, Reasa? It would probably be best not to head south though."

Thereasa couldn't believe what she was hearing. Not only was Liam giving her permission to wander around alone but also his parents weren't objecting. Could she really walk around unescorted? Would this be her opportunity to slip away unseen while their guard was lowered? Just the thought of disappearing made her want to weep but knowing the harm coming their way made her heart break even more. She couldn't allow Louis to hurt any member of this pack because of her.

"If that would be permissible, I would like to see more of the pack," she answered, keeping her voice carefully modulated not to show any sign of her tumultuous emotions.

"Just don't go too far," Liam answered, his smile widening. "There are patrols around all the boundary lines so if you see any wolves out there, do what they indicate they want you to do."

His caution made sense, though she was going to do her best to avoid any wolves she came across. If luck was on her side she could slip passed them. Thanking Ashleigh for breakfast, Reasa kept her emotions locked down tight and headed outside with Liam, walking with him to the Alpha's house.

"I may be a while," he told her. "Despite the few hotheads around, my pack mates are pretty decent people. Enjoy your walk, and if you feel uncomfortable at all just head back to our place. You'll be fine there."

Now the moment was on her Reasa didn't want to leave. Staring up into Liam's smiling face her hand itched to reach up and touch him, to pull his head down and taste his lips once more. There was total trust in his eyes and she was about to break that trust. Even though she knew it was for the best, it didn't hurt any less. "I will not go far," she lied, holding her breath while she waited for him to acknowledge her words.

Liam nodded, heading into the Alpha's house, as Reasa turned towards the tree line. Her feet felt leaden but she took the first step, forcing herself to keep moving. There would likely be no better opportunity than this one and she had to keep going. She brushed a hand over her wet face, lowering her head and disappearing into the trees.

How far had she travelled already? Had she passed the boundary line? She'd been walking for close to half an hour, being careful to hide her tracks as best as she could. If the wolves came looking for her they would probably find her in the forest, but if she could make it to a road and hitch a lift into the city, then there was a good chance she could evade them.

A sound to the left startled Reasa, and she froze in her tracks. Something or someone was close by, and she hadn't seen any sign of them approaching. Could she outrun them? Had they even seen her? Perhaps if she stayed silent long enough they would leave? Any hope of that happening was dispelled when a male voice whispered close to her ear.

"You've made my job so much easier, Thereasa."

She screamed, but a hand clamped over her mouth, a thick arm snaking around her body to hold her pinned to a wide chest. The arm was naked, and as she struggled against him she realised he was completely naked which meant he was most likely a wolf as opposed to a vampire. It still made his next whisper so much more confusing...

"Michael sends his regards..."

Astonishment stilled her movements, dread washing over her. Michael? What was he doing aligning himself with wolves of all things? He detested all Weres as did the majority of European vampires. This man was certainly a Were. There was no reason for a vampire to run around a forest unclothed.

The moment of surprise passed, and her fear escalated. Michael excelled at being a vampire. His penchant for cruelty was almost as legendary as Louis', and he had no love for her. If her former coven leader had sent him then that was to be part of her punishment. He wanted her to die in the most excruciating manner possible.

Reasa started struggling again, kicking behind her to try to catch her captor off-guard. Her blows were ineffectual though. She was human now and so very weak.

The Were threw her to the ground, slapping her face as she tried to rise. His blow was hard but controlled. It was enough to cause her head to snap back against the bark of a tree, pain blossoming at the base of her skull. Crying out, she slumped to the ground in a wave of dizziness.

So, this was what her end would finally be? All it took was one slap to subdue her? Hysterical laughter bubbled up inside even as tears began to flow. They said pride came before a fall, and Reasa was honest enough with herself to admit that the ease of her defeat rankled as much as being caught. When she had been a vampire she could have killed the wolf with one bite, now she was watching him through hazy vision pulling on a pair of sweatpants and reaching for what looked like a phone.

"The bitch came to me... " he was saying into the device and she knew he was talking to Michael. He appeared certain she'd be of no further trouble to him and that fuelled her inner rage.

Reasa wouldn't go down without a fight. She wouldn't be delivered into Michael's hands. Grasping at a nearby rock, she rose unsteadily and threw herself at the half-clad male.

"Stay down!" he growled, backhanding her again.

Blood welled up in her mouth as she crumpled in a heap at his feet.

"No...it's nothing. Stupid bitch tried to attack me. I thought you said she was a vampire? She smells human... "

Reasa's ears were ringing from the second blow, so much so that it took a moment to realise that something was very wrong. Struggling to fight off her disorientation, she opened her eyes, trying to raise her head up from the ground. Red...all she could see was red. It took another moment to realise what her brain was trying to grasp, and when she did, she rolled forward and vomited up her recently eaten breakfast.

* * * * *

Fucking Alpha! Reading him the riot act. Glaring at him with eyes full of condemnation. He could have snipped those eyes out with a flick of one talon. He could have made Rafe Armand-Hanlon weep for death. He hadn't though, he had been a good boy. He had obeyed his parents as they'd asked of him, even though Rafe was the reason they weren't with him.

He was still furious, still itching to take apart something or someone. So he had headed into the forest away from the compound, where he could destroy something without causing any harm to the pack. Dara had tried to stop him, his beautiful angel. She had tempted him and he'd almost given in but he was too close to the edge, too afraid he would do something to hurt her.

He could still see the confusion in her eyes, still see the hurt on her face as the words had spewed from his mouth. "Stop following me around like a bitch on heat. Don't you have enough wolves to whore yourself with? I'm not interested in sloppy seconds, Dara...or in your case that would be sloppy hundreds, wouldn't it?"

So much pain crossing her beautiful face, and then the expected shadow as the light died in her eyes and any compassion she'd ever harboured towards him extinguished. His own pain was like razors scraping down his skin, and he knew he would cut himself a thousand times to try to alleviate that feeling. He deserved it too, for hurting his angel as he had.

"Fuck you, Kothari." Her voice had been winter frost. "As if I'd ever look at you in that way. It will be a cold day in hell before I ever stoop that low. I'm done with putting up with your shit. I don't care what you do anymore; just stay the fuck away from me from now on."

He'd given her his best smile, the one that told a person that they were visiting at the insane asylum and if they were very lucky...they may get out of it alive. "You're the one following me with your tongue hanging out, wolf. I can't shake you off no matter how blunt I am. Are you really that desperate? You should have some pride in yourself, Dara."

She had turned around and walked away without another word and she'd taken his heart with her. Only she would never know that now. He had destroyed any chance he may ever have had with her. That fuelled his rage as much as his dressing down by Rafe had. That he'd deserved both was a moot point. Everything was spiralling and he was losing all control. He had no anchor to keep him in check and he was so very, very afraid...

He heard the voices in the distance and he shadowed himself from view in an instant. No one was supposed to be out this way...it was why he always headed in this direction when his beast rose. The sound of skin on skin assaulted his acute hearing, and a woman's cry was heard. Kothari took off silently in the direction of the disturbance the last of his control ebbing as he moved.

The girl was lying on the ground when he entered the clearing, her caramel skin bathed in blood. The left side of her cheek was scraped raw, her bottom lip split and oozing blood into her mouth. He knew her from the pack compound. She was Liam's mate...the one who had come to kill them. There was no sign of the other Varcolac, there was only a strange wolf talking on a cell phone.

"No...it's nothing. Stupid bitch tried to attack me. I thought you said she was a vampire? She smells human... "

Kothari's control snapped in that moment and he flowed into the clearing...

He took the male's arm first, slicing it off at the shoulder. The phone was still clutched in the dismembered limb's grasp as it fell to the forest floor, the wolf's blood splashing all over his face. Kothari licked at the hot nectar, vaguely aware of the other male screaming and spinning away from him. The girl was moaning in shock, vomiting onto the dry dirt but he ignored her and concentrated on his prey.

Moving at supernatural speed, he sliced through a kneecap, glee rising up inside as the wolf howled and dropped to the floor beside the girl. Had the stranger been thinking of raping Liam's mate? Kothari wasn't sure but he took care of that issue with his next cut. The stranger was screaming mindlessly now and it was the sweetest symphony Kothari had ever heard. He would leave his neck until last...so he could enjoy the music.

Another leg...and then the other arm, he was coated in blood by the time the male was just a head attached to a bleeding torso. The stranger wasn't screaming anymore which was mildly disappointing. Instead, he was uttering a pathetic mewling noise as his chest heaved for air.

Straddling the prone form, Kothi leaned forward, his breath caressing an ear that was still attached to the body. He giggled softly, rapture running through him as the male stilled completely and the acrid scent of terror filled his nostrils. "If you go down to the woods today, you're in for a big surprise...
"

He giggled again as he let the ditty trail off, running his tongue over one blood splattered cheek. "This is my forest, wolf, and that is my pack mate you decided to play with. You should have stayed at home today, stupid boy, but then, I suppose if you had I wouldn't have had so much fun or dined so well... "

Kothari slit the wolf's throat with a talon, opening his mouth over the wound and swallowing down the last of the dying male's blood.

* * * * *

Thereasa gagged again, and again, until all she could do was dry heave. She had seen many horrifying things in her time but nothing compared to watching her captor being dismembered by a ghost. Her brain tried to tell her that it had to be one of the Varcolac that was doing the damage she'd witnessed, however the sheer brutality on show overwhelmed any reason and all she could do was pray she wouldn't be next.

When she heard the giggling and sing-song voice, all breath left her body and her blood froze in terror. She was afraid to look up, afraid to see the madman turn in her direction. Instead, she curled up in the foetal position and prayed that her end would come quickly.

"Are you seriously hurt or is it just cuts and bruises?" The seemingly normal tone of voice was at odds with what she'd just witnessed.

"Liam's mate, do you require serious healing?"

There was impatience in his tone now but still a hint of sanity. Taking a deep breath Reasa opened her eyes slowly, pushing her sore body up into a sitting position. Hunkered down beside her was Kothari, his clothes and skin drenched in blood. She had warned Liam about this male only a handful of hours ago. She had been correct in her warning and she feared what he may yet do.

"It's just cuts," she finally answered, her voice sounding weak and small. Her throat was also sore from all the vomiting she'd done, which didn't help her sound confident either.

Kothari was silent for a long moment and then he reached out to touch her sore cheek, running his thumb against her bottom lip. "Drink."

She was too afraid to disobey him, surprised to realise that he had nicked a cut on his thumb and it was his blood she was swallowing. He was healing her.

"You shouldn't be so far from the pack, Thereasa. You have no inkling of the dangers that are out here." His said the words conversationally, though there was weight behind them.

He was warning her againIst himself but that was at odds with his current actions. "Why did you help me?" Now that he didn't appear to be ready to kill her too, her curiosity was breaking through her fear.

Kothi cocked his head to the side, as if he too, was trying to figure that one out. "I owed Liam," he finally answered, nodding his head as he spoke. "I hurt him when we sparred. I needed to atone for that."

When she didn't respond, he reached up and took off his glasses, and speared her with a gaze that was a kaleidoscope of red and silver swirls. "Tell no one what you witnessed here today, and I will tell no one that you tried to run. You won't make that mistake again...will you, Thereasa?"

There was no escaping the implied threat in his voice and it sent a shiver down her spine. She tried to answer him but no words would come out so she settled with nodding her head. Her compliance appeared to please him because he rose and the air shimmered around him. When it cleared he was impeccably dressed in black T-shirt and jeans, no trace of blood to be seen. He placed a fresh pair of sunglasses over his eyes and then motioned to her right.

"I guessed your size but those should fit. Stay away from the corpse and get changed. I will be in those trees while you do."

He strode away as her gaze turned where he pointed, shock rocking through her as she saw a complete duplicate set of her clothes folded neatly in the dirt to her right. How the hell... ? Reasa shivered and swung her gaze back to where Kothari had vanished. Someone had to warn the pack about him but she couldn't say anything without giving herself away. Perhaps she could tell Liam. Perhaps he would understand why she'd done what she had.

Stripping off quickly, she wiped away a couple of small specks of blood from her shoulder and dressed in the clothes the Varcolac had provided. They were a perfect fit and for some reason she found that even creepier than anything else she'd just witnessed. She didn't want Kothari to know her that well.

A sound intruded as she went to rise after slipping on her sneakers. For a moment she couldn't work out what it was and then she realised it was coming from the severed hand still clutching the cell phone...

* * * * *

Michael had listened to everything that had happened. Each scream had sent a shiver down his spine and he'd known he would have to tell the Master about it. The hybrids were more dangerous than they had first thought, but with enough warning, his Master would be able to neutralise them.

He whispered into the phone when it became apparent the hybrid had moved some distance away, trying to attract Thereasa's attention. He repeated the words endlessly until it got his desired result.

"Do not say anything, Thereasa, merely breathe twice into the mouthpiece..."

After whispering for almost five minutes, he heard two breaths ring in his ear. Hatred washed through him, but Dante's words were still rattling around in his brain. It was now apparent that his former coven member was too well protected at the pack compound so he would have to get to her another way. If it had just been a case of killing her, he would have risked a pack attack, however maybe Dante was right and there was intelligence to be learned from her?

The wolf had said she scented as human...that would be something his Master would be interested in and he'd only be able to learn what had happened if he talked to Thereasa before she died. "Do not speak, just breath once for no and twice for yes. If you alert your companion that anything untoward is happening, I swear to you a thousand vampires will die. Do you understand, Thereasa?"

Two breaths resounded once more, and a smile slowly spread over his face. He had the bitch now, and one way or another she would pay for her betrayal. "I have Louis' best soldiers with me and they're spread out all over this city. Some are even scattered throughout other cities where vampires make their home. Each one of them has enough Amort to kill hundreds of our kind. One word from me and the killing starts, and I know how much you wouldn't want that to happen, Thereasa. Would you?"

One breath, as he had expected. Sentimentality towards other vampires had always been her weak spot, though she had counted it as a strength. He had known that one day it would play into his hands..."Then listen very carefully...this is what you need to do to prevent that from happening... "

*****

Kothari returned to the clearing, his bloodlust abated by the slaughter of the wolf. He found Reasa standing beside one of the tall oak trees, her expression wan despite her bronzed complexion. For a moment he felt a tinge of pity for the girl. How she remained sane after all she had been through was beyond him. Then the moment passed, and he slipped back into the coldness of his soul.

Checking that there was no visible signs of what she'd endured he stepped back and let his gaze run over the clearing. He would fix the mess when she had gone. No one would ever know what had transpired here this day.

"Go back to the pack, Thereasa, and stay there. You are Liam's mate and as such, you belong at his side. If you ever do anything to hurt him again, I will make you regret it. Are we clear on this?"

Dumbly she nodded, and he gestured her away. He didn't watch her leave, instead he waited ten minutes and scented the air. She was far from the area when he took off his glasses and narrowed his gaze on the wolf's corpse. White fire bled from his eyes, incinerating the body and all the other evidence in the clearing...

Rayne let out a slow release of breath as the train rocked to a halt in Braşov station. For too many centuries she had avoided returning to where her life had first begun. Now she was a step closer to her beginnings, and she couldn't deny the feeling of homecoming that assaulted her.

She hadn't expected to have this reaction to being back in Romania and she wondered if Gard felt the same. Turning to look at him, she saw his gaze peering out to the station interior as they waited for the other travellers to alight. "When were you last here?"

He turned to smile at her, a soft glow in his eyes. "Not that very long ago," he admitted. This is where I tracked down Caleb and released Callain back into this world. He had left Annie briefly in Bucharest while he was meeting with Joshua here about his first stirrings of unease over Europe. I didn't know who Caleb was with at the time but I know now since our trip to Scotland. They were playing at being tourists. It was quite fun to watch them thinking they were being so clever when all the while I was following them."

"Caleb was aware something wasn't right that far back?" She was surprised to learn that.

Her mate shrugged. "I don't think it was anything definite at that point, just a faint tendril of speculation on his part from something a friend of Joshua's had imparted. Nothing tangible came of their meeting, and Caleb returned to Annie none the wiser that he had met me. I have a little skill in dream walking myself though it exhausts me so much I prefer not to do it. It took me three days to recover from our meeting and awakening Callain. I had to hide my identity from Caleb's mind until the time was right."

Rayne arched an eyebrow at him, mock-resignation crossing her face. "And I am only just learning this now? I think I may have to teach you the true definition of what being mates is supposed to mean." She was teasing him, enjoying seeing a flash of concern twinkle in his eyes before he realised that was her intention and he wagged a finger at her.

Her thoughts were already wandering though, and a speculative gleam entered her green eyes. "Do you think Joshua was alerted by Dante?"

CHAPTER 2

Her question earned her a light chuckle. "You noticed that too then? Dante didn't appear the least surprised to see us show up at Louis' place. Given we managed to slip passed all the other vampires looking out for someone arriving in Europe, that could only have meant that he had been given a head's up by Joshua."

"And here was I thinking you were just a pretty face," Rayne laughed, winking at his mock- outrage. "Yes, I would say Dante and Joshua are known to each other, though I don't think Louis is in on that secret."

The passengers had all left the train, so they rose and exited onto the outdoor platform. Rayne admired the curving rooftop, the organic shape appealing to her ascetically. Inhaling deeply, she closed her eyes and let out a long slow breath. "You can smell it in the air," she sighed, a beatific smile gracing her lips. "The sweet scent of home."

"We're not quite there yet," he countered, reaching for her hand to pull her into the main building. "We still have a fair few miles to go yet, but I know what you mean. The air smells so much sweeter here. I suppose it always will."

Rayne smiled at the excitement in his tone, turning back to the earlier conversation as they headed out of the station. "Do you think Caleb knows Dante? Joshua is someone he trusts so there could be precedence that he may."

Gard pondered the question for a moment and then shook his head. "He would have mentioned him at some point. I think

Dante is acting for reasons that only he truly understands. They just happen to coincide with our goals at the moment."

"I liked him, and Joshua." Rayne grinned at the narrowed glance her mate shot her way.

"Yes...I noticed. Perhaps you are the one who needs some further instruction on what a true mate should be."

"Why, Kothari senior...I do believe you are jealous." She burst out laughing at the dark glare he gave her, her amusement cutting off as he dragged her into a nearby alleyway and pinned her against the wall.

"Keep it up woman and I swear I'll take you right here and now and to hell if anyone might walk past. Oh, and call me that again, and I will not only take my sweet time about it, I'll make you beg for everyone to hear." He sealed his threat with a hot, wet kiss that stole her breath away.

"Hmmm, yes dear," she whispered into his mouth, giggling as he palmed her breast and gave it a gentle squeeze.

He kissed her again and then they pulled apart, sharing a glance that told the whole world just how they felt about each other. Gard looped an arm over her shoulder and they headed back onto the street.

"Do you think he's okay?" Rayne asked after they'd walked a mile or so. Her gaze was flittering from face to face and then the surrounding buildings, but her mate knew exactly who she was referring to.

"He has to fly the nest at some point, Sarayne. Now is as good a time as any." Though he tried to sound convincing, he knew she could hear underlying concern in his voice.

"I keep wondering what we did wrong," she admitted, her voice low. "Did we try hard enough? Was there something we could have done differently?"

Stopping, Gard ignored an angry mutter from a passer-by who almost barrelled into him. He gathered his mate close, kissing the top of her head, as he ran a soothing hand down her back. "We have loved our son with everything that we are, Rayne. We have protected him as best we could and been there whenever he has needed us. There isn't anything else we could have done differently than to love him as we have. He will find his way, my heart. His journey may just be a bit rockier than most others."

He had told her the same thing countless times and she could only hope that it was the truth. It was so hard not to wonder, not to worry about the beautiful son she had brought into this world though. She ached for him to be happy, for him to one day find that other half of his soul and never be alone again.

"Come on, the sooner we get this mission over with the sooner we will be back home with Kothari." Gard released her but retained hold of her hand, pulling her along the busy streets towards their goal.

After a while, Rayne came out of whatever thoughts had been dominating her mind, a perplexed look crossing her face. Ahead of them were scores of people all dressed in black gothic attire, all heading in the same direction. "Is there a convention or something on in the city?"

Gard laughed, genuine amusement shining in his eyes. "Ahh those are the vampire groupies," he chuckled. He pointed to a building up high, thick trees and bushes at its base, its red brick rooftops and steepled tower glistening in the sunlight. "They're headed to Bran Castle to see where Vlad the Impaler was purported to live."

His amusement rubbed off on her, shaking away her gloomy thoughts. "Seriously? They genuinely believe that Dracula lived there out in the open among humans?" No self-respecting vampire would ever have allowed humans to know of their existence, even in centuries gone past. Although, she supposed maybe back then there hadn't been a whole lot of options available to Gard's people.

"No vampire ever lived in that Castle," her mate answered, a smile still playing across his lips. "Doesn't hurt tourism though to let people think that he was real and foster the myth Bram Stoker created with his book. The Council had a long talk with the vampire who revealed our existence to the author back then. They decided to let him off with it after the way the myths and legends grew and covered our tracks."

Rayne laughed, shaking her head. "If only they knew what they were seeking was actually walking beside them right now," she whispered, as they skirted around particularly large group of tourists.

"They'd wet their pants," Gard growled, causing her to laugh louder.

A few people turned to look at them, quickly turning away again and hurrying forward towards the fabled Castle. Gard and Rayne turned in the opposite direction, heading further away from the seat of civilisation.

"There are no trails where we're going anymore," Gard said, his eyes drawn to the Southern Carpathians that were looming ahead of them. "The trees and vegetation have overgrown everything so we'll have to take to the skyline to get there."

"If it's so difficult to reach now then is it the place we're looking for?" Rayne asked, a frown marring her brow.

"It's difficult for humans to reach, even possibly Weres, but not to vampires. We're lucky you're a cat and like climbing trees. I think a wolf would have a devil of a time trying to get through the underbrush."

The smugness of his tone had her laughing. "Yes, you were very smart to pick a panther for your mate," she agreed.

He shot her a grin, picking up his step as anticipation washed over them. Now they were so close to home, it was impossible not to rush forward. "Come on, let's go. I'm suddenly very antsy to see what's left of the Palace."

A few hours later, and far off the beaten track, a sleek black panther sailed from one treetop across to another, closely followed by a redheaded vampire. The cat expertly dug claws into a branch, drawing its hind legs up to balance on the thick limb. Gard hadn't been kidding when he said the trail was overgrown. It was nigh on impossible to continue by foot as they wound their way higher and higher up the Carpathians.

Rayne uttered a small purring sound as her mate ran his hands down her back, inwardly smiling at the sheer joy on his face. The closer they came to their goal, the more charged he became, his excitement rippling down their mate bond.

"We're close," he breathed out, his lavender eyes almost glowing with anticipation. "Only a few more miles now, but we need to head east. Can you make that tree over there or do you want me to carry you?"

The tree in question was quite far even for her panther to leap, but she was reasonably confident she could make it. She'd only had to shift back to human form twice so far when the distance had been too great for her panther, and that had only been because Gard had refused to take a minor detour.

"You just like rubbing your body against mine and being the knight in shining armour," she answered telepathically, injecting humour into her words. "I can make the jump but you go first just in case I need any assistance." There was no harm in being pragmatic.

"You'd better not," Gard growled, eyeing the waiting tree to their right. He dropped down a few branches beneath her, and then sprang forward.

Rayne watched her mate glide effortlessly through the air. She could tell he'd used all of his supernatural reflexes for his push off the lower branch to counter the loss of momentum he had from stopping. That didn't bode that well for her if he'd had to use all his resources. Though, he did almost overshoot the Oak tree so perhaps it wouldn't be as bad as she first thought.

Gard had deliberately placed himself lower down on the waiting tree. If she failed to make the jump then she would start to fall downwards and he would want to be lower to enable him to react in time if needed. He was a smart male and she couldn't help grinning with pride.

"Panthers are so not supposed to smile, Sarayne," he called across the expanse. "It's downright creepy."

Shaking her head, she judged the distance to the branches above him, her hind legs coiling ready to spring. Rayne pushed off with all her strength, arching her back to increase her forward motion. She knew instantly that she wasn't going to make it but she didn't panic. Instead, she made her body as aerodynamic as possible, giving herself as much of a chance as possible.

"Sarayne!"

Gard's furious yell echoed through the trees as she began to plummet downward. Her stomach lurched and her front paws began to scramble in the air for purchase that she knew wasn't there. She shifted in mid-air, knowing her panther's body was much heavier than her human form. At least this way she would fall at the slightly slower pace, and it would be easier for Gard to catch her.

If she hit the ground it was going to hurt and there was a good chance it could kill her. There were far too many branches out there that could take her head at the velocity she was falling. For the first time ever, Rayne considered the possibility that she might actually die. Gard would murder her if she let that happen though...the fact that she would already be dead being a bit of a moot point.

Pain rattled through her side as a moving object crashed into her halting her fall. The pain increased as she was suddenly propelled sideways at such speed she caught a thick branch to her midriff, her breath cutting off at the hard impact. It hurt to breathe; it hurt to move, but she was alive and draped rather inelegantly face forward over a branch.

"Ouch!" She shrieked as a hand connected with her upturned backside. "I'm injured here!"

"You're damned lucky to be alive, woman," Gard retorted, fury lacing his tone. "I've a good mind to spank your bottom harder and for at least a week. I swear you just took a thousand years off my life."

Despite his ire, she could hear the concern and relief in his voice. She could only imagine what he must have gone through seeing her fall like that. "You're immortal," she snorted, pulling herself up so she could straddle the branch facing him. She needed a few moments to allow her body to heal, and from the look on her mate's face, he needed a few to calm his racing heart.

Looking up, she realised just how far she'd fallen. It was a miracle Gard had managed to get to her in time. Turning her gaze back to his ashen face, she reached out to place a hand on his chest. His heart was racing so fast it was a wonder he wasn't hyperventilating. "I'm fine, Gard."

"Only because I caught you in time," he growled, a faint trace of panic still shining in his eyes. He pulled her into his arms, his hold so tight she thought he would crack a couple of her ribs. "Don't you ever do that to me again, Sarayne. I swear I will make you regret it for at least a millennia if you do."

She hid her smile in the crook of his neck, sending love and reassurance down their mate bond and allowing him to threaten her with whatever dire retribution he needed. If it helped to calm him anxiety levels down she could put up with it. "I'm fine," she reiterated, rubbing her lips against his neck. "I'm safe."

She kissed up his jaw, sighing when he turned his head and plundered her mouth in a kiss so desperate it brought tears to her eyes. She returned his kiss, allowing him to ground himself in her touch until his heart finally began to slow its erratic beat and his touch gentled.

"I love you more than life itself, Sarayne," Gard whispered against her lips. "I am nothing without you, my heart. Please don't ever scare me that way again."

"I promise I will do my very best, my darling, but we are living in dangerous times. Please don't hold it against me if I can't keep to that." She would never lie to him or give him empty reassurances. He wouldn't want them from her anyway.

Gard lowered his forehead against hers, a rueful smile crossing his handsome face. "I guess that is the best I can ever hope for," he sighed, his hands slowly trailing down her back, his fingers tracing her spine. "Are you healed?"

"Good as new," she answered, smiling to lend weight to her words. He would be giving himself a hard time that he'd hurt her while rescuing her and she needed to divert him before he went down that path. "Though you and I are going to be having a discussion about you hitting me, Mister..."

It had the desired effect, his lavender gaze turning resolute. "You deserved that spanking."

"Remember those words when I turn them back around on you one day," she countered, moving away to look at the next grouping of trees. "I think you forget that I am Varcolac sometimes, Gard, and so very much stronger than you when I want to be." She gave him a saucy wink.

Throwing his head back, he laughed loudly. The sound startled some nearby birds and sent them fluttering into the evening sky. "Bring it on, woman. I'm not afraid of you." He rose beside her and examined their route. The distance between trees appeared fairly uniform.

Glancing to the side, he captured her gaze. "We should get a good run at this last section, our forward momentum making the jumps easy. Is there anything that concerns you?"

She shook her head, in full agreement with him. Her panther shouldn't have any issues, but she didn't want him to be second guessing her abilities. "Just for the sake of your piece of mind, why don't you go first and I'll follow at five second intervals? I'm sure my panther can make each jump but there is no harm in being cautious."

His answer was to smile and nod his head. "That was just what I was going to suggest."

It was Rayne's turn to laugh now and she rolled her eyes. "Men..." she muttered under her breath, but her vampire was already leaping into the next treetop and it was time for her to shift back to panther form and follow his lead.

It wasn't long before she could detect a break in the treeline up ahead, a sign that they were closing in on their location. A handful more leaps and then Gard was waiting for her as she reached the last tree.

"We're here," he breathed softly, reverence in his tone. "We can continue on foot from here."

It was easier for her to make her way down the tree in panther form, so she waited until they touched down on the mossy ground before she shifted back to human. The trees and foliage were still relatively thick where they'd come down so she made sure her clothing was sufficient for the terrain so her skin didn't get too nicked. Her long black hair she quickly plaited down her back, so it wouldn't get in the way.

Gard was retying his dark auburn locks at his nape with a leather thong, his gaze alert as he surveyed the area. "I don't see any obvious signs of disturbance," he mused. "Might not be a bad idea to check a little further afield before we head deeper in towards the Palace."

Rayne didn't recognise this part of her former homeland. She had been found on the western side of the Palace and had lived most of her younger life in two of the villages leading away from the vampire court. From what she could remember, most of the Romany settlers had moved as far away from the court as if they could sense the danger that was brewing at that time. Any folklore that they may have had about this area, had been carefully wiped out of existence within two generations. She was probably the only person outwith the Triumvirate who still remembered any of the history of this place.

"I'll take the left," she answered crossing to his other side.

"You were already on the right side," he grumbled with no real heat in his tone.

"I know; I just felt like taking the left side. Sue me."

"Some days I think you just like teasing me, woman."

"Of course," she laughed, "Isn't that my job?"

He grinned back at her, rolling his eyes in mock exasperation, before his expression turned serious. "If you see anything even remotely suspicious don't investigate it on your own. Come and find me."

"Ditto," she shot back, giving him a broad smile. "Meet back here in half an hour?"

Gard nodded, stealing a quick kiss. "Don't do anything foolish," he breathed against her lips, causing her to laugh once more.

"Like I said...ditto," she quipped back, turning to head into the closest treeline.

Gard watched her go before he turned to his path and vanished into the waiting trees.

Rayne alternated between both her forms to traverse her section of the mountain forest. Sometimes it was simply easier to be a panther to get through a particularly densely packed area. She completed her sweep, her innate ability to tell time alerting her to the fact she had to head back. She didn't encounter anything out of the ordinary so she was relaxed as she returned back to her mate.

"All clear my end," she announced as she exited the trees to where he was waiting for her.

"Same here," he answered, his gaze already sliding from hers as if irresistibly drawn to the hidden structure waiting for them. "Time to go home," he murmured, and she followed him forward towards where the Vampire Queen had once held her court.

The decay of thousands of years couldn't diminish the beauty of his former home. Everywhere Gard's gaze fell, he remembered another time and the magnificence that was his Queen's Palace. As he and Rayne threaded their way passed thick foliage into the clearing that had once been the Palace's great courtyard, he slipped back in time to see the breath-taking vision it had once been.

They halted by a crumbling wall that was now at mere ankle height, however his mind's eye saw the gracefully curving crescent moon construction that had been three feet high and made of the palest limestone. In a hushed voice he spoke, bringing to life an era long passed to his silent mate. "The crescent moon was our family's crest. All who saw it knew it signified the Royal House of Ardweni, our great grandmother, and the first of the Vampire Queens. It was the symbol of all that was right in our world, of all that was good about our people."

He breathed deeply, closing his eyes as he let it out slowly. "This wall here used to stand three feet high. It curved towards the main door to the palace and was flanked by urns full of the most beautiful flowers to scent the air. Many a night Anakatrine and I sat on that very wall, mapping out the stars above, as night bled into early dawn."

His lips quirked in an affectionate smile, reliving memories long passed but still greatly treasured. "Ana was fascinated with the sky above us, she couldn't get enough of it. She used to lament often that she couldn't soar through the skies like a birds above, and I had to often remind her that it would be considered unseemly for a Queen to frolic in the air."

Rayne laughed quietly, threading her arm through his and resting her head on his shoulder. "How old was she at the time?"

"She was six." He sighed as he said it, a trace of sadness in his voice. "It was after our mother had passed and Ana had ascended to the throne. I was barely a man at the time, and yet I had more freedom then than she would ever have again. I tried to give her as many moments where she could be just a child, but often my role was always to remind her she was a Queen. She did not have much of a childhood."

"I'm sure whatever childhood she had with you was treasured, my love. She would not have turned out to be one of the greatest living Queens if that had not been the case. I am sure that even at that young age she was aware that she was speaking flights of fancy. That you would sit with her and listen shows that you were the perfect Guardian for your young Queen."

"I loved to hear her laugh," he admitted, smiling down at her. "If only you could have known her, Rayne, and heard her laughter. That one day when you did meet, Ana was so full of sorrow at what was to come. You would have loved her and she you, I am certain of that."

When she merely smiled, his gaze turned back to the courtyard. "You can just about make out the grid pattern the mosaic tiles were set in leading up to the main door." He pointed to the ground and she could almost make out what he meant though time had done too much damage to get a clear picture.

"The tiles were blues and greens with accents of silver and golds," he continued. "Each tile was a mini image in itself but grouped together they created an underwater vista of what life must have looked like beneath the waves of the sea. In those days our people were very artistic."

"It sounds amazing." For some unknown reason Rayne found she couldn't speak in anything above a near whisper. The expression on her mate's face was so full of awe it touched her heart that he was sharing this part of his life with her. It seemed out of place to talk normally and she didn't want to break the spell he was weaving all around them.

"There were two great pillars beside the entrance into the hallway. The Roman's adopted the same style later on, but I'm sure there was a vampire at the heart of that architecture." Gard was standing by a crumbled wall so decayed it was hard to see there had ever been a doorway there. He walked forward, onto a large expense of moss that was growing unevenly.

"Beneath our feet were more limestone tiles in fractal patterns. They were shades of reds, pinks and purples. Visitors often stood in the hallway for hours at time just admiring the many different hues. Our mother eventually placed seating in the hallways for those guests who took their time appreciating the beauty that surrounded them."

His hand swept to the left, to the largest shell of wall that still remained standing. "The staircase ran up the left wall, to the Royal suits. It was always guarded fore none could ascend without express Royal permission. Each tread was of the shiniest white marble, a lavender runner lining the middle so no one would accidentally fall down them. Ana loved to sit at the very top peering down at Mother's guests as they arrived. She was impossible to keep in bed when she was a child."

Rayne could see the vista in her mind's eye, a mental image of a little redheaded girl so full of excitement as exotic guests arrived at her home. The wealth of love in Gard's voice was unmistakable, and she was now beginning to understand why he had searched so long for his beloved Anakatrine to be reborn.

He appeared to shake himself out of his reverie for a moment, turning to smile at her and gather her close to his side. "Come, the throne room was this way." Gard led them forward into another overgrown moss area, only this time the walls on either side of them appeared to be more stable.

"Have those walls been pointed?"

Her mate's smile broadened, happiness exuding from his big frame. "When I first awakened Callain I came here," he breathed softly. "I knew Anakatrine would return soon and I longed for our old life together. I started rebuilding the throne room one brick at a time. I wanted her to have her home back once more."

Silence hung around the open room as he stopped talking and Rayne let her eyes sweep across the huge area. "You didn't finish your task though. Why did you stop?"

For the first time since they'd arrived a shadow crossed Gard's face. "I realised that though Ana had returned, she was but an echo of a time long past, and I was holding onto memories that would never come again. Annie isn't Ana, they just share a body and mind. She doesn't want to live up here in the ruins of a Palace long buried, and why should she? Annie's life is with Caleb and the pack. It was wrong of me to presume that she would ever want to stay here."

"I'm sure one day Annie would love to come here, Gard. She would come for Anakatrine so the vampire Queen might one day relive her life here with you."

He shook his head, his smile turning resigned. "No, that life has passed now. I am content with the life that I now live. How could I not be? I have the best of both worlds."

The kiss he gave told her how much he loved her and that he meant everything that he said. When they broke apart, they shared a smile and then her gaze turned back to the room before them. "Tell me of the throne room. Is that a tapestry I see over there?" Rayne truly did want to hear more of the world her mate had loved so much before they had come to know each other.

Gard's smile was once more that of excitement, lighting up his face and making him more beautiful if that was humanly possible. "All the great vampire houses had their own banners. This one is all that remains and it's of the Royal house of Ardweni. I was astounded to find it still in existence after all this time. Ana must have placed a preservation spell on it though it appears to have faded."

Leaning down they stared at the faded cloth. "Can you see the crescent moon shape at the top?" he asked, his fingers hovering a bare inch above the fabric. "Behind the two thrones was a wall of clear glass. Above them was a skylight shaped in the crescent moon. To either side of the audience chamber, the seating also curved in that same crescent moon shape. It was the emblem of the Royal house and just about every area within the throne room echoed with that design."

Rayne gasped, startled eyes flowing to meet his. "The Council chambers...its seating is in the same design... "

Gard laughed, a soft sound echoing through the crumbling walls. "You see what thousands of vampires have never seen despite looking at it each day." His voice was warm with approval and more than a hint of pride. "Yes, my heart, they are unaware but they still hold to traditions of long passed. The vampire nation still bows to the Royal House of Ardweni though they are unaware."

Rayne laughed with him...it was hard not to as she imagined some of the more traditional, hidebound vampires sitting there with all their pomp and arrogance. In their ignorance, they were completely unaware that they had retained a symbol of the most precious thing they had ever lost, their Queen. "Do you think they will ever learn the truth, Gard?"

He was silent for a long moment and then he shrugged his shoulders. "I have no idea what Anakatrine's plans are, though I am fairly certain she has one. She always did know far too much than any one person ever should have. It was what made her the greatest ever vampire Queen and why our people never deserved to have her grace our world."

Rising, Gard let his gaze swing around the room once more and then held out his hand. "While reminiscing is fun, it's not getting the job done we came here to do. Come on, let's check out the area behind the Palace."

"It doesn't look as dense out there," Rayne mused, scanning the area quickly. "Is that normal?" If Gard had been visiting from the main entrance, which would be the norm for him as that would be the route he was used to entering the site; possibly he may not have approached from the rear.

It appeared her train of thought was echoing in his mind because he tensed a little, a frown on his face. "On the contrary, it should be more overgrown," he muttered, starting to walk forward. "Stay close, Rayne."

She wanted to roll her eyes and make a smart quip about being overprotected, however his tense demeanour dampened down any words she may have uttered. There was a silence about the mountain that didn't feel natural, as if the animals knew something was out there that shouldn't be. Following his lead, she stepped back out into the forest, moving to the left as he signalled his movement to the right.

"Keep in touch at all times. Alert me the instant you see anything that doesn't feel right."

"Maybe we should stay together? If you're so concerned." She didn't asked the question because she was afraid, but more because she knew his focus would be split if he was worrying about her safety.

We'll cover more ground this way," he answered telepathically.

It made sense so she concentrated on her surroundings, looking for any signs of tracks that would indicate anyone had visited the site recently. Rayne had made her way a circuitous route of about a mile from the Palace when she noticed the first indication of trees having been chopped down. The trees had been removed a good fifty or so years ago but given the remoteness of the spot, it was still highly suspicious.

"Gard, I have evidence of someone being here." She expected an instant response and held her breath when all she received was silence. "Gard?"

Again, there was nothing but silence and shiver of unease trickled down her spine. Gard would never leave her alone, especially when what they were tracking was a direct threat to everything they held dear. Had something happened to him and that was why he didn't answer? He'd given her no warning that anything was amiss.

More unease overwhelmed her as she was struck by a sudden thought. Their failsafe! She had to check it was still in place. Turning her thoughts inward, she searched for the great tree she'd placed at the very forefront of her mental defences, and what she found brought her feet to a dead halt. It was gone! In its place was barely a mark that it had ever existed.

Someone had been inside her mind and tampered with her defences. He or she had to be powerful to breach them, and also very close by. Had they gotten to her mate yet, or was he still safe? If Gard tried to reach her and couldn't find her he'd come looking and then they'd be in serious trouble. Spinning on her heels Rayne took off back the way she'd come only she didn't make it two steps before something bit her on the neck and her feet stumbled over a tree root.

She fell forward as her legs gave out, barely able to stop her forehead smashing off the ground as she landed in a heap. Her vision began swimming in an instant, and the strength in her arms gave out as she tried to pull herself up from the ground. "Gard, run!" she screamed in her mind, because her voice wouldn't work despite how hard she tried to make it.

"Trap!" She tried again, knowing that she was close to losing consciousness and he most likely couldn't hear her. Blackness descended though she fought it every step of the way, her heart hammering wildly as she tried to reach her mate. "Run, Gard...run..."

Something wasn't right, he could feel it with every step he took. The area he was traversing was too pristine, too devoid of all tracks. There should have been animal droppings, some indication that something had travelled over the ground and yet there were none and their lack was every bit of a warning sign than if he'd detected footprints.

Gard was certain no one had actually stepped foot on the Palace site but the further he walked towards the rear the more sure he was that someone had visited the area in the last century. He wanted to kick himself for not checking this far back the last time he'd been there but then he supposed he'd had no call to at the time. Now, all he could think about was getting back to the Palace and his mate. They were far too vulnerable up here on their own when they knew nothing of what may be waiting for them.

"Sarayne, head back to the Palace."

He took a couple of steps backwards and then he froze on the spot. "Sarayne!"

Gard spun to his left and took off at supernatural speed. It was the fastest route to her last known location. Dread filled his soul, fear clogging his throat as he ran. There was no way in hell she wouldn't answer him when he called. Something had to have happened to her.

"Sarayne! Answer me!"

Total silence greeted him, and he realised that he could barely feel their mate bond. It was as if someone or something was muting the bond but he knew that was an impossibility. Only they could do that, or Rafe, and their Alpha was thousands of miles away. "Sarayne, where are you?"

All contact with his mate cut off a split second after something stung him in the neck. The huge vampire fell forward with a loud crash, a branch spearing him in the shoulder as he fell. Gard roared out in fury as he toppled forward, fear for Rayne the only thing he could think of. They had been ambushed, of that he was now certain, lulled into a false sense of security at finding the Palace site and front entrance completely undisturbed.

Darkness was descending and he shook his head to try to clear it. He couldn't pass out, not here and now, not when Rayne needed him. "Rayne...Rayne..." Gard lost his fight to stay conscious, inky blackness claiming his last thought of his missing mate.

*****

A cloaked figure entered the cave, his tall frame concealed by the charcoal grey garment. Outside were close to a hundred elder vampires. Inside, were two prone figures bound in chains so thick it would have taken all the assembled vampires to break them. The figure stood peering down at their prey, his lips stretching in the rictus of a smile. It was the only part of the male that could be seen, his hood concealing the majority of his face.

"You have done well," he said telepathically to the lone vampire in the cave with him.

"The formula you provided made the task easy, Master," the bald-headed male replied, bowing low.

"It certainly did work to subdue them; however I will test to ensure that it dulls their magical abilities too. All this will be pointless if the toxin is ineffectual against that." Hunching down beside the bound couple, the Master danced inside their sleeping minds, his psyche flowing down the pristine corridors within until he found the area he was looking for.

The girl's abilities were of the lesser in offensive terms, but he still placed a block around her ability to shadow and shapeshift. As long as she remained dosed with enough of the toxin he'd formulated, she wouldn't be able to break through his block.

Next, he turned his attention to the male, reaching out a gloved hand to brush away a lock of auburn hair that partly obscured his face. He had seen this one around over the centuries and knew that he was a force to be reckoned with. "Well met, Guardian," he whispered tracing a long finger over a chiselled cheekbone. "Long have I yearned for this moment, though I did not expect it to be so soon. I am not yet ready to play my final hand, old one, though I will enjoy watching the chaos your disappearance engenders."

It was the first time the vampire beside him had heard his Master's true voice, and it caused tears of adoration to flow down his face at the sheer beauty of its tone.

With no further words, he entered the Guardian's mind, finding his place of magic and bolting the door firmly shut. It would be disastrous should the male be able to unlock the door while in captivity. His wrath would be like none other and should he escape his bonds...the Master would lose many of his followers should that occur.

He would have to ensure that didn't happen, and made a mental note to stay close until he could determine how long the toxin would keep the couple unconscious.

"No one enters the cave," he instructed the vampire at his side. "No one speaks to them, no one interacts with them. And most definitely no one who has a key to their bonds comes within a hundred feet of this cave. I will remain for another few hours but then I must leave this place. After that, you are in charge of the prisoners, Heathen. Should they escape, your life will be forfeit. Are we clear on that?"

The vampire fell to his knees, fierce determination shining from his mind. "Yes, Master. It will be as you instruct. No one will enter the cave except to administer the toxin."

The cloaked figure stifled down a grimace of disgust at the zeal in the vampire's mental tone. Weaker minds were much easier to subdue but they burnt out faster than he would have liked. He would have to cultivate another to take Heathen's place if the vampire continued down his current rate of decay.

Sweeping passed the kneeling male, the Master strode out of cave and into the early evening air. A hundred vampires all knelt as one, his love, and approval bathing them where they knelt. This was as it should be. This was as it always should have been. Soon now, it would be his time, and the world would quake in fear at his very name.

* * * * *

Thousands of miles away a deep male voice cried out, frantic brown eyes opening in a gasp of pain.

"Rafe?! What's wrong?" Lacey sat up beside her mate, her hands automatically coming around to clutch at her abdomen.

"Gard...Rayne...I can't sense them anymore, Lace. I can't feel them down my Alpha bond!"

"No!" The word choked out, tears filling Lacey's eyes as she stared at her mate. "Are they...?" She couldn't say the word that filled her soul with dread.

The huge Alpha turned anguished eyes to meet hers, unshed tears brimming in their depths. "I don't know," he whispered. "I just know I can't feel them anymore. Something has gone wrong in Europe, something terrible has happened there."

Throwing her arms around him, she wept against his shoulder, her tears coming out in loud sobs. The impact this would have on the pack was devastating. The impact it would have on Annie was catastrophic. "What can we do, Rafe?"

He was already gentling prising her arms from him, climbing naked from their bed. "We need to let Caleb and Annie know, and someone needs to check in on Kothari. I don't know if it's just my Alpha bond that's been cut or if it's his familial bond too. If he senses they're gone...I have no idea what he'll do, Lacey. He was barely in check earlier when I had to come down on him over his fight with Liam."

She was getting up too, hastily pulling on jeans and a sweater while he dressed. "Kallum's still up at the Praetorian compound. Kothi's close to Dara, maybe it would be best to have her check in with him?"

Now that the initial panic was starting to wear off, Rafe tested his Alpha bond with the Varcolac, his big frame relaxing a tad. "Kothari is sleeping and his bond feels calm," he told her, sighing with relief as he spoke. "He doesn't appear to be aware of anything at the moment so it looks like we have some time in hand. Let's contact Annie and Caleb first before we disturb anyone else's sleep. Maybe they'll have an idea on how best to support Kothi through this crisis."

It made sense if the danger point wasn't with them at the moment, and yet, Lacey felt uneasy about not being more proactive. There was no telling when Kothari might become aware that something had happened to his parents. They should have a contingency plan in place for that moment. "Are you sure, Rafe?"

It wasn't often that she questioned her mate on pack decisions so he took a moment to think through the issue. "We need to try to have answers for him when he becomes aware, Lace. If he suspects we have no idea what to do, he's more likely to go off half-cocked and we will have no way of countering his reaction. Let's take the time that we have to be as prepared as we can be."

Lacey nodded her agreement, following Rafe from their bedroom. They had a few hours in hand. With luck, they would have a plan of action that would satisfy the erratic Varcolac and all hell wouldn't break loose, as she feared it would.

Rafe was hitting the speed dial on his phone as he entered his study and Lacey headed to the kitchen to get some coffee brewing. "You know...?" she heard him saying before his voice was cut off, and her heart went out to his sister on the other end of the phone. Losing Gard would crush Rhianna, and most probably bring out Anakatrine in all her fury. While they had been discussing Kothi's reaction to what had happened, neither of them had considered what reaction the vampire Queen would have to the news...

Reasa had hurried back to the compound hours earlier, her thoughts in complete chaos. She hadn't been sure what had frightened her more, Kothari's obvious insanity or the words Michael had spoken to her on the phone. There had been no mistaking what she had to do, and yet, now the time had come she didn't want to do it.

She was in love with Liam Eriksson, and she couldn't deny that any longer. She also couldn't be with him, that simply wasn't an option. If she chose to ignore Michael's message then thousands of vampires would die. She'd caused enough damage as it was. She just couldn't be responsible for more deaths.

It had seemed a cruel twist of fate that Liam had been leaving his Alpha's house as she'd re-entered the compound. His expression had lit up at seeing her, and any last lingering thoughts of denial had melted away as she watched him. He was quite simply the most magnificent male she had ever seen. The compassionate, humble side to him, a true balance to the wonderful vampire she had glimpsed in his mind. He was a male worthy of loving, and now she had found him, she had to leave him.

If he'd found it odd in the least that she had wanted to spend so much time with him, he had never mentioned it. Instead, he had basked in her presence, showing her around the compound as he welcomed her to his home. Even the brief moment when Cassia and Pietro had pulled into the compound late afternoon hadn't dampened the bubbling happiness emanating from Liam.

No words had been spoken that she was aware of, though the vampire had studiously ignored her. Pietro had nodded in Liam's direction, her redheaded male inclining his head in acknowledgement. No doubt Liam had been thinking that this was a good sign, and that with time, they would be able to live in harmony within the pack. His thoughts couldn't have been further from the truth, though Reasa couldn't tell him that. He would never let her out of his sight if she did.

Now she was lying beside him, listening to his deep breathing and knowing that a handful of hours from now he would wake to find her gone. A lone tear escaped and trickled down her cheek, her heart feeling as if it was about to split in two.

"Reasa?" Liam murmured her name, and she couldn't resist twisting her body into his. Thick arms wrapped her securely to his chest, a thigh hooking around hers. "Why aren't you sleeping?" he asked sleepily, his eyes opening as he pulled her close.

"You snore," she answered, though it was a lie, but it brought a wry chuckle from the man beside her.

"Do not," he laughed, "though if we're on that topic of nocturnal noises, you have this habit of making a little mewling sound every now and then."

She doubted that very much, but she smiled at his quick comeback. "You're not very good at telling fibs, Liam. You wouldn't last long in Europe."

In answer, he rolled over until she was beneath him, supporting his weight on bent elbows. He was more fully awake now, and the gleam she could see in his eyes from the crescent moon's light told her he had other nocturnal activities in mind. She should stop this right now, and yet, he felt so good covering her body. She had an hour before she needed to make her move. That should be plenty of time.

"Just as well I have no plans to go to Europe," he quipped back, his body moving helplessly against hers as he let out a low groan. "Tell me to stop now, Reasa, otherwise I have other plans that you may not approve of."

It would be that easy, of that she had no doubt. All she had to do was tell him to leave her alone and they would once more be lying platonically beside each other. She didn't want to though, so she wound her arms around his neck and pulled his head down to hers. "I don't want you to stop, Liam."

His big frame tensed in surprise, and she could feel his eyes burning into hers. "Reasa? Are you sure, because I can wait for however long you want. There is no rush to be together. I am willing to wait."

She uttered a resigned sigh, amusement lacing her voice. "First you want to kiss me when I don't want you to and now when I tell you that I do, you decide to question me? Just kiss me, Liam Eriksson. I have a need that only you can assuage."

It was all he needed to hear, his head lowering the last few inches to hers. His lips brushed hers tentatively at first, a slow, lingering, gentle kiss so full of love it made the ache in her heart flare brighter. This beautiful male loved her with a passion so fierce it was staggering, and she was planning to leave him as soon as she could slip away.

It was wrong of her for wanting this moment with him, when she knew she couldn't give him what he so richly deserved. It was weak and selfish, but if she was going to die this night then she wanted to know what it was like to love with the man who had been fated to be hers since the moment they had both been born.

CHAPTER 3

Reasa opened her mouth to him, feeling the ache of having denied them both for so long. Every night they had lain together she had fought her own desire, listening to him sleep until she was too exhausted to keep her eyes open. If only she hadn't been so foolish. They could have had nights like this so many times if she'd only let down her defences and allowed Liam into her heart where he belonged.

Her kiss tasted of that knowledge, desperation creeping into her response as she arched her body into his. She asked him for more without words, but he kept his touch gentle, soothing her desperation with tenderness until she wanted to weep.

Liam pulled his mouth from hers; tracing tiny kisses along her jaw and down her neck. "Your skin feels like satin, so smooth and soft. I've dreamt of this for what feels like forever, Reasa, and your taste surpasses everything I've ever imagined."

They were the sweetest, most heartfelt words she had ever heard. They made tears gather in her eyes, which she swallowed back. No one had ever loved her with such conviction before. She didn't deserve to have Liam's love but she would take this moment and treasure it for however long she might still walk this world.

"Love me, Liam," she whispered, threading her hands in his auburn hair as he suckled at her neck sending liquid fire racing through her veins.

"I do, Thereasa," he groaned, his lips moving back to her mouth, the heat of passion in his next kiss. "I love you with every fibre of my being," he breathed into her mouth. "You are my heartbeat and my every breath. You are my soul mate."

How could any woman not love a male who was so tender and compassionate in one breath, and yet, who was darkness and danger hidden beneath his soul? This glorious male would take on the world to protect her even as his fingers trailed down her arm in a touch so tender it was a light as a feather.

He made her burn with a desire so hot she felt as if she would explode. He teased her with tenderness so sweet it tugged at the softer part of her soul that had only ever craved to be loved. She ached to feel him inside her, to know what it was like to be adored by her beautiful Liam Eriksson. He was intent on taking his time with her. She was intent on disabusing himself of that notion.

Winding her legs around him, she pressed the very heart of her body against the hard, thick shaft that moved restlessly against her. She gasped out aloud and arched again, dragging a tortured groan from her lover.

"Reasa...stop that. I want this to be...Reasa!"

"I want you, Liam, all of you. I will not break. You will not hurt me. You will love me as a woman and not as a china doll you're afraid to break."

He stilled and looked down at her, moving to the right so he could reach out and turn on the bedside lamp. He didn't need the additional light to see her, but was aware that she did. Chocolate brown eyes traced every feature on her face, desire brimming in their smoky depths. "I want this to be perfect," he said softly, trembling fingers brushing down one cheek.

She smiled at him, grinding her lower body against his and thrilling at the way his jaw clenched and his nostrils flared. "How could it not be?" she asked, her need echoing in her voice. "I want you, Liam. I need you. Please love me."

His answering smile was so lascivious she shivered with anticipation. Had she just tempted that delicious vampiric side to him or was she about to get his lusty wolf. Whichever it was she was sure she was about to be loved within an inch of her life.

"So be it, beautiful," he breathed out, a split second before she felt her nightgown tear and he tossed the remnants aside. Sitting up astride her body, he let his greedy gaze wander over her nakedness, his hands coming to cup her tight breasts. "So beautiful," he murmured, leaning down to capture one hard peak in his mouth.

Reasa gasped as wet heat closed over her breast and Liam suckled hard. He tugged at her swollen peak sending tiny sparks of pure electricity shooting down her body to pool in the juncture of her thighs. She had never known her breasts to be this sensitive before, but then she hadn't had Liam laving them with such intent before. Each lick was pure heaven. Each suckle was another jolt of pure pleasure.

She moaned and writhed beneath him, her thighs aching to open to admit him, but they were clamped shut by his thick thighs sitting astride her. Liam teased her mercilessly, until she was sure she was making that mewling noise he'd mentioned earlier. His soft laughter told her he was thinking the same thing, and she would have given him a smack if he wasn't holding her wrists bound above her head with one hand.

"Tease," she groaned out, her heart thumping wildly as the ache between her legs grew unbearably.

"I can be," he breathed softly, releasing her breasts to slide lower. He trailed wet kisses over her quivering abdomen, continuing lower until he was kissing her mound and her inner thighs, deliberately staying away from where she wanted him most.

"Liam!"

"So impatient," he laughed, hooking one of her thighs over his shoulder. One large hand pressed her other thigh apart, pinning her in place so she was open to his greedy gaze. "Dear God, you're stunning," he whispered, his breath tickling against her flesh.

Reasa tried to press herself towards his mouth but he held her still, blowing gently against her heated flesh.

"So wet," he whispered. "So perfect. All mine." His tongue rasped over her before he had fully finished speaking and it was so unexpected she cried out.

Oh crap, she was getting the wolf. There was no denying that; not from the way he nuzzled at her body, or the long, slow licks he subjected her to. He was taking his sweet time, tasting her essence, scything his tongue over every inch of her sex until she shuddered in a hot mess.

He flicked at her apex, teased the tiny bundle of nerves that set her blood on fire. She was panting, writhing, aching to feel him buried deep inside her. "Liam...Liam...please."

His throaty growl was all the warning she got before he suckled against her clit, pushing her that last short distance to her climax. Reasa shattered in a million pieces, bliss making her body tremble as her heart tried to climb out of her chest. She cried out, moving against his wicked mouth, climaxing in mindless pleasure as he lapped against her body.

It was the most spellbindingly erotic climax she'd ever had and it took her a few long moments to come down from the heady bliss he'd engendered. When she opened her eyes, Liam was naked above her and she swallowed hard as she let her eyes travel down to the thick shaft standing proudly between his legs.

"Uhm...everything about you is oversized, I see," she managed to get out, a faint feeling of concern colouring her words. She was human now and he was huge with a capital H. Perhaps she should have let him take his time.

"The human body is an amazing thing," Liam sighed, his fingers moving to rub against her sex. "It's very adaptable once you play it perfectly." Two thick fingers slid inside her, and she arched towards their wonderful intrusion. "That's it, beautiful girl, enjoy my fingers. Just like that..."

Liam pressed his fingers in and out slowly, building up the pace as she closed her eyes and allowed her body to be guided by his. It felt so good feeling him inside her, preparing her for his cock, widening her so she would be ready to take all of him.

Three fingers speared her and she gasped loudly. His thumb rubbed against her clit as his fingers picked up speed. She was mindless, helpless against him, moaning and writhing, as he loved her with his hands. Her breath caught as he pinched her clit hard, another climax rolling over her with such ferocity she was fighting to breathe.

"Reasa, sweet Reasa...look at me..."

Her eyes fluttered open to meet his, her breath trapped in her chest at the open adoration she saw in his gaze. "I love you, Thereasa." His cock pressed against her opening, an inch sliding slowly inside.

"I love you, Liam," she gasped, arching up as he pressed down.

He eased deep within her body, sheathing himself in her wet heat and stilling his movements when they were joined. His hands ran up her arms to gather her wrists together above her head, his free hand gently stroking down her cheek to her collarbone. "Mine," he growled softly, flecks of amber shining in his eyes.

She knew that he wanted to mate with her, and it hurt that she would have to deny him this. "Too soon," she whispered, seeing the slight hint of hurt that he couldn't conceal fast enough. "Liam... "

"It's okay," he reassured her, a soft smile crossing his face as he leaned down for a slow kiss. "One step at a time, my love. I can wait." He withdrew and slid back inside her, his thickness stretching her in delicious ways.

"Oh God," she moaned bucking her hips to meet him. "It's so good..."

He laughed and it was so full of male satisfaction she had to laugh too. Males were universal the world over, and couldn't help being smug when they loved their women to perfection. "Don't let it go to your head," she teased stifling down another moan.

"No...I'm about to go to your head," he quipped back, flexing his hips and driving himself hard into her waiting body.

Reasa's toes curled, her breath caught and she was certain stars danced before her eyes. Before she had time to recover he was thrusting deep again and she was helpless against his assault. Her body moved in time to his. He teased her in a dance that alternated between hard and forceful, to soft and gentle. Each time she thought she had detected his rhythm he switched it up again until she was a mindless, quivering wreck beneath him.

"Liam... I need... I need... "

"What do you need, dear heart? Tell me what you want and it's yours."

The deep huskiness of his voice told her that he wasn't unaffected by the sweet torture he was subjecting them to. His own desire was at fever pitch and he needed his release as much as she did.

"I need to come," she gasped, rolling her hips in such a way that his next thrust into her teased him and made him growl loudly. She did it again, and again until he lost control and was taking her hard and fast, pushing her towards that perfect moment of union that was theirs and theirs alone.

Reasa climaxed hard, crying out and shuddering beneath Liam as he growled his own pleasure into the night air, his neck straining as he pulsed deep inside her and bathed her with his pleasure. She couldn't think, couldn't breathe, all she could do was soar on a wave of ecstasy that felt as if it would never end.

When reason finally returned she was cradled on her side in Liam's embrace, their hearts beating loudly and their skin slickened with sweat. His breathing was as erratic as hers was, and for a long time she just lay there listening to his heart slow down, a feeling of complete safety overcoming her as she lay in his arms. It was without a doubt the most beautiful, staggering lovemaking she had ever had, and she was glad she had taken this moment with him, no matter what the future may hold.

"You're incredible," Liam murmured against her hair, cuddling closer as their skin cooled down on the early morning air.

"You're not so bad yourself," she quipped back, giggling when he gave her a soft pat on her backside.

"Not so bad? Talk like that will get you into trouble, wench."

His laughter was low and happy, and it wrenched at her heart. She managed to keep her tone light, hiding her sadness from this beautiful male who wanted nothing more out of life but to love her. "Yes, I tend to excel at that," she answered, faking a wide yawn.

It had the desired effect, Liam reaching for the rumpled coverlet to pull over them. "You're exhausted. You need to sleep."

"It's so hot too," she groaned, and he placed a few inches between their bodies, as she suspected he would. He always put her needs before his, and her eyes filled with tears as he ran a hand down her back as she faced away from him towards the window.

"Sleep, love," he whispered, a yawn escaping him. "I want you rested for tomorrow so we can do that again, it was so totally amazing."

"It was," she whispered back, fighting the tears that threatened to fall. She wouldn't be here when he woke and that would truly break his heart. She deserved every single bit of what was heading her way. Maybe then she would have atoned for all the wrong she had done to this wonderful male and his pack...

Reasa evened out her breathing, simulating falling asleep as best she could. It must have worked because he fell asleep within a few minutes, but she lay there an additional ten before she climbed out of the bed as soundlessly as she could. While she may not be a vampire any longer she still retained a lot of her previous skill set, like how to move silently.

Liam muttered in his sleep and rolled over, but he didn't wake. Breathing out a sigh of relief, she gathered her jeans and T-shirt, collecting her jacket as she headed into the adjoining bathroom.

Dressing in there served a dual purpose; if Liam woke, it wouldn't be unusual that she be in the bathroom, and there was also a door out to the hallway from this particular room. It was kept locked for the most part, though Liam had told her that when family was visiting from the Hanlon pack, it was open to the rest of the house if required.

Now she carefully turned the key in the lock and cracked the door open. The house was silent but she maintained her stealth as she crept down the stairs and made her way to the back door. It was a testament to the trust the house's occupants had placed in her that no one stirred as she let herself out. That was another black mark on her soul, but then, she had so many now what would one more really matter? Ashleigh's talk with her came to mind and she swallowed hard. Perhaps that black mark did matter just as much as the rest of them.

Taking a shaky breath, Reasa slipped into the trees behind the Eriksson house. There was no turning back from this, thousands of lives depended on her. She had no doubt that Michael would do exactly what he said he would. If she didn't hand herself over to him, a full assault would break out on the North American vampires and countless of them would die from Amort poisoning before the pack and Council could mobilise fast enough to give them the newfound cure. She couldn't be responsible for that, she just couldn't. She hoped Liam would understand...he had to.

She moved east slowly, making sure to stop and listen as she went. There would be wolves out there patrolling and she had to make it to the rendezvous point unseen. A sound echoed off to her left and she froze in her tracks, holding her breath. She waited a full five minutes before she moved again, certain it must have been an animal she'd heard. If it had been a pack member then they would have dragged her kicking and screaming back to the pack.

She was almost at the road when she heard another noise. This time it didn't fade when she stopped, and her heart sank as she spun around to see who was pursuing her.

"There is some satisfaction in being proven right though I admit in this instance I wish I had been proven wrong for Liam's sake," Pietro hissed, fury dancing in his mismatched eyes.

Reasa's heart leapt in her chest, dismay overwhelming her as she gazed at the scarred vampire. "No! You can't be here. Go back, Pietro. Now!"

His face twisted into a grimace, his scar stretching as his eyes bled black. "And let you get away?" he sneered, loathing dripping from every word. "It's a shame Liam has to learn what a treacherous bitch you are, Thereasa. He deserves so much better than you. Fate has truly fucked with his life."

She had to make him leave but she didn't know how. If he was here when Michael arrived, there was no telling what would happen. "Please, Pietro. Please. For Cassia, for Liam and the rest of the pack. You must go back. You must let me go."

"The only place you're going is back to the pack, so get used to that. Now move, Thereasa."

"No...you don't understand!" She tried again, urgency making her words tumble over each other. "You're in danger, Pietro. You have to leave here right now. Please...before it's too late."

Michael's cold words echoed around them, and Pietro spun around, talons at the ready. They were completely encircled by close to two dozen elder vampires, the blond vampire lounging against a large tree trunk.

Reasa moaned in fear, her gaze flickering frantically around them for some avenue of escape. There was none, and no matter how good Pietro was, there was no way in hell he could take on all of the vampires and win.

"I didn't tell you to bring a friend, Thereasa."

She moved to Pietro's side, her gaze locking with her former coven member. "He followed me. He isn't supposed to be here. Forget about him, Michael. I'm the one you want."

The blond vampire moved forward, amusement shining from his eyes. "You still try to protect this vampire? I never understood why you were so intent on protecting him in Europe and here you are doing the very same thing. Are you fucking him?"

Pietro hissed revulsion crossing his face. "I am mated," he growled, appearing more incensed at being linked with Reasa than being surrounded by so many enemies.

"Our mission wasn't to kill him," Reasa spat out, ignoring Pietro's outburst. "It was information gathering only. You broke Louis' command. You should have been punished as Bruce was. I was weak to leave you alive."

"No, you were too busy following your own agenda and betraying your coven," Michael hissed back, venom in every word. "You've gone from hero to zero, Thereasa. Louis has sanctioned your death." He laughed at her expression, glee blazing from his eyes. "Yes, you no longer have his protection. You're mine to do with as I please."

Reasa swallowed down her fear, keeping Michael focused on her and away from Pietro. "So be it," she answered, her voice calm despite the fear threatening to overwhelm her. "You know how Louis feels about his coven members taking the law into their own hands. My own situation is testament to that. If you harm this vampire beside me and bring his friends to Louis' door, your death will be a certainty."

She could see that had him thinking so she pressed on. "Think about it, Michael. You know what I say is true. Let Pietro go and you can do whatever you want with me." She could feel a subtle tensing of the vampire beside her, and knew without looking that he had glanced down at her. She had to keep Michael engaged though, so she stared straight ahead.

She thought she had him for a moment and then his expression hardened. "Do you think me stupid, Thereasa? Do you think I am gullible enough to allow him to leave and bring the rest of his pack down on my head? No, he chose to follow you so he will meet your fate. He should have died in Europe anyway. It's obscene to know one scarred such as he sullies our people."

"Michael...Michael, please don't do this. I'm begging you. You don't want to do this." Reasa knew it would appeal to him to have her beg. It would buy her a little time...time enough to try to save Pietro. As she spoke she pulled on her newly learned dream walking skills. She slid into the mind of the vampire standing at her side, whispering a mental apology that she was once more invading his soul.

"Pietro...we have little time. Forgive me for doing this..."

"NO!" he roared, pushing at her psychic form, trying to dislodge her from his mind.

"I'm sorry...I'm so sorry but you must call to Cassia. I am too far from Liam to reach him but you have the mate link now with Cassia. Call to her, Pietro. Warn her of this danger, and then try to fight your way through them. I will do my best to keep Michael occupied." She slipped from his mind before he could answer, praying he would do as she asked.

Michael was laughing loudly, his confidence so high he didn't consider that possibly there could be wolves close by to hear. "Oh, you beg so sweetly. I find I like hearing you beg, Thereasa. Are you sure you're not fucking Pietro because you plead for his life as if you were." His laughter cut off, cruelty replacing his amusement. "I think we shall kill him first...seeing as you're so partial to him."

He signalled to his men, and a handful of them raised their arms. Reasa stared mutely at them for a second, her terrified mind trying to register what they held in their hands.

"I came prepared with Amort." Michael's smile was nothing short of insane. "I really liked watching the flesh putrefy on Pietro's body. I want to see it again."

Pietro moved then, a bellow of utter rage dragged from the depths of his soul. At supernatural speed he incapacitated two vampires, throwing hacked off arms at a third and decapitating the fourth.

Michael sprang out of his reach, roaring at his men. "Kill him!"

Three vampires flew at Pietro, knocking him to the ground. Reasa jumped on one of their backs, holding on as he tried to shake her off. He shook her so hard her teeth rattled but she held on like grim death, trying to buy Pietro some time to defend himself. Sharp talons sliced her thigh and she screamed in pain, releasing her hold and rolling to the forest floor.

The pain was excruciating but it wasn't half as terrifying as seeing blood spurt all over her and chunks of flesh being ripped from Pietro's body. He was outnumbered and outmatched. There was no way he could fight them all off though he was able to inflict some damage. She prayed he had listened and got a call out to Cassia, because it was only a matter of seconds before they were both done for.

"Enough!" Michael roared, and the vampires peeled away to leave them lying bleeding on the ground.

Reasa spared a glance at Pietro, tears falling as she saw the damage to his body. His arms and legs were mangled, and it looked like his spine had been crushed. He would never heal in time; the damage was far too great. She had tried to protect him, tried to atone for her past sins and now she was taking him to her grave.

"I'm so sorry," she wept, dizziness threatening as the blood pumped too quickly from her leg wound. Her human body was letting her down, and if her last words were to be to this wounded warrior, then she wanted him to know that she was sorry for all the harm she had ever done to him.

Puzzled, pain filled eyes met hers, confusion warring with his hatred. Pietro stared up at her, willing his body to heal, frowning as he saw her vision blur as tears fell down her cheeks. "Thereasa?"

"Oh, how touching." Michael's tone was bored as well as amused his expression a twisted, ugly mask of sincerity. "Let's end this, shall we?" He picked up one of the fallen guns, smiling as he pointed it at them. "Stay with me a little longer, Thereasa. There is enough Amort on these bullets to eat Pietro alive in a matter of minutes. It will be such fun to witness."

The gun cocked, and time seemed to stand still. There was no question in her mind, no second-guessing of what she must do. It felt as if she had waited for this moment to come, so that she might buy him some extra time and she might find some peace in the afterlife. "Forgive me," Thereasa whispered, throwing her body forward as the bullet fired.

"NO!" Pietro screamed, his arms coming up to catch her as she fell forward onto his chest, the bullet striking her squarely in the back. Hot, wet, sticky blood coated his hands, Reasa's breath rushing out as her head fell against his neck. Pietro screamed again, and then again, his voice joining with the screams surrounding him.

Breath brushed his neck weakly; a heart beat against his chest slowly. He could hear his name being called. He could hear frantic cries for Reasa, but all he could do was lay there, as a heart slowed with each beat and a breath caught with each gasp. "No," he whispered, tears blurring his vision. "Stay with me, Reasa, please stay with me. I forgive you. I forgive you... "

* * * * *

Cassia flew out of bed, terror filling her soul. "Pietro! Where are you?"

"East quadrant, beside the road. Two dozen vampires...Reasa is here. Am hurt. Hurry!"

"Mom! Dad!" Cassia ran from her room tears running down her face. "Pietro and Reasa are being attacked!"

Her parents were already grabbing clothes as she ran from the house hurrying to Rafe's. She was so distraught she didn't even noticed there were lights on or question why Caleb and Annie were there. "Pietro...Reasa...the east quadrant. Vampire attack!" She gasped the words out, stumbling as she swung around and fled back outside.

"Aaron, lock down the pack now!" Rafe roared, flying from the house with his sister and her mate beside him. He shifted to wolf form as he leapt down the stairs running at full speed towards the attack. He didn't stop to see what the rest of the pack was up to. They were well trained and knew what to do in the face of an attack. Instead, he ran, fury filling his soul that someone would dare harm his pack.

The scene was carnage when he arrived, body pieces everywhere, Andrei and Alexei reigning death down on all they could reach. Wolves were hacking at fallen vampires, working in concert to take heads while avoiding being bitten. Off to the right he could hear more vampires arriving, the Varcolac and Praetorians were on their way.

"Reasa! Reasa!" Liam's anguished scream cut through the night and his head swung to the right so see figures lying on the ground.

The pack appeared to have the vampires under control, so he shifted back to his human form, kneeling down beside Liam. "Oh God, no," he breathed out, sorrow filling his soul as he stared at the woman cradled in Liam's arms. "Liam...Liam...she's gone, son. She's gone."

"NO!" Liam screamed, holding her close, rocking her body against his as tears rolled down his face. His anguish was transmitting to everyone present, his grief causing tears to fall down everyone's faces. "She's not gone, Rafe. She's not gone. She can't be. She can't be!"

Frantic eyes searched wildly, finding the one person he sought. "Help her, Annie. Help her. Make her wake up again...please."

The redhead knelt beside him, gently pushing the Alpha to the side. "Oh, Liam...I wish I could, sweetheart. I truly do..."

"She's there, Annie, I can feel her still there," he wept, his eyes pleading with her. "I can feel her in there, she isn't gone."

"Let me through," Mallen ordered, the doctor pulling open his bag as he joined the group. "If Liam says she's there then I'm not going to argue with him, not after he just brought six seemingly dead vampires back to life. So, I'll work on the physical side and you can do your mental shit. Come on, people, we don't have a lot of time here." His stoic pragmatism seemed to shake off some of the stunned grief they were experiencing and the group parted to give them room.

"Clear up this mess and then do a sweep to make sure we got them all."

Pietro gently disentangled himself from the bear hug Cassia had wrapped him in since she'd found him among the melee of body parts. Keeping a hold of her hand as he sat up gingerly, his body protested the movement but he had to see the bodies. "There's no sign of Michael," he hissed out, fury invading him that the main instigator had gotten away.

"Fan out, do a full search of the area," Rafe ordered. His gaze fell on Mac who was staring down at Reasa's body. "Mac, can the Praetorians run a sweep of the city? I don't want any of the pack away from our borders until we're certain the coast is clear."

"We're on it," the Praetorian leader answered, glancing down at his mate.

"I want to stay with Liam," Lily said quietly, scrubbing at her wet cheeks.

"Is that wise?" "He just made us cry a little," she sighed, leaning in to give him a hug. "Liam's in control, Mac. Nothing bad will happen."

Her mate wasn't so sure of that but he had to go with what she wanted. Her pack needed her right now, so this was her place to be. "Stay here until I come get you." He kissed her lightly and then turned to gather his people. If this Michael was anywhere in the city to find, then they would find him.

* * * * *

The pain was gone and it felt so amazing. Reasa slowly opened her eyes, blinking against the harsh whiteness that surrounded her. Where was she? Glancing around in confusion, she tried to clear her head but it felt kind of fuzzy, as if what she was looking at wasn't real. The last thing she remembered was being in the forest and the next she was here. Was this what the afterlife looked like?

Michael had shot her at point blank range. There was no way her fragile human body could have survived that kind of trauma. She only hoped that her sacrifice had given Pietro the precious seconds he'd needed to heal enough to protect himself. Maybe it had been enough time for the pack to get there and help him...if he had called to Cassia as she'd told him.

"Was it a hard choice?"

Reasa spun around, her mouth opening in surprise as she stared at the beautiful woman standing watching her. Her thick red hair was pulled up in an intricate design, and she wore a flowing deep purple gown cinched at the waist by an ornate silver belt with a crescent moon clasp. Reasa was certain she'd never seen the other woman before and yet, she appeared familiar somehow.

"Annie?" Even as she breathed the name, she knew it wasn't Rhianna standing there. They shared the same colouring but their faces were different.

"Was it a hard choice?" the woman asked again and this time Reasa listened to her words, understanding what she wanted to know.

"No," she answered quietly, reliving that moment in the forest once more and knowing if she had to do it over again she would make the same choice.

"Do you know who I am, Thereasa?"

Knowledge came to her in an instant, awe overwhelming her. "You are Anakatrine, last of the great Vampire Queens." Tears came unbidden and the need to subjugate herself to the woman who had taken everything from her and yet, in the process, had given her back her most precious possession. Reasa knelt down on both knees, bowing her head. "Thank you, my Queen, for the gift of my soul. I didn't deserve it but I am grateful for your generosity."

The Vampire Queen let out an inelegant snort, so surprising Reasa's head shot up to see open amusement on the other woman's face. "Oh, stand up, child," Anakatrine laughed, holding out a hand. "Do you want to know a secret that only Callain and Gard know? I used to bespell my audience chamber to turn the tiles into cushioned pillows. It still looked like it was tiled but it was soft when my subjects knelt. It used to confuse the hell out of them but I always worried that their knees would get sore with all that kneeling. I never could abide all that kneeling malarkey."

When Reasa only gaped at her open-mouthed, she laughed again, pulling her to her feet. "What? I'm not what you expect of a Queen? I can be many things dependant on the circumstances. Sometimes I am benevolent, others I am a warrior. There are times when I must make the most painful of decisions and then there are times like these, when I can just be one woman talking to another."

"I don't understand what's happening here," Reasa whispered, her confusion absolute. "Am I dead like you are, living in someone else's mind?"

Anakatrine's gaze turned serious, her hands squeezing Reasa's tightly. "You are between worlds...in a place only Callain or I can walk. Unfortunately, we cannot walk in the same moment here, but I can feel an echo of him behind me sometimes."

She waved her hand at nowhere in particular, a graceful arching of a limb that was so beautiful it made Reasa catch her breath. "Out there, Mallen is working to stabilise your body with the Varcolac donating their blood to help repair the damage. In your mind, Liam is wading through your shattered hallway, searching desperately for the pieces of your psyche to hold your mind together as they work. In here, it is just you and I, two women having a pleasant talk. Why don't we sit for a while? You've had a busy night and must be weary."

Bright red, high-backed armchairs appeared out of nowhere, and Reasa allowed herself to sink into one as the vampire Queen settled into the other. "Why am I here, Anakatrine? Why are we here?" It seemed like the most important question in the world, one that she had to have answered.

"Why do you think, Thereasa?" Was the cryptic response, confusing her further and yet, opening up her thoughts too.

"I am being judged."

Anakatrine snorted once more, laughter dancing across her face. "I am not judging you, child, I am merely spending some time with you while you make your decision."

What was she talking about? What decision was she required to make? "Please...I don't understand...can't you talk without riddles."

The smile the vampire queen gave her was one of fondness though there was more than a hint of ruefulness about it. "I have spent eons talking in riddles, child. Sometimes it is hard to break the habit. When I stripped you of your immortality, I told you that you had three souls to save, Thereasa. Name those souls and our time here is done."

Everything Rhianna had told her was true, it had been the vampire queen who had taken her immortality. She had known it at the time, known it when she knelt before this woman, and she now knew the answer to the question just posed to her. "Liam," she breathed seeing his beautiful face as if he was standing before her.

"I forgive you..." a voice echoed in her mind, the last sound she could remember hearing. "Pietro..." Tears fell down her cheeks, the emotions within demanding an outlet.

"Was it a hard choice...?" The question from the vampire queen, the one she had answered without needing to think..."No... "

Anakatrine was watching her closely, glowing lavender eyes brimming with a love that was so fierce it was incandescent.

"Thank you for my soul..." Reasa's voice, her words uttered only a few breaths before as she knelt before this wondrous being...

"My soul..."

Heat radiated throughout her body, a soft warm glow that wrapped her up and embraced her in a safe cocoon. She wasn't afraid of it, she didn't understand it, she just knew that it would do her no harm.

"Thank you for Liam's soul, sweet child. Thank you for Pietro's soul, fierce vampire. While I grieved that I had to take such dire steps to lead you home, I had faith that you would one day find your own soul once more. Never forget who you are, Thereasa. Never let mistakes of the past define you. This is who you are now, a woman who has saved countless innocent lives. A woman who was willing to give her life to save another. Welcome home, child."

The heat intensified until it was all around her. "Anakatrine...I'm afraid." She couldn't see the Queen anymore, she couldn't drag her eyes open or stop the dizziness from enveloping her.

"Anakatrine... "

"Reasa...Oh god, Reasa!" Liam's tears were covering her face, her body protesting as he rocked her against him ignoring the irate bellows from the doctor at her side.

"Liam, let her go... "

"No..." she murmured, forcing her eyes to open, to see her mate's beautiful face above her, tears of joy streaming down his cheeks. She didn't want him to let her go, she wanted to be in his arms forever. "I dreamed of the vampire queen," she whispered, tears falling from her eyes. "She was so beautiful, Liam. So kind and loving. She helped me find my soul...she helped me..." Her words trailed off, her body needing the rest, her mind so tired all she wanted to do was sleep.

"Oh my god...do you see that?" Mallen's stammer had everyone turning to look at him in surprise. He was pointing at Reasa, at the gaping wound on her leg. "She's healing herself...
"

Caleb turned to Rhianna, shooting her a puzzled glance. She was pale and looked exhausted, but she was smiling so widely he knew she'd been up to something. He'd known something was happening when she'd told him to hold her and not to let go no matter what happened. Nothing had appeared to be happening so he'd been a but perplexed by her request but he'd done as she asked. "Annie?"

She yawned, snuggling against his chest as Liam dragged his gaze from his mate to look at them. "Thereasa saved her three souls. Her penance is over." Her lavender gaze connected with the Varcolac, a happy smile gracing her face. "Anakatrine returned Reasa's immortality, Liam. She will heal herself in good time now, though it would probably be more comfortable if she wasn't left lying on the forest floor while she did."

A hush fell over the clearing, all eyes staring at them. "Do you mean it, Annie?" Liam whispered, hope in his voice. "Reasa is a vampire once more?"

CHAPTER 4

Her smile widened if that was possible and she rose to her feet with Caleb at her side. "She is a vampire once more," she agreed placing a hand on his shoulder. "Take her home now, Liam. Cassia, take Pietro home too. There has been enough drama this night. Let's care for those we can and find a way to help those we can't."

Caleb gathered her to his side, knowing her thoughts were travelling back to Europe and to what could have happened to her brother and his mate. The rest of the pack wasn't aware of that turn of events as yet, and it appeared they would try to limit that knowledge to those who needed to know for the time being.

"Back to Rafe's?" he asked, and she shook her head as she looked at her brother. The Alpha's attention was on his pack at the moment, and the ones he could do something to help.

"Tomorrow," she answered, her heart heavy as her eyes turned to stare off into the distance. "Be safe," she whispered for only Caleb to hear. "Be safe, brother of my heart. Your work here is not yet done."

* * * * *

"Will you mate with me, Reasa?"

How could she deny her fierce male when he looked at her with such adoration on his face? As soon as her body had healed he had loved her with no holds barred, and it had been even more exquisite than their first time together. He hadn't needed to be gentle because she was human. He had been lustful and strong, demanding and tender at the same time. Now they lay together joined, welcoming the dawn's first rays through their open window, her glorious male was asking to join with her forever.

Reaching up a hand, she brushed aside his long, auburn locks, drinking in his beauty and wondering how she had ever deserved to know such happiness. Anakatrine's words whispered through her mind and she pushed away the last lingering self-doubt that she had. She deserved this because she had earned it, with every tear that had been wrung from her soul.

"I have walked through fire to be with you, Liam Eriksson. I have known my greatest weaknesses and shame, and I have known my greatest strengths and compassion. I am honoured to be yours for eternity. Yes, I will mate with you."

The joy on his face brought tears to her eyes, and she let them flow as he moved inside her body, his lips plundering hers, his body worshiping her with his love. Now that she was free from the past, there was hope for this future with her redheaded Varcolac, and she was taking it while it was on offer. Nothing and no one would deny her.

"Liam...my beautiful Liam...I love you so much." The words were ripped from her soul as her body soared in ecstasy, and her fangs sank into the side of his neck to nourish her second lust.

She could feel his life essence filling her body... both his blood and his seed claiming her. It made her heart thud wildly, it beating racing as his teeth sank into her collarbone and he claimed her as his mate. Nothing had felt so good, and she doubted anything ever would. Nothing could ever compare to this perfect moment of being claimed by her magnificent mate, and now she was a vampire once more, it would be a memory that would never pale.

They danced together in their rhythm of love, true mates joining in a perfect moment of bliss. he gave her his strength and she gave him hers. They were one heart beating, one breath echoing in the early morning air.

"I love you, my sweet, sweet Thereasa. Now and forever," Liam whispered the words with tears of joy in his eyes, complete for the very first time in his life. It hadn't been an easy journey, but he would have walked through endless trials to win his mate's love. She was worth every single tear he'd shed, every single missed heart beat when he thought he had lost her. He was probably going to be a tad overprotective for a little while until the terror of seeing her lying in the forest so lifeless diminished, but he expected she would understand that.

"Thank you for not giving up on me, Liam. For believing in me when I doubted myself. Fate blessed me when it chose you for my mate. I will do my utmost to be everything you ever dreamed of."

"Silly," he chuckled, kissing the side of her neck as he gathered her close. "You already are and always were, Thereasa. With you I am complete and I can't wait to spend the rest of my existence with you. Thank you for trying to kill me."

"Liam!" She groaned as he brought that up, shame running through her at the mere mention of it. She tried to hide her face but he wouldn't allow her to, tilted her chin up so their eyes could meet.

"Do not hide from the past, love. It is what brought you into my life and what helped us learn that the Varcolac were immune to the toxin. In a roundabout way, it was also what pointed towards the antidote for Amort too. It happened and it's unescapable, but we can look to the good that came of it and not to the misguided thoughts that created the situation."

"You have a novel way of looking at things, my mate," she sighed, a half-smile curving her lips. "I will try to see things from your perspective. I guess old habits die hard sometimes."

He rolled over on top of her once more, his body hardening as he rubbed against her. "I could always think of novel ways to re-educate you when you have a lapse..." He gave her his best leer and she burst out laughing.

"I'd hold that thought if I were you. If my newly reacquired senses are correct, I think we may have some early morning visitors."

"What the hell? Who would be calling at this time of the morning? It's barely dawn... " Liam's grumble came to a halt as he scented their visitors, his gaze swinging away from the bedroom door and back to his mate. "Are you okay with this?"

Reasa sat up reaching for a dressing gown and sliding it on. "I think I need this, Liam. We need to know if this is going to work."

The soft tap on the door interrupted them, and Liam shrugged into a pair of silk PJ bottoms as it swung open.

"Hope you two are decent," Cassia called out a bare second before her head peeked around the door. She was smiling and looked slightly tousled, but her body language was completely relaxed. "Sorry for the early hour but Pietro was being a complete pain. He insisted we come over to see how Reasa was."

It was all the woman in question could do not to gasp in astonishment as the door opened wider and the other couple entered. Pietro's mismatched gaze went immediately to hers, and she wondered what he was thinking behind the carefully neutral expression on his face.

"Liam...would you and Cassia mind?"

Her mate shot her a perturbed glance, but she smiled at him to reassure him. With a pointed look at Pietro who smiled innocently, Liam allowed himself to be escorted from the room by Cassia.

"He won't harm her..." she heard the blonde Varcolac say as the door closed behind them and she was left alone with Pietro, who remained where he had stopped in the room.

"Are you well?" he asked, when the silence lengthened.

Reasa nodded, unsure what to say to the vampire who had almost died twice because of her actions. In her mind she could still hear his voice in the forest, but she didn't dare hope that he had come to repeat those words.

"You were human. You knew that shot would have been fatal. Why did you do it, Thereasa?" There was honest confusion in his voice, a need for understanding in his eyes.

"I couldn't allow you to die because of my actions," she answered, fighting to keep her voice from shaking from the wealth of emotions that were suddenly building up within her. "I erred in Europe and you suffered something so horrific that no one should ever have had to suffer. Whether or not it was I who administered the Amort was a moot point. I was in charge of that mission and you almost lost your life because of my mistake. I could not allow that to happen a second time."

His eyes pinned her so she couldn't look away, his expression one she couldn't quite make out. "You weren't running to Michael for rescue last night, were you? You were trying to save the lives of your people even though your own immortality had been stripped from you." He paused, taking a few steps closer to the bed. "You knew Michael was here to kill you, didn't you?"

"What is one life when a thousand could possibly be saved?" she asked, her hand touching the cover, inviting him closer. "Would you not have done the same thing, Pietro de la Rios?"

Yes, he would have, if that had been the only option open to him. Staring down at Reasa, he could see that she had honestly believed that had been her only choice, and he felt a kinship with her that he'd never felt before. She was what he knew, a fierce vampire willing to lay down her life for her people. Yes, she had made mistakes and he had paid for some of them, but deep in her heart, she was of his heart and mind. She would die for those under her protection, or those she classed as being hers to protect.

He took the two final steps to the bed, sitting down on the edge, as he kept their gazes locked. "I hated you so much," he ground out, his voice rough with emotion. "You knew that and yet you still threw yourself in front of a bullet meant for me. Do you have any idea how raw it scrapes the inside of your soul to know the person you have hated most in this world would die for you?"

"I will answer that should Michael ever choose to die for me," she replied, a poignant smile on her face because she knew that day would never come. Michael's soul was lost forever and she would rip his head off before she ever allowed him to try to redeem himself in her eyes. She wondered if that was how the vampire watching her felt...if he wished she hadn't acted as she had.

"My soul has been crying out since that day we met in Europe, Thereasa," Pietro whispered. "It has shrieked and raged. It has demanded vengeance and retribution. That agony almost lost me Cassia, and despite mating with her, it still cried out. I didn't think it would ever stop, not as long as you walked this planet. But...last night as I held you, as your blood coated my hands and I listened to your heart slow and felt your breath stutter against my neck...my soul shrieked once more and it had everything to do with you. It cried out No. It wept for the fragile human woman who would give her life for me knowing I hated her. You have no debt left to repay me, Reasa. I forgive you."

The entire time he spoke her tears fell and she didn't try to hide them. Though he cried his own tears and his voice was raw with his emotions, there was such peace on his face. "I'm sorry, Pietro, so very sorry for the hurt I have brought to you." She reached out tentatively, touching the scar on his cheek when he didn't pull away.

He gave a shaky laugh, clearly trying to lighten the moment. "Cassia is very partial to my scars," he admitted with a small smile. "And they freak the vamps out at the Dive which is also a lot of fun."

His expression turned serious once more and he placed his hand over hers and held it to his cheek. "We have both walked different roads, Thereasa. Each of us has been damaged in our own different ways, but we have found something amazing along the way. We have found Cassia and Liam, and we have found a new home where we are welcomed and loved. We have both fallen, but we have risen back up. It's time to put the past behind us and concentrate on the glorious futures we have ahead of us. I am willing to do this. Are you?"

"Yes, oh yes, Pietro, I am so ready for that." On impulse she threw herself into his arms, hugging him tightly when he enveloped her in his embrace and held her close. "To new beginnings, Reasa."

"To new beginnings, Pietro."

*****

"Do you think I should go up there?" Liam's gaze slid to the kitchen door earning him a snort from his friend.

"I told you, they're fine...for now." Cassia laughed as his head spun around, his expression startled.

"Well there's no telling what Rafe is going to have to say to them both about why they managed to land themselves into their predicament in the first place," she pointed out, though something told her their Alpha was preoccupied elsewhere at the moment. "Seriously, Liam...what Reasa did for Pietro last night, it changed everything."

As if on cue, the dark-haired vampire appeared in the kitchen, smiling as he crossed to Cassia and gave her a resounding kiss. All the tension had left his body and even Liam could see that he was at peace with his soul. If he hadn't seen it he had felt it the instant the other male had entered the kitchen.

Reasa followed him in a few seconds later, sliding into Liam's embrace as if it was the most natural thing in the world. The smile she gave him was beatific and he kissed her, holding her tightly as she laughed at his anxiety.

"Do males ever grow up?" She asked Cassia who was also smiling.

"I'll let you know if mine ever does," the blond wolf quipped back, earning her a harrumph from her mate.

"Did anyone see Kothari last night?" Liam suddenly asked, his brow drawing down in a frown. In all the chaos that had happened, he didn't recall seeing the reticent Varcolac, and for some reason that made him feel uneasy.

"I don't think so, but then I was more interested in the fact my mate was lying in pieces and you were with Reasa. He had to have been there though; a full pack alert had gone out." Even as Cassia spoke, whatever unease had been trickling down Liam's spine was transmitting to her.

"He feels so calm," Liam whispered, his frown deepening. "Too calm... "

"Dara's agitated," Cassia exclaimed, her gaze turning to Pietro. "Something's very wrong...we need to find Dara right now..."

* * * * *

Dara was pissed with a capital P. She couldn't believe she had allowed Kothari to manipulate her as he had the day before. He had deliberately pushed her buttons, being a complete pig and calling her names to get rid of her. She'd fallen for it too, and that was why she was so mad. She was angry at herself and furious at Kothi. He hadn't shown up for the pack alert and when she got her hands on him she was going to give him a piece of her mind.

Stomping up to his house, she was pissed that she'd had to walk half a mile too. Why the hell couldn't he live closer to the main compound? That was something else she would give him a piece of her mind about and to hell if it wasn't really his fault. He was a grown man for God's sake. He didn't have to live with his parents. The fact that she still lived with hers was a moot point.

"Kothari, get your ass out here now!" she yelled, standing with her hands on her hips outside his front door. All the lights were on in the house so she knew he was awake. "Kothari, I mean it! If I have to come in there!"

Silence greeted her, an eerie silence that sent a shiver down her spine. Why were all the lights on? That didn't make sense. Neither, did Kothi ignoring a pack alert. Had something happened to him? What if some of the vampires had doubled back and attacked him while the rest of them were concentrated elsewhere?

"Kothi?" Dara walked up the three steps to the door, her breath catching when she saw it was open a fraction. With a hesitant hand she let it swing open, fear clogging her throat as the main living area came into view. Everything was in complete disarray, every piece of furniture smashed into pieces. The curtains were ripped from the windows, jagged holes in the glass on the back wall.

"Kothi? Answer me!" Panic laced her voice as she entered the wrecked room. There was no sign of any blood or body parts, the house just appeared as if a cyclone had taken place inside it.

Dara ran into the kitchen to find it wrecked, fear clogging her throat at the destruction. She didn't stop there, she turned and took the stairs two at a time, the same chaos echoed in every room she checked. There was only one exception, and it appeared odd that it remained so pristine. Gard and Rayne's bedroom remained untouched, the only evidence that someone had been there, a leather bound journal resting on the middle of the bed.

"What did you do, Kothi? What did you do?" Dara whispered the words, as she reached for the journal, opening it up to the first page...

July 8th

Dear Journal,

Mommy told me to write what's wrong with me. That letting it out in some way was better then not at all. Something is wrong with me. I hear mommy & daddy whispering at night when they think I'm sleeping, even with Antie Annie and Uncle Kaleb.

What's wrong with me?

Dara's heart clenched as she read the first entry, the lost cry of a little boy who knew that he was different even when he was so young. It was hard not to feel empathy for that little boy despite the wanton destruction in the house. Something had happened to push Kothi over the edge. Maybe there was some clue to what it was in his journal. She turned more pages trying to find some evidence of what had set him off. Her breath caught as she read, her heart pounding as she stopped at an entry...

DEAR AGONY

YOUR HURT HER, YOU HURT OUR ANGEL!! HOW COULD YOU HURT HER.

YOU HURT HER YOU HURT HER WE HURT HER WE HURT HER...

Dear God, he was talking of himself as two separate entities! He'd even named the other part of himself...Agony. Who had Agony hurt? Why had it distressed Kothari so much? There were no reports about any pack member being hurt. In fact, the only thing that came to mind was when she'd been with Kothi and he'd lost control. Was he talking about her? She leafed back a couple of pages, re-reading some entries about Kothi's Angel. Did he mean her? It appeared to tie together but maybe she was imagining it.

She paged forward to the end of the journal, and promptly ran out of the room and threw up in the hallway. The last two entries...oh sweet Jesus...if he wrote them after destroying the house...

GONE!!

THEY ARE GONE!!

Deep scores lined the page, the words carved into the paper. But it wasn't that which made her throw up...no that was bad enough, but it wasn't that which had turned her blood to ice. It was the very last entry, written so neatly and precisely...

Dear Kothari...

I'm here

THE END